THE SECOND CHAPTER OF A
BAD DREAM

THE SECOND CHAPTER OF A
BAD DREAM

GARY WATSON

authorHOUSE®

AuthorHouse™
1663 Liberty Drive
Bloomington, IN 47403
www.authorhouse.com
Phone: 1-800-839-8640

Published by AuthorHouse   01/18/2013

ISBN: 978-1-4817-0564-6 (sc)
ISBN: 978-1-4817-0604-9 (e)

DEDICATION

To My Family

Suzanne

Kelli and Hayley

David and Matthew

Tandy and Clinton

CHAPTER ONE

"Things like this just don't happen here!"

Police Chief Edgar Quinn's only response to his officer's distraught declaration was a shrug of the shoulders. Blinking because of the intense red and blue strobe lights, Quinn strode briskly past the ambulance and coroner's van parked in the driveway of the two story colonial at 237 Cotton Gin Lane and stopped to comfort a red-eyed, puffy-faced, pony-tailed teenage girl wrapped in a hunter green fleece blanket on a chilly March evening.

Quinn hugged the sobbing girl and wiped away a tear that was rolling down her cheek. "I'm sorry about your Dad, Hannah. He was a good man. I know how proud he was of you. He talked about you all the time. I'm not going to ask you a lot of questions right now, but if you can, I need you to tell me a little bit about tonight."

The slender brunette wiped away another tear and cleared her throat. "My last mid-term at Florida State was cancelled, so I got to come home from school a day early. I didn't bother to call the house. When I got here, Dad's car was in the garage. He wasn't downstairs, so I assumed he was upstairs reading or using his laptop. He does that a lot. I was going to tell him I was home. I knocked on the door to mom's and Dad's bedroom, and when he didn't answer, I stuck my head in. That's when I found him. I threw up in the floor." The girl wiped more free-flowing tears from her eyes.

1

"We'll clean up. Where's your mom?" Quinn reached into his shirt pocket and pulled out a stick of Black Jack chewing gum for Hannah.

"In Augusta with my aunt who had cancer surgery a few days ago. I've called her. She's on her way home." She unwrapped the gum and began chewing it vigorously.

"Hannah, it's going to be busy around here for a few hours. Is there someone you can stay with until your mom gets here?"

"My best friend Claire should be here any minute. I'm going to her house."

"Good." Again, Quinn hugged the girl, who was trembling despite being wrapped in the blanket. "I'm going to have Officer Landry stay with you until Claire gets here. You take care, all right? We'll get to the bottom of this."

Having given Officer Landry his orders, Quinn followed his assistant chief Sam Rogers into the pricey house belonging to the president of Sanderson State Bank, the oldest and more established of the town's two financial institutions. Quinn, a few pounds overweight and certainly not a poster boy for physical fitness, groaned as he contemplated the long staircase leading to the second floor bedrooms. Puffing with every step, he paused at the top to catch his breath before walking the final few feet to the master suite. "Yep," Quinn admitted, sucking air as he stepped inside. "This kind of thing doesn't happen around here." He tiptoed around Hannah's voluminous patch of vomit to get closer to the bed.

Gregory Carson, fifty-three year old banking executive, civic leader and former Chamber of Commerce Citizen of the Year, was sprawled naked on his back, his hands and feet tied with seamed black nylon stockings to the king-size four poster cherry bed. "I wonder what his fellow Rotary Club members will say about this," Quinn, his breathing almost back to normal, mumbled to himself.

"No sign of trauma to the body, chief. No blood, no bullet holes, no knife wounds," Assistant Chief Rogers reported.

"And no obvious sign of forced entry into the house. Is anything missing?" Quinn asked, looking down on the bed.

"Hannah doesn't think so, but she's not in any shape to give us a detailed inventory. Gregory's wallet is still in his pants. It's got five hundred dollars in it."

With his eyes still locked on the bed and Gregory Carson's body, Quinn announced, "I know what happened. We'll perform an autopsy and run toxicology tests to determine the cause of death, but I know what happened. While we're waiting for the results, we'll try to find out who his bondage partner was. We'll talk briefly with Sarah and tell her what we know as soon as she arrives from Augusta. The important thing is to get her and Hannah settled in for the night—away from this house. There will be plenty of time for questions and filling in the blanks tomorrow. All right, Lawson," Quinn nodded to the county coroner who was standing out of the way in a corner of the spacious tray-ceiling room scribbling notes. "He's yours now."

"So, what happened?" Sam Rogers asked his boss.

"Too much of a good thing, Sam. Too much of a good thing. Let me know when Sarah gets back in town. And make sure you clean up that pile of throw-up."

Quinn was tired and his breathing became labored again as he walked out of the house. His day had been long. Confident that his officers and Lawson Lockridge would properly wrap up processing the site, he wearily slipped into his white police cruiser, ready to go home, kick off his boots, pop a beer, chill out for a few minutes and try to get a little rest before meeting with Sarah Carson. Backing out of the driveway, Quinn had to slam on the brakes when a green Ford Expedition recklessly pulled in, blocking his way. Miffed, Quinn hopped out of his car. "Damn it, Stephen, how about moving so I can get out of here!"

"Don't leave just yet, Quinn! Tell me what's going on!"

"Gregory Carson's daughter came home and found him dead. I thought you would have left town by now."

"Hopefully I'll be gone in a few days, maybe a week. Gregory's dead? My God! That's horrible! What happened?"

"Too much of a good thing."

"Would you like to explain?"

"Gregory was tied to his bed, naked. My guess is the old boy's heart gave out on him during some kinky sex."

"Come on Quinn. You've got to be kidding. Gregory? Straight-laced Gregory? Coat and tie Gregory? At church every time the doors open Gregory? I don't believe it."

"Well, believe it. Everyone has skeletons in their closet, Stephen, even here in Sanderson. Unfortunately, Gregory had a kinky one in his that turned out to be deadly."

"I would have never pictured Gregory and Sarah into that kind of stuff."

"You're half right. Sarah wasn't at home."

"You've got to be kidding! I don't believe it! This family? Gregory cheating on his wife? Who the heck was with him?"

"We don't know. With him tied to the bed the way he was, it appears to be a case of 'sit and run.' I think his partner panicked when she realized he was having a heart attack. She hopped off

Gregory and hightailed it out. We'll find out who it was. What they will be charged with, if anything, is another matter."

"Sit and run? That's bad, Quinn. How's Hannah?"

"Numb. Finding your father dead is bad enough. Finding him this way is a real shock to the system. Doesn't do a lot for the family's social standing either."

"Mind if I take a few photos? I still can't believe this. Poor Sarah. Poor Hannah."

"You ought to be saying poor Gregory. He's the one who died with his pants down and his pecker up." Quinn looked back at the house. "Yeah, take your photos. Just stay out of the way. Don't go inside. Lawson Lockridge is finishing up and I'm going home. There's nothing else I can do here tonight. And by the way, Stephen. The stuff I just told you? You didn't hear it. Got that? Check with me tomorrow. Late tomorrow. That's when you can hear what I just told you." Quinn was in no hurry to flesh out the details of this night to the owner/reporter of the Sanderson Sentinel. He and the rest of the little town would find out soon enough.

CHAPTER TWO

J ake Martin grudgingly eyeballed the surroundings as his three
year old black Nissan Maxima rolled slowly past the small
nondescript black and white sign announcing *Sanderson City
Limit.*

Nothing. That's what he saw. Nothing. Like the sign, nondescript.

No people. No cars. Only a few old rundown houses and mobile
homes and several small deserted, dilapidated commercial buildings
that looked like they had not served a customer in fifty years. Jake
wondered if some wicked viral plague had wiped out the entire town
or if one of south Georgia's spring tornadoes had blown through and
sucked everyone up into the humid blue sky that was dotted with
dirty white clouds and whisked them away to Oz. Jake was already
getting depressed, or more accurately, more depressed.

Driving deeper into the community hidden in the southwest
corner of the state, Jake began noticing signs of civilization and
he let out a deep sigh of relief. On the east side of Highway 99 he
passed the cluttered Kountry Kitchen convenience store, offering
Georgia Lottery tickets, ice cold drinks for seventy-five cents
and milk for three twenty-five a gallon. Business looked slow at
Jabbo's Auto Repairs, housed in an old converted barn that was in
considerable need of repair itself. A bit farther down the highway,
Jake managed a smile when he noticed a familiar friend on one
corner of an otherwise barren crossroads. "This place can't be all

bad. At least they have a Waffle House," he said thankfully, fondly visualizing a plateful of cheese and eggs, raisin toast and hash browns.

As in most small towns, no matter their geography, the highway soon became Main Street, a narrow venue with one traffic light, lined with dogwood trees in distressed wood planters. Most of the stores were moms and pops in old buildings, well-maintained but definitely showing their age. A dress boutique, a barbecue joint, an antique shop and a Western Auto on the right side of the street first caught Jake's attention. The city government complex, a set of two aging brick buildings that included the police department, was on the opposite side of the street. Charming was the word that came to Jake's mind as he continued down Main Street. Charming sounded better than antiquated. This was a town of the 1960s, the type of wide spot in the road he vaguely remembered from childhood trips with his family and coffee table books, an abundance of which his mother always had scattered throughout their house. Jake knew the people here would be pleasant and hospitable and happy with their lives. Sanderson certainly would be a nice place to visit, but he wasn't crazy with the idea of having to live here. A more appropriate name for the tiny town would be The Sticks. It was 40 miles from the nearest interstate highway, and 50 miles from a town large enough to have its name in bold letters on the state map.

Looking for the office of the Sanderson Sentinel, Jake poked along Main Street much slower than the posted 25 miles an hour. If he drove any faster, he would miss the newspaper office and be headed out of town. "There it is," he said to himself while pulling his Maxima into an angled parking space between two dirty, dented pickup trucks. The thin Sentinel storefront was flanked by T.J.'s Pawn Shop on the right, and Hansen's Farm Bureau Insurance Agency on the left. With both hands gripping the steering wheel, Jake sat motionless for five minutes, seriously contemplating cranking the Maxima and fleeing, but he knew he couldn't. He had no one to blame but himself for this predicament, and the Sanderson Sentinel offered his best, his only option.

Jake ran his fingers through his closely cropped brown hair that was showing specks of gray, took a deep breath and again talking to himself, urged, "Let's do this!" Stepping out of the car and on to the sidewalk, he was passed by a middle-aged woman with her headful of brown hair wadded in a tight bun. She offered a smile and a cheerful "Hello" as she walked by. Jake nodded and proceeded to the door of the Sentinel office. With his hand on the metal push bar of the glass door, he paused for a moment before going in.

Jake had barely set foot inside before he was greeted with another cheerful "Hello" by a bespectacled smiling older woman with a chubby face and silver hair. She was sitting at an uncluttered desk toward the back of the narrow front office which had brick walls painted ugly olive green. One wall was lined with old photos and certificates and plaques the Sentinel had received down through the years. The room had a definite newsprint scent.

"I'm Jake Martin. I'm here to see Mr. House."

The woman got up, walked around to the front of her desk and extended her hand to Jake. "Nice to meet you Mr. Martin. I'm Hazel Jennings. Mr. House is expecting you. Come with me." She led Jake down a short narrow hallway to an office whose door was open. "Mr. House, Mr. Martin is here to see you."

Jake was surprised. Stephen House couldn't be older than 28 or 29. His blond hair was a little too long and he was wearing an open collar, short sleeve pale blue oxford cloth shirt, khaki pants and penny loafers without socks. Jake was expecting someone much older and much less contemporary. House shook Jake's hand and invited him to sit down. Hazel excused herself, saying she would be back shortly with glasses of ice tea. Jake took a moment to study the young man's office. A three shelf oak bookcase was three-quarters full with novels, biographies and self-help guides, and a letter-size wire tray on the corner of his desk was filled with unopened mail. The burgundy sofa and two matching upholstered side chairs looked like they had been there awhile. The only adornment on one of the off-white walls was a large gold-framed portrait of a stately old gentleman. The opposite wall held Stephen House's University of Georgia diploma and several University of Georgia Bulldog plaques.

"Did you enjoy your drive down Main Street? All ten seconds worth?" House asked, a sizable grin spreading across his face.

"Looks like a nice little town."

"It is. How long did it take you to get down here?"

"About five and a half hours. But I took my time. This is new territory for me."

"It's not Atlanta, is it?"

"That's for sure."

"It's a different lifestyle here. Things are real laid back, real slow. But the people are really nice. You won't find better people anywhere than the folks here in Sanderson."

"I don't doubt that at all."

Hazel arrived with the tea and Jake and Stephen both took long sips. She stood in the room, waiting for the verdict on her beverage.

"This is great! Sweetened just right," Jake nodded appreciatively.

Hazel smiled, nodded in return and started to leave the room. "Thank you Hazel," Stephen told her.

Jake took another swallow. "This may be the best tea I've ever had," he told Stephen.

"Just wait till you taste her cooking. You'll have to push yourself away from the table. You'll gain weight. Eating her cooking is how

9

I got this gut," Stephen said, patting his stomach that Jake thought looked as flat as most of the abs in the cheesy television infomercials for exercise equipment.

"She's your receptionist?"

"And a little bit of everything else too. This place couldn't run without her. You're going to like working with her. You *are* going to take the job, aren't you?"

Jake's eyes bulged at Stephen's question. "Aren't you supposed to interview me first, ask me some questions, make sure I'm the right person for the job?"

"Nah. You can do this job in your sleep. In fact, you're way too qualified for this job. I'm surprised you even came down here. But I'm glad you did."

Jake didn't know what to think about Stephen offering him the job so quickly. "Uh, well, if you don't have any questions for me, can I ask you a few?"

"Sure. Ask away."

"The ad said you needed a publisher, slash, editor, slash reporter."

"Yeah, you'll be doing everything. I want someone who can come in and run the Sentinel. Reporting, designing pages, making editorial decisions, making sure we're not spending more money than we're making, helping Hazel with the day-to-day operation. You'll definitely be hands-on."

"I can do that. It might take me a few days to get up to speed, but I can do that. Let me guess," Jake paused. "You grew up around this newspaper and you've been taking care of all of those things."

Stephen smiled and took another sip of tea. He smiled at Jake again. "This is my father's paper," he started, nodding in the direction of the portrait hanging on the wall. "He spent 50 years building this paper. Dad died last fall."

"I'm sorry."

"Thanks. He dropped dead of a heart attack one night during a city council meeting. He'd gotten really upset at the mayor during the meeting. The doctor doesn't know if that had anything to do with the heart attack, but as crazy as this sounds, it was appropriate that Dad died that way. Cowboys die with their boots on. Dad died with his pocket tape recorder on. He was always passionate about this town and this newspaper. I'm thankful he went like that instead of cancer eating at him for months or Alzheimer's taking his mind. I don't know if I could have handled that."

"And now you are taking over for your father and need some help?"

"Not exactly." House got up from his chair and sat on the corner of his desk to be closer to Jake. "Dad left me the Sentinel in his will, but I don't want it. I know he always wanted me to take over. That was his plan from the time I wrote my first story in crayon in Mrs. Smith's second grade class. That's why he insisted I go to the University of Georgia and study mass communications." House paused and looked at the portrait of Stephen Henderson House, Esquire. "I loved my Dad and I still miss him. A lot. You'll never meet a finer man. But I don't want this newspaper. What I want to do is get away from this place a year or two so I can decide on my own what to do."

Jake looked at the elder House's portrait. "Sounds reasonable to me."

"There's another reason I want to leave. You probably know what it is. I don't want to be compared to my father. There is no comparison. He was an icon in this town. I don't want to follow in his footsteps. Not here, anyway. The people here expect me to be my Dad, and I'm not."

"That's a tough spot to be in. What about your mother? What does she think? Any brothers or sisters who want the paper?"

"Mom died three years ago. I'm an only child."

"Can't you just sell it? I'm sure there are some media groups that would love to have the Sentinel."

"I wish I could. Dad was smart and crafty. That's why he was so successful. His will states that I can't sell the Sentinel for five years. I guess he figured that if I had to stay around that long, I might decide that running the Sentinel isn't all that bad, and I would change my mind. I checked with lawyers. The will's ironclad. But it doesn't say that I can't pay someone to come in and run the Sentinel for me while I'm off on my vision quest. That's where you come in."

"I'm flattered, but moving here would be a huge change for me."

"City boy in the country, right?"

"Right . . ." Jake hesitated. ". . . and there's some things I need to tell you."

"You don't have to tell me anything."

"I need to . . ."

"No you don't. It's in the past."

Jake was puzzled. "Why me? This state is full of good newspaper people, and I am certain some of them applied for this job. Why me, with all my baggage?"

"Why not you? Trust me, Jake, this is not a decision I made on a whim. I've done my due diligence. You're good at what you do, aren't you?"

"At one time I was."

"I think you still are. And I think that right now, you need someone to believe in you."

Jake felt the flush inching across his face. "I can't argue with that."

"I may not want to run the Sentinel, but that doesn't mean I don't care about it. I do. It's been a big part of my life. It has provided a wonderful living for my family and put me in a position to where I can leave and roam around for a long time without having to worry about money. I want someone here who will care about this newspaper as much as I do. I know your background. I know when you were starting out, you spent some time at small newspapers in small towns, maybe not as isolated or as small as we are here, but you know the small town dynamics. I think going back to your roots will do you good. And obviously, I think it will be good for the Sentinel."

Jake was touched by Stephen's passion and insight, which to him, showed a maturity not evident by his appearance and age.

"You *are* right," Jake admitted after a quick moment of reflection. "I do know a little about small town newspapers. And I know most of them don't have much of a staff. Sometimes it's a one-man show. What about here?"

"You've got a good staff. It's not big, but it's adequate. Hazel handles the classifieds and keeps the books. She's been here forever. Millard Lancaster sells advertising. He's worked for us almost as long as Hazel. Kenny Richards is a student at the community college over in Freeburg and helps with sports and general news. You'll find out quickly that high school sports are big around here. Heck, it's our major form of entertainment. Kenny's good. He'll be a big help to you. And we've got Mr. Abner, a retiree, who helps us deliver papers to the post office and our retail outlets."

"What's the circulation?"

13

"Less than 2,000. But I guarantee you every one of those 2,000 people read every word of that paper when they get it every Thursday. People will stop you on the street, and they will be able to talk to you about every line you've written."

Jake studied Stephen's youthful face and took a moment to digest what he had heard. He appreciated Stephen's sincere desire to find the right caretaker for the Sentinel, but was this what he really wanted to do? Then again, did he have any other choice? He glanced down at the floor and then looked directly at Stephen who was still sitting on the corner of his desk. Jake took a visibly deep breath and asked, "What about money?" If Jake admitted the truth, he was hoping Stephen would make such a lowball offer there would be no way he could take the job. After all, small town newspapers have the well-deserved reputation of paying peanuts.

Stephen smiled, slipped off the desk and sat back in his chair. He leaned back and locked his fingers behind his head. "Tell you what," he started. "I'll let you decide what you make. You get with Hazel, look at the books and come up with a number that's O.K. with you and is something we can handle." Stephen leaned forward, crossed his forearms and propped them on his desk. "I'll make the pot even sweeter. You stay here five years, work hard to raise the value of the Sentinel, and I'll cut you in on five percent of what I sell it for."

Jake was flabbergasted by Stephen's offer. Five years was a long time, but Jake knew that even small papers in small towns bring a nice price. A five percent cut could be substantial, perhaps helping to set him up for an early retirement in Key West or the mountains of east Tennessee. "Are you sure about this?" Jake asked Stephen.

"I'll have my lawyer draw up a contract."

Jake squirmed in his chair and looked at the young man who seemed so confident and assured about what he was doing. "Mr. House," Jake started following a pensive pause. "You've got yourself an editor—and a reporter—and a publisher!"

"Terrific!" Stephen's eyes brightened. "When can you start?"

"How about in the next five minutes?"

"Don't you have to go back to Atlanta for your things?"

"All I have is in my car. I travel light."

Stephen chuckled. "I'll cut you some slack. You can start tomorrow. There's an extended stay lodge down the street. It stays full with migrant farm workers, but that might be a good place for you to stay temporarily. Talk to Hazel. She may know some places that are for rent. If you're wanting to buy, especially something new, I'm afraid the choices are slim. Down here we don't have a new subdivision on every corner like you do in Atlanta."

"Renting is fine for the time being. I don't need anything big and fancy."

Stephen smiled again. "That's good, because there's not very much down here that's big and fancy unless you're a banker or one of the bigger farmers. Just good hard working folks who are living day to day, harvest to harvest."

"I really appreciate all of this. I'm not sure what to say, except thank you," Jake said as he rose from his chair.

"No, thank you," Stephen responded quickly. "I know you're going to do a great job for us, and I really believe you'll like living here. It'll take a little adjusting, but you can do it."

Jake nodded. The two men shook hands. The realization struck Jake that, at age 45, he was starting over from scratch at a little paper in a little town in a God-forsaken patch of Georgia. At least he was getting a second chance. And whom did he have to thank? A kid who was young enough to be his son.

15

CHAPTER THREE

The Sentinel, the little newspaper in the little town where matters of consequence seldom occurred, kept Jake busy during his first week. A procession of visitors, many of whom were local merchants hoping for a free plug for their enterprises from the new editor, kept Jake from getting much done during the day, meaning he had to work evenings, which was hardly an inconvenience, considering that Sanderson's limited night life revolved around high school activities, Wednesday night prayer meeting at the local churches and Thursday night BINGO at the American Legion. Hazel's matronly friends made certain Jake was fed well, deluging him with pot roast, fried chicken, squash casserole and banana pudding. Jake joked with Hazel that if the food continued flowing, his expanding waist would quickly outgrow the claustrophobic office he had chosen down the narrow hall from Stephen House's more spacious domain. Five minutes into Jake's first day on the job, Robert McIntire, one of the town's three Realtors, dropped in, offering a welcome basket of fresh fruit, his business card and assistance in helping Jake find a residence. Following Stephen's advice, Jake had rented a room at the extended stay lodge on the south side of town. The place wasn't very clean and he wasn't impressed with his fellow lodgers, who left early every morning and arrived back late, but it would do for a few days. McIntire, a tall balding fellow, had his sales spiel cut short by Charles Chambers, gregarious president of the Sanderson Rotary Club who arrived to invite Jake to their noon meeting the following day. Shortly thereafter, soft-spoken, gray-haired Stanley Allen, long-time pastor of Sanderson First Baptist Church, came through, inviting Jake to the Sunday 11 a.m. worship service. Other visitors were steady and frequent. Jake appreciated their hospitality, and he greeted them all with grace and humility, but he quickly grew weary. He was ready to get down to work. He had much to learn about the Sentinel.

As eager as Stephen was to leave town, he was prepared to stay and tutor Jake until he was comfortable enough to run the paper on his own. Jake was impressed with his boss' knowledge and patience in going over hundreds of details, and how smoothly and efficiently the newspaper operated. There was an air of professionalism at the Sentinel, something that Jake had noticed missing with many small town papers and even larger publications.

With Stephen doing most of the work and Jake looking over his shoulder, the duo put together the next issue of the Sentinel. The headline front page article was about the death of banker Gregory Carson, which, for one of the few times in the Sentinel's history, resulted in every single copy being sold, even with a press run of 500 extra copies. Most readers were disappointed. Police Chief Edgar Quinn had admitted little for publication other than the death was still being investigated, which was somewhat pointless since many of the details surrounding the death had already circulated through the local gossip pipeline. Following a gentleman's agreement that had been forged shortly after Quinn took over as chief, Stephen printed only what Quinn told him he could print. Jake didn't agree with that arrangement, but it was the relationship many small town papers grudgingly accepted to keep from alienating one of their biggest news sources—the local police chief or sheriff. And if that is what Stephen House and Quinn had settled on, Jake was certainly too new in Sanderson to start rocking a steadily sailing ship. So, while the breakfast club at Waffle House and the ladies getting their hair done at the Style Shop were speculating about Gregory's lover, the Sentinel dutifully and boringly extolled his community involvement. His most recent project was working with the city council to lure a small sign making company that was considering locating in the decaying ten acre industrial park on the west outskirts of town. Sanderson needed new jobs to lessen the dependence on the local farming economy. But even with the weak story about Gregory Carson and having to coddle Quinn, whom he had yet to meet, Jake was happy with his first week on the job.

With his first Sentinel on the streets, Jake had a day to catch his breath, go over a few more details of the paper's operation with Hazel and reflect on his first week in Sanderson. He had no complaints. The people were friendly, almost too friendly, the staff at the Sentinel had made him feel comfortable and welcome, and he had been too busy to get bored or depressed. Now, he wanted to spend some time looking over the town, learning where everything was, and finding a more permanent place of residence—on his own, without the help of Robert McIntire. His plans for the day changed when Kenny Richards asked him to tag along for a story at Barber County High School and the afternoon baseball clash between the Barber County Pirates and their hated rivals, the Eagleton Eagles from adjoining Okefenokee County.

Jake had quickly learned how valuable Kenny Richards was to the Sentinel. A life-long resident of Sanderson, he knew everyone and everything that was going on. He eagerly tackled any assignment and showed quality writing for a 20 year-old who was still two months away from an associate degree at the nearby community college. He did good work, covering everything from council meetings to cattle sales, but his passion was sports. He had earned letters in football, basketball and track at Barber County High, but readily admitted his athletic career was undistinguished, due mainly to his size, or more appropriately, lack of it. He only weighed 145 after eating a big meal, and his height might hit 5-7, if he had not had a hair cut in a month or so. A fourth place finish in the region hundred meters was the highlight of his career. Despite never logging much playing time, he was a team player, always cheering for his teammates, working hard in practice, doing whatever the coaches asked of him. Realizing he wasn't physically talented enough to earn an athletic scholarship to college, Kenny had turned to writing, intending to transfer to the University of Georgia for the upcoming fall semester and land a spot on the sports staff of The Red and Black, the student newspaper. Jake's first impression was that Kenny had a bright future in journalism and indeed, one day, would be covering the University of Georgia Bulldogs or the Atlanta Braves for a major daily.

But today his assignment was a cooking competition in Mrs. Hampton's home economics class at Barber County High School. Jake eagerly accepted Kenny's invitation to be a sidekick. Since so much of the town's activities centered on the school, Jake wanted to learn more about it and the teachers and students. Besides, the cooking competition sounded like fun and Kenny had excitedly told him they would get to sample the wares. Another tidbit Jake was quickly realizing: Sanderson's females, young and old, knew how to cook.

Pulling into the front parking lot of Barber County High School, Jake thought he was back in metro Atlanta. Instead of the three room, wood-sided, tin roofed, no air conditioning country school he had conjured up with his snooty, big city bias, Jake discovered a contemporary brick and sandstone one-story structure that would fit in nicely in any of Atlanta's smarmy suburban neighborhoods. When Jake admitted his off-target perception, Kenny quickly retorted, "You mean you haven't heard? When we built this new school a few years ago, we wanted to do something to pay tribute to our old school, which was exactly like you described. So, the school board chose to keep the toilets outdoors. Saved us money installing a sewer system too. By the way Jake. You haven't lived until you've pulled splinters from your butt after using the outhouse!"

"Oh? So you're a comedian as well as a reporter," Jake said, mocking Kenny's tale. "That joke stinks so badly it belongs in an outhouse."

"You think I'm joking? Wait until you see the pig pen in back of the school."

"I get the idea," Jake smiled. "Despite my delusions, you folks down here are living in the twenty-first century."

Kenny responded seriously, "I'm not kidding about the pig pen."

"Yeah, right. Maybe you should consider writing comedy instead of sports."

"Seriously, we do have a pig pen. There is one in back of the school—way back—for the Future Farmers." He laughed, admitted he was joking and motioned Jake to follow him into the school.

They walked through the front door into a spacious, open circular common area that had three hallways extending like spokes. The administrative offices were to the left, with a sign that prominently requested *Visitors, Please Sign In At The Office.* Kenny started walking down a hallway toward classrooms when Jake grabbed him by the shirt and asked, "Don't we need to check in?"

"They know what we're here for," Kenny replied assuredly. He waved at two ladies sitting at desks in the glass-encased office and they waved back. Jake waved too, even though he had no idea who the women were and they waved back. They smiled and Jake smiled back and he followed Kenny down the hallway. The wonderful aromas of food got more intense. "Man, that smells good!" Jake said in admiration as the scent of freshly baked bread wafted through the hallway.

They reached the Home Economics suite which was crowded with girls putting the final touches on their creations. Jake was impressed to see three male students in the mix, seriously and painstakingly working on precisely the right presentation for their culinary delights.

"Everyone looks so young," Jake said, shaking his head.

"They *are* young," Kenny explained to him.

"Yeah, I guess they are," is all Jake could reply. He realized how many years had passed since he set foot in a high school, even as a reporter.

Kenny introduced Jake to Maddie Hampton, the long-time home economics teacher. Jake thought she was a nice-looking woman, perhaps a couple of years younger than him, four or five inches shorter than his 5-11, with short brunette hair and green eyes. She thanked Jake and Kenny for coming, urged them to sample all the contest entries, and excused herself to welcome parents and faculty members and get the program started. Jake stood in a corner and waited until most everyone had filled their plates before getting in line. Kenny was busy snapping photos and talking to some of the young chefs about their recipes.

Jake loaded his plate and found an unoccupied table. He didn't want to think about the grams of fat and carbohydrates that were in the fried chicken and pasta salad, bread and strawberry cheesecake he had mounded on his plate. A hefty glass of sugar-laden ice tea helped send Jake's caloric intake off the chart. But as guilty as he felt, he still ate every bite. The seemingly endless supply of food from the well-intentioned folks in Sanderson was putting Jake's goal of maintaining his weight at 190 in serious jeopardy.

He was contemplating going after another dessert selection when Maddie Hampton joined him at the table. Jake glanced across the room and smiled when he saw Kenny with one of the female contestants. Jake didn't think Kenny was working at that moment. He was flirting with the cute leggy blonde in the short denim skirt.

"So, what do you think of our young chefs?" Mrs. Hampton asked before taking a bite of a chocolate chip cookie.

"They're very good. I offer you my plate as evidence," Jake replied while waving his hand toward the few crumbs that remained.

"These are all juniors and seniors. They've got some experience. Now, the freshmen and sophomores, the freshmen especially . . ." Mrs. Hampton stopped to smile. ". . . for instance, have you ever sampled salmon and eggs?"

"Uh, no. That, I believe I will pass on."

"Kenny says you're taking over the Sentinel so Stephen can satisfy his wanderlust."

"That's right."

"We all knew Stephen wanted to leave. I don't blame him. In fact, I admire him. Here, he'd always be in his Dad's shadow. Mr. House was revered in this town. Stephen needs to go some place where he can be his own man."

"I hope he finds what he's looking for."

Mrs. Hampton finished off the cookie before asking Jake, "Is Sanderson what you're looking for? How in the world did you manage to find your way to our quaint little village?"

"The story's too long to tell. Let's just say I'm thankful for the opportunity Stephen has given me."

"Where are you from?"

"I've spent a lot of time in the Atlanta area."

"Atlanta? Wow! I guess you're experiencing culture shock."

"A little bit, but this is a nice place. The people are great."

"Yes, they are. This is a wonderful little town. I've lived here all my life."

"You've never had the itch to go somewhere bigger, with a few more things to offer, like job opportunities?"

Before she could answer, two bubbly coeds rushed up to the table. "Mrs. Hampton, may Emily and I leave a few minutes early?" asked one of the girls, a wispy non-stop talker with too much makeup and a mop of brown ringlets. "We've got some spirit signs we want to put up at the baseball field."

"Sure Laura," Mrs. Hampton smiled. "As long as you've cleaned up your mess."

"Thanks," replied the other girl, taller and more filled out and deserving of a second look, thanks to a tight-fitting red shirt. Both girls took time to hug Mrs. Hampton before bouncing away.

"That's why I'm still in Sanderson," the teacher explained. "I thought about leaving a few years ago when my husband died, and once, after that, but it didn't take long for me to realize this is where I belong. All my friends are here, my mom and Dad live down the street from me, and I've got the greatest job in the world. I've known all these children I'm teaching since they were born. They never give me any trouble."

"I'm sorry about your husband."

"He was killed by a drunk driver. John was coming home from Destin, Florida. He had been deep sea fishing with an old friend. The other driver came across the center line and hit John head on. He died on the spot. The drunk walked away with a few scratches and a broken arm."

"I don't know what to say. I'm truly sorry for your loss."

Maddie replied to Jake with an expression that to him seemed much too peaceful for someone who had suffered such a tragedy. She smiled. "I try to find something good out of every situation. "Yes, I lost my husband, but a drunk driver went to jail for a very long time, meaning he won't hurt anyone else. And the accident caused some of my students to reassess their driving—and drinking—habits. So yes, I did have a tragic personal loss, but other people benefited."

Jake could only shake his head in admiration. "It's wonderful you can see things that way. I wouldn't be able to."

"Yes you could, if you put your trust in God. What about you? Any family?"

"I'm divorced. No kids. They never were a priority. Do you have children?"

"I've got one, a son. Robbie can tell you about wanderlust. He went off to college last year—to the University of Hawaii. Talk about getting as far away from home as you can!"

Jake smiled in reply and looked at Kenny who was still talking to the blonde girl. Mrs. Hampton noticed Jake sneaking a peak at the young reporter. "Kenny's smitten with her," she explained. "He's working hard to grow their relationship, but it has been difficult. She's shy and not very sociable. It's ironic that her name is Sunny, because that's not her personality. I don't think her home life is very good. She's starting to blossom a bit. I've tried to pay her some extra attention, and so have Kenny and Janet Wayne, the manager of our public library."

"She's a pretty girl. I can understand why Kenny would be attracted to her." Jake changed the subject as Kenny started toward him and Mrs. Hampton.

"Had enough to eat?" Kenny asked Jake.

"Too much. I need a nap."

"No time to nap. The game starts in thirty minutes. We need to get to the field, or we won't find a seat."

"Did you know that Kenny was an excellent home economics student?" Mrs. Hampton smiled, first at Kenny and then at Jake.

"Kenny? No, I didn't know that. He neglected to tell me."

"Yeah, I'm awesome at boiling hot dogs. The only reason I took the class was I needed an elective."

Mrs. Hampton immediately refuted Kenny. "He's being too modest," she explained. "His senior year he finished second in our end-of-school cook-off. His chicken and rice casserole was marvelous!"

"Can we go on to the game?" Kenny requested.

"Before you go," Mrs. Hampton interrupted. "We have these cook-offs regularly. Would you like to be added to the list of judges?" she asked Jake.

"Absolutely, provided you tell me there's a gym around here somewhere so I can work off all the calories you'll be feeding me."

"I'm sure Coach Vaught won't mind you using the football team's weight room. I'll call you."

Jake and Kenny left the home economics room and headed down a back hallway to the baseball field. "That'd be something if you and Mrs. Hampton hooked up," Kenny suggested to Jake's surprise.

"I'm not interested in hooking up with anyone. Right now, I've got my hands full trying to take care of me. But what about you? The little blonde's a cutie."

"She's a sweet girl. She's just got some issues to work through right now. As much as anything, she needs a friend, and that's what I am right now, her friend."

"Bull crap! You expect me to believe that? As difficult as you may find this to believe, I was once a hormone-ravaged teenage boy. A girl that cute, all I would be thinking about is getting in her pants. To heck with this friend stuff." Jake cringed as the last word came out of his mouth. He didn't know Kenny well enough to say something like that, even as a joke.

Kenny put his hand to his heart in fake indignation. "I assure you, Mr. Martin, that my intentions toward the young lady are totally honorable. But if she and I are ever together and she asks if she can give me a hand—with my homework or whatever—I'm not going to object."

"How noble of you," Jake grinned. "This fair maiden of yours, what grade is she in?"

"She's a senior. I'm trying to talk her into going to the University of Georgia. She's got the grades. I think it would be good for her to get away from home. Her father is a jerk. No, he's more than that. He's an asshole."

"Tell me how you really feel about him. And the fact that you're going to transfer to Georgia doesn't have anything to do with your suggestion that she go there, right?"

Kenny smiled. "What do you think?" he asked Jake. Before Jake could answer, Kenny added, "Hey, you want to make a friendly wager on this game, say for lunch one day?"

"I don't think so. Besides, if we did, I would be at a competitive disadvantage. You know all there is to know about these two teams. I don't know anything about them. You wouldn't be trying to pull a fast one on me, would you Kenny?"

"No sir, just trying to supplement my severely insufficient salary from the Sentinel. You know, a young man about town like me needs some operating cash."

"Yeah, there's so much here in Sanderson to spend it on. Just be careful with your friendly wagers."

"It's harmless. A bunch of us guys do it all the time. Look at how packed this place is," Kenny pointed out as they walked out of the school building and got a first glimpse at the field.

Jake quickly had another of his rural perceptions shattered. Three hundred fans, a crowd many of the larger Atlanta high school teams could only dream of and hope for, had gathered for this battle between two long-time rivals in Georgia's classification of its smallest schools. From his earlier—much earlier—life as a sports reporter, Jake knew few other high schools and many of the state's small colleges did not have fields as nice as Barber County's, which had a double-decker brick press box and concession stand, a nine inning electronic scoreboard and aluminum seating that created quite a racket when spectators stomped their feet.

Barber County and Eagleton, thirteen miles apart, were bitter adversaries in sports, debate, even band. Off the field, the kids got along well, many attending the same churches and showing up at the same parties. On the field, friendships were forgotten. The rivalry was intense, usually fueled by the impact the contests had on the region standings. Nine years out of ten, either Barber County or Eagleton was region champ, particularly in baseball or basketball.

Jake immediately sensed the depth of the rivalry. Fans from both teams were screaming before the first pitch was thrown, and they got louder inning by inning. Kenny was doing his share of the yelling. Jake tried to explain to him a reporter is supposed to be neutral and not be hollering louder than the fans, but Kenny's reply was, "No way! Not when we're playing Eagleton!"

The game seesawed back and forth, the teams swapping the lead several times with the fans continually trading insults. Trailing 7-6, the Pirates brought the home fans to their feet in the bottom of the fifth inning when their skinny shortstop, displaying surprising power, connected solidly with a fastball, drilling a line drive that one-hopped against the chain link fence in centerfield, sending the runner from first base blazing toward home plate with the run that would tie the game.

The ball and the runner arrived at the burly Eagleton catcher at the same time. Ignoring Georgia High School Association rules, the runner crashed into the catcher, causing the ball to fly toward the backstop and his mask toward the first base dugout. The collision knocked both players down and created a cloud of dust. After a quick moment to get their bearings, both players hopped to their feet and

27

the Barber County runner rushed the Eagleton catcher, sending him back to the ground with a form tackle Coach Vaught and the football team would have loved. With the crowd screaming, both benches emptied and players engaged in several small shoving matches that featured language harsher than the shoves. The spectators were more serious. Two dozen fans streamed out of the stands and were soon on the field tossing punches and demonstrating headlocks and other holds they had learned from Saturday Night Wrestling on cable TV. Twice Kenny had attempted to leap over the fence and join the fray, but both times, Jake grabbed him by the shirt tail and chided, "No way. You *are* staying impartial in all of this." It was an ugly, ugly scene, particularly two profanity-spewing Daddies in blue jeans and t-shirts who were entwined, flailing away at each other, some of their punches connecting and others missing wildly. Coaches from the two teams managed to separate their players, but considerable jawing was still going on. The spectators and parents continued screaming at each other, ready to resume fighting if provoked just the slightest bit more.

Two shotgun blasts rattled the air, causing the majority of the combatants to stop. The two foul-mouthed Daddies didn't. Their confrontation was getting more intense, more violent. One of the Daddies was big and chiseled, with a body an Atlanta Falcons' lineman would envy. The other was short and as thin as a drinking straw, but was fighting with the ferocity of a feral cat that is about to be put down at the animal shelter.

Two more shotgun blasts rang across the field. "All right, people. Enough is enough!" Chief Edgar Quinn commanded in a deep voice. Quinn, thick in the waist, six feet tall and, red-headed, usually didn't have to give orders more than once for them to be obeyed. He headed purposefully to the two combative Daddies and pulled them apart.

"You son of a bitch! I'll kill you. First chance I get, I'm going to kill you!" the bigger Daddy screamed at the other Daddy. Blood from a scratch on his forehead was trickling down his right cheek. He lunged toward his opponent, but Quinn pulled him back.

"You're not killing anybody, Joe Lambert!" Quinn scolded. "Now get your sorry ass out of here before I put it in jail. Same for you, Todd. Go home! The rest of you too. This game is over!"

"But we need to finish this game Chief," pleaded the frazzled Barber County coach, his white jersey stretched and pulled out of his pants. Winner is in first in the region."

"I don't give a damn if the winner gets to play the New York Yankees in the World Series! Game's over. I'll let the high school association deal with the two teams. Right, Mr. Ump?" Quinn asked as he glanced at the dazed and confused home plate umpire who was standing by himself on the pitcher's mound.

"Uh, that's right Chief. I'll have to file a report."

"Well, you go file your report. The rest of you, go home!" Quinn had his right hand clamped firmly on the back of the neck of Joe Lambert, the goliath who was squirming to get free and still swearing at tiny but tough Todd Monroe. "Damn you! Ow!" Lambert screamed as the chief dug his fingers deeper into his neck.

"Am I going to have to throw you in jail, Joe?" Quinn asked.

Lambert quit struggling. "No," he replied in a calmer voice. "But that son of a bitch's boy didn't have any business bowling over my boy like that. It's against the rules!"

"Since when did playing by the rules mean anything to either one of you? Now get the hell out of here!" Quinn barked.

Todd Monroe, sporting a large welt under his right eye, wasn't ready to shut up. "You're right Chief. That bastard or anyone in his family has never played by the rules. They're a bunch of cheats and backstabbers!"

Lambert screamed and jerked out of Quinn's grasp. Quinn deftly stuck out his foot, tripping Lambert and causing him to fall face flat on the ground. Quinn grabbed the man by the hair and jerked him to his feet. Todd Monroe, who had stepped forward itching to resume the fight, stopped dead in his tracks when Quinn warned, "Don't you even think about it!" Monroe mumbled something under his breath and walked away.

Back on his feet, Joe Lambert wiped dirt off his shirt and, escorted by Officer Landry, spouted every cuss word known to man as he walked to his pickup truck. He sped off, his tires leaving black rubber marks in the parking lot. The crowd had scattered and order had been restored.

Jake was standing by the third base fence, taking in the way the police chief had diffused the situation and keeping a hand on Kenny who still wanted to put his two cents worth into the fracas. "He has a way of getting your attention and making people listen. He must be a strong son of a gun to be able to clamp on to that big dude the way he did," Jake said in admiration.

"That's Chief Quinn. He's pretty easy-going, but when he tells you to do something, you'd better do it," Kenny explained. "Now can I go talk to some people and get some information for a story on all of this?"

"Yeah, go ahead. Just stay out of trouble yourself. You're working, remember," Jake warned as he began walking toward Chief Quinn who had just patted Barber County Principal Connery on the shoulder, sending her home as well.

"Whose parent are you?" Quinn grumbled as Jake approached. Quinn took two sticks of Black Jack chewing gum out of his shirt pocket, stuffed them in his mouth and wadded up the wrappers before sticking them back in his pocket.

"I don't have a dog in this fight. I'm Jake Martin with the Sentinel."

"Oh, the new guy. Nice to meet you," Quinn said as he extended his hand.

"Same here. You did a fantastic job dismantling this melee. I was afraid someone was going to get hurt."

"Thanks. I hope this didn't give you too bad a first impression of our town. Folks here are actually pretty nice. They just take their high school sports way too seriously." Quinn was giving the chewing gum a pounding.

"So I noticed. It's not that way where I'm from."

"Where's that?"

"Atlanta."

"Atlanta? Big city boy, huh? How in the heck did you end up here?"

"It's a long story."

"I'd like to hear it some time."

"Maybe. How about you? Are you a local?"

"Heck no. Charlotte."

"Charlotte? Big city boy, huh? How in the heck did you end up here?"

"It's a long story."

"I'd like to hear it some time."

"Call me. We'll go over to the Waffle House and compare stories."

"Sounds good. I'll buy. Tell me, Chief. Does this school have a pig pen?"

Quinn grunted and walked off the field. Jake stood at third base, thinking little ole Sanderson might not be so boring after all.

CHAPTER FOUR

The baseball brawl captured the attention of everyone in Sanderson and the High School Athletic Association one hundred miles to the north. For three days, Jake and Kenny spent an inordinate amount of their time writing about and rehashing the incident with mammas and Daddies and fans who were concerned that the high school governing body would come down hard on both teams, levying heavy fines or perhaps suspending play for the rest of the season. The fine, no matter how large, would not be a problem. The townsfolk would raise the money in a matter of hours. Ending the season would be a bitter pill for Barber County to swallow, since the Pirates would likely win the region and stood a good chance to go deep in the state playoffs. Jake was amazed that no one was apologizing for what took place. They were behaving as if the brawl was a normal part of the competition. Jake just knew he was tired of hearing so many people whine about a high school baseball game, and he was ready for the high school association to render its ruling. Or maybe he wasn't ready for that. If the decision was to take away the Pirates' opportunity to play, then all the phone calls, visits and letters to the editor would start all over, but at an even more intense level.

Stephen House walked into Jake's office, and before he could say anything, Jake cracked at him, "If you're here to talk about that stupid baseball game, I don't want to hear it!"

Stephen laughed and sat down in front of Jake's desk. "I told you these folks take their high school sports seriously," he said.

"I believe you now. It's a miracle someone didn't come away from all of that with major league injuries. Especially Mr. Dumb and Mr. Dumber. What is it with those guys?"

"Ah, Joe Lambert and Todd Monroe. There's always been bad blood between them. Their Daddies got tangled up in a bad business deal that left a lot of hard feelings, and now their sons are bitter enemies. Trey Lambert should be going to school at Barber County, but his Dad makes him go to Eagleton because Nick Monroe is at Barber County. For the most part, all they do is a lot of mouthing off, but Joe does have a bad temper."

"They were doing more than mouthing off that day. One of them might have done something they would regret later if Quinn hadn't shown up."

"Quinn doesn't take foolishness off anyone. But around here, a fight at a baseball game or some high school kids drag racing is about all he has to deal with. Sanderson isn't exactly the Crime Capitol of the United States. Gregory Carson's little fatal adventure was the most excitement we've had around here in a long time."

"How did Quinn end up here in Sanderson?"

"Talk to him some time. You two have a lot in common. So, what do you think about our little town?"

"It certainly hasn't been boring. Between learning what I'm supposed to be doing here at the Sentinel, trying to calm everyone down about that brawl, and keeping up with all the gossip about the banker and the bondage queen, I haven't had time to be bored. The people here are nice. Gossipy, but nice."

"I'm glad you're feeling comfortable, because I'm about to leave you. I'm driving up to Atlanta tomorrow, selling my car, and catching a plane to the west coast. I don't know when I'll be back."

Jake took a deep breath. "Well, I think I can handle everything, but I wish you'd stay a while longer. What if I decide I don't fit in here? Or what if I botch things up?"

"You won't botch things up, and you fit in here. I can already tell. Besides, if you don't make it here, where else would you go?"

"You've got a point," Jake admitted humbly as he dropped his head.

"Don't take what I said the wrong way," Stephen assured. "I firmly believe this is the place you're supposed to be at this point in your life. Good things are going to happen to you. You deserve that."

"Thanks. I hope you're right. I know I appreciate your trust in me."

"No, thank you. You're doing me a great favor. I feel very confident leaving the Sentinel in your hands so I can go off on my great journey."

"I wish you the best. I hope you find what you're looking for."

"So do I. I'm going to leave my cell phone number with Hazel, but I don't want to be bothered. Run this place the way you want to. I may call every now and then to see how things are going, but then again, I may not. Have you found a place to live yet?"

"I'm still at the extended stay lodge. I've been meaning to look, but I've been too busy."

"Good. Listen, I want you to stay at my house. I'm not going to sell it, not right this moment, any way, and I really don't want to rent it. You can stay there free, as long as you take care of the place, regular maintenance and that kind of stuff."

Jake looked at Stephen with disbelief. "That's incredibly gracious of you. Why are you being so good to me?"

"Oh this is a business arrangement. I expect you to take good care of my place."

"Thank you, Stephen. I'm speechless."

"That's good. I'm not paying you to talk. I'm paying you to write, and you do that well."

Their conversation ceased as Kenny rushed into Jake's office. "The high school association has made its ruling," the young reporter huffed. "A thousand dollar fine for each school and Trey Lambert and Nick Monroe have been suspended for the rest of the season. We can live with that. It could have been a lot worse. We'll miss Nick, but we'll get by. We can still win region and go to the playoffs."

"Good," Jake said with a sigh of relief. "I'm glad this whole mess is over."

"So am I," Stephen replied. He got out of his chair and shook Jake's hand. "Good luck," Stephen said.

"Same to you, Mr. House. Same to you." Jake said sincerely and with appreciation.

"And keep Kenny straight too," Stephen smiled.

"It's the other way around. I'm going to need Kenny to keep me straight. He's the one who knows everyone and everything."

Kenny blushed at the compliment. He didn't say anything.

"The boy does have a great future. He's great at schmoozing and shooting the bull. He would make a great politician," Stephen kidded. "Seriously, good luck Kenny."

"Thanks Mr. House. I'll miss you."

Stephen shook Kenny's hand, patted him on the shoulder, and shook Jake's hand again. He left and Kenny and Jake began talking. "I'm nervous," Jake admitted to Kenny.

"Nervous?"

"Yeah. Nervous. It's been a long time since I've been totally in charge of running a newspaper. I'm afraid I'll mess up."

"You won't mess up, Mr. Martin. And even if you do, so what? This isn't Atlanta. Not that many people would know. Shoot, there's not enough that happens around here for you to mess up unless you get the guest speaker's name wrong at the next garden club meeting."

Jake smiled. "You've got a point. So, do you think the high school association's ruling was reasonable?"

"Real reasonable. I think we got off easy. I was really worried that we'd have to forfeit the rest of the season. Everyone's relieved."

"Go ahead and start on the story for Thursday's paper. Be sure and get quotes from the coaches and school administrators. By the way, how's Sunny?"

"She's all right, I guess. I haven't talked to her in a few days."

"She's a cute girl. I'm sorry about the crude remark I made, you know, about getting into her . . ."

"No big deal. I know you were kidding. I'll admit my blood starts pumping a little faster when I look at her, especially those long legs, but seriously, we're just friends. She's very shy. I'm one of the few people she'll talk to."

"I understand," Jake responded. "My wife was shy when we first met." Realizing he had brought up a subject he didn't want to expand on, he quickly changed subjects. "Stephen is letting me stay at his house, but he didn't tell me where it is. Got time to taxi me there?"

"Sure. It's nice and has plenty of room. It's outside the city, sort of sits out by itself. You won't be bothered by neighbors." They were about to leave but Jake stopped to answer his phone. He looked seriously at Kenny as he listened intently to the caller. "Where?" Jake asked the caller. "Thanks," he said after having his question answered.

He looked at Kenny again. "I thought you said nothing ever happens around here."

"Nothing ever does."

"You might want to rethink that. The caller was suggesting we get out to Silver Lake. There's been a murder."

Kenny was out the door almost before Jake finished his sentence. Jake was right behind him.

CHAPTER FIVE

During the ten minute drive to Silver Lake, Kenny tried to recall the last murder in Sanderson and he couldn't. He wasn't counting Gregory Carson, because the conclusion was he had died of natural causes. The little town simply didn't have any violent crime. "Man, this is my first murder!" Kenny chirped with excitement. "Who was the caller? Did they say how the victim was killed?"

"The caller didn't identify themselves, and no, they didn't give any details. Calm down. This isn't like covering the Super Bowl or Final Four. Someone has died."

"You're right. I'm sorry. Do you remember your first murder?"

"No, but I'm certain I'll remember this one. Nothing bad is ever supposed to happen in this little town. Yeah, right!"

Following Kenny's directions, Jake continued to drive several miles until turning down a muddy dirt road into thick woods. The lake was on private property and a chain that usually blocked the road was down. The ride got bumpier as Jake's Maxima hit the ruts and rocks in the narrow road which seemed to go on forever. Finally, Jake spotted two Sanderson police cars, Quinn's unmarked cruiser and the coroner's van and pulled in behind them. He didn't know how any of the vehicles would get out, because there was no place to back up or turn around and the road was muddy from recent rains.

"This is a great place to dump a body," Jake admitted to Kenny as they got out of the car and started looking for Quinn. "Talk about being off the beaten path."

"The Taylors don't like people being on their property. They won't let anyone fish in the lake. I wonder who found the body."

"That's one of the things Quinn can tell us . . . if we can find him." Jake and Kenny stopped after a few steps to listen. They heard faint voices coming from a barely visible trail leading off the left of the road. "This way," Jake motioned to Kenny and they proceeded down the trail, having to push away briars and small trees with their hands. The wet ground squished under their feet. The voices got louder and thirty yards later, Jake and Kenny came to a small clearing. They both gasped. The nude body of a man was tied to the trunk of a dead pine tree that had fallen at a 45 degree angle. Quinn, Sam Rogers and Lawson Lockridge, all wearing blue latex gloves, were standing by the body. Quinn turned around when he heard the noise made by Jake stepping on a twig.

"What the hell are you two doing here?" Quinn asked in surprise and annoyance as he walked up to Jake and Kenny.

"It would be better for us to ask what you're doing here," Jake replied.

"Who told you we were here?"

"I got a phone call," Jake said as he and Kenny walked closer. Kenny's eyes were bulging.

"Who called?"

"I don't know. They didn't say."

"You shouldn't be here. This is a crime scene. We don't want anything disturbed."

"We won't get in your way. I promise."

Jake and Kenny weren't close enough to the body yet to distinguish facial details, but already Kenny had nervous beads of sweat popping up on his forehead. "This is the first time I've ever seen a real live dead person," he admitted nervously.

"A real live dead person?" Jake asked.

"Oh brother, I think I'm gonna barf!" Kenny put his hand to his stomach.

"Here chew this," Quinn said, offering Kenny two sticks of Black Jack gum. Quinn started chewing on a couple of sticks of the gum himself.

"Thanks," Kenny, breathing hard, said. His jaws began working double time. He started to toss the wrappers on the ground, but a dirty glance from Quinn made him choose instead to tuck them in his pants pocket.

"Martin, did you ever see anything like this in the big city?" Quinn asked while motioning Jake and Kenny closer. The corpse was tied with thin rope to the tree at the ankles, waist and hands, with his hands stretched over his head. The feet and hands were covered with blood. After a few seconds of studying the body, Jake realized that both of the man's big toes and thumbs had been cut off—raggedly. "God! What a mess!" Jake said, turning his head for a second to regain his composure from the wave of nausea roaring in his belly.

"That's Todd Monroe!" Kenny cried, his voice cracking. "I'm gonna throw up!" Kenny turned away and the vomit rolled.

"Damn it Kenny!" Quinn roared. "Don't puke on my crime scene!" Kenny was still bent forward with his hands resting on his knees, waiting for the second wave to come, and it did shortly. He managed to compose himself after a short rest and turned around to face Quinn and Jake. His face was red and tears were rolling down his cheeks. Quinn reached in the back pocket of his uniform pants and tossed Kenny a handkerchief.

"I suspect this poor son of a bitch bled to death," Quinn said, looking back at the bound body.

Jake, who was still fighting off nausea himself, studied the corpse's face. "This was one of the guys in the brawl at the baseball game. You folks do take your high school sports seriously."

"I doubt this had anything to do with that damn ball game." Having said that, Quinn quickly added, "But the first person I am going to talk to about this is Joe Lambert."

"They don't like each other," Kenny offered, his red, swollen eyes still glued to the lifeless body. "Oh man, I can't believe this. Got any more gum chief?" Quinn tossed him his last two sticks.

"How long has the body been here? Got another stick of gum?" Jake asked.

"Sorry. I'm out. A few hours. My guess is this happened sometime last night." Quinn looked at Jake. "I can't tell you anything right now. We need to get one last close look at the body before we get it down and then go over this scene with a fine tooth comb."

"I've got to ask," Jake said to Quinn. "I know how you found the banker—tied to his bed. Now we find this guy strapped to a tree. Any connection between the two?"

"I don't think so," Quinn quickly responded. "Gregory Carson wasn't mutilated like this. We will check for a connection, though. Anyway, I need the two of you to leave. I'll talk to you tomorrow. Don't talk to anyone about this, got it? Word will get out quick enough as it is and everybody *will* think we've got a damn serial killer running loose around here. We don't need that. Do I have your promise to keep quiet? Cooperate and I'll give you some good information for your next paper."

"Yeah Quinn. I'll cooperate, as long as you promise to give me *all* the details," Jake said as he and Kenny started walking away. Quinn mumbled something that, to Jake, sounded like "All right." Kenny, trying his best not to get sick again, was quiet during the short walk back to the car. Jake managed to get his car turned around, but in doing so swiped a small pine tree and put a three inch scratch in the left rear panel. "Damn!" he fussed.

"My uncle's got a body shop. We can get him to buff that out for you. He won't charge," Kenny told him. After that offer, which greatly pleased Jake, Kenny got quiet again, not saying anything for the next five minutes. Jake sensed that while Kenny's body was in the car, his mind was still back at the crime scene with the bloody corpse.

"You just lost your virginity, you know that, don't you?" Jake said to him. Kenny responded with a confused glance.

"You just saw your first dead body, I mean your first that wasn't at a funeral home, right?"

"Right."

"What did you think?" Jake asked, wanting Kenny to talk about what he had seen, rather than replay it over and over in his mind.

"The fact that I threw up twice is a pretty good indication of what I think," Kenny confessed.

"Don't worry about it. I've done it too. In fact, I'm not sure how I kept from throwing up back there. I've got a weak stomach. I can't ride a roller coaster without getting sick."

"I always figured my first would be the victim of an auto accident, or maybe a shooting, not some naked guy tied to a tree with his big toes and thumbs cut off. But why the thumbs and big toes, Jake? For something like this, I would have guessed it would be his dick that was sawed off. You know, by a jealous girlfriend or a vengeful husband who caught this guy humping his wife."

"Not a bad theory, but I don't have the answer to your question. The one thing I do know is you started off with a bang. A lot of reporters go all their lives and never see anything close to what you saw today. It was a shocker, even for me, and I've seen my share of dead bodies down through the years."

"Who would do something like that, Jake? Tie someone to a tree and cut them up like that? No one deserves to die that way. It's awful. It's sick!"

"The killer wanted to make a point to the victim and to the rest of us."

"What kind of point?"

"Who knows? That's one thing Quinn will be trying to figure out during his investigation."

"Man, I can't believe this has happened right here in Sanderson. Nothing this wild or exciting ever happens here."

"Nothing this wild ever happens in most towns. Lots better than a baseball brawl, huh?"

"Not for Todd Monroe."

"Well, between the brawl and what we've just seen, you and I are going to be very busy the next few days. Our next issue is going to be great. My guess is we may set an all-time sales record. Tell you what. I'll take care of the murder and Quinn's investigation and you do the story on the high school association ruling and the local reaction. That's still a big story, a story that a lot of people will probably be more interested in than the murder."

"Oh, I don't know about that, but I like your plan. I'm not sure I'm ready to tackle a murder story."

"You could handle it, but you know the background on all the baseball stuff. Who knows, the brawl and this murder may end up being tied together."

"You really think so?"

"It's an interesting theory to ponder. In fact, we can let our minds run wild and theorize on several tie-ins—the banker, the brawl, what we've just seen. It seems like a big coincidence to me that a few days after this guy, what's his name? Todd Monroe? And another guy who hates his guts are involved in a fight, Monroe ends up dead. And what are the odds in a little town like this of two people being found tied up and dead within days of each other without the two incidents being connected? We'll see. We'll see what Quinn comes up with in his investigation."

By the next morning, Quinn's frustration was showing. He and Sam Rogers had spent two hours questioning Joe Lambert about Todd Monroe's death, and had come up empty-handed. Lambert claimed he was sleeping off a hangover at his house the night before, but he had no one to back up his story. His son Trey had spent the night with a teammate, something he did often to keep his distance from his alcoholic, volatile Dad, and admitted to Quinn he had no idea if his Dad was home or not. Everyone knew about the bad blood between Lambert and Monroe, and that Lambert had blatantly threatened Monroe during the baseball brawl. Quinn pressed Lambert, trying to goad him into confessing that he had gotten drunk, abpackinged Monroe and taken him to the isolated spot on Silver Lake and killed him. Although he expressed no regret at Monroe's demise, Lambert swore his innocence and firmly and continually told Quinn he couldn't provide any information about the murder. Quinn didn't have enough evidence to hold Lambert, so he let him go, with the standard "Don't leave town" warning and added, "Stay away from the booze too. I need your mind clear."

"Hell, Chief! The baseball playoffs are coming up. You don't expect me to miss them, do you?" Lambert asked with a fanatical father's sincerity and a disbelief that Quinn would think for a minute he would miss the ball games.

"No, Joe," Quinn sighed. "I don't expect you to miss the playoffs. And I'm sorry Trey got suspended."

"We're still gonna win. To hell with Barber County!" Lambert blurted out. He quickly exited police headquarters.

Quinn shook his head. He walked out of the small interrogation room and toward his office. Jake had just walked through the front door, checked in with the receptionist and was headed back to see Quinn. "Got any news for me today?" Jake asked the chief.

"Yeah. It's hot as hell and the baseball playoffs are about to start."

Jake laughed. "It is hot. Let's walk over to the barbecue place. I'll buy you a Coke and some lunch."

Quinn readily accepted Jake's offer and they started their short walk across the street to the little joint that had excellent sliced pork sandwiches, pastries and ice cream. "So, do you think Lambert had anything to do with the killing?" Jake asked.

"Nope. Joe's nothing but a hot-headed redneck. He's all talk and no action. Besides, I don't think he's smart enough to pull off what we saw. That wasn't your typical flying into a rage and killing someone."

"I don't suppose you've got any idea about the deal with the thumbs and toes being cut off."

"None at all, but I will find the son of a bitch who did this."

"Well, apparently there's someone around here who's not the innocent little country bumpkin everyone tries to act like."

"Now don't go off on these people down here," Quinn chided. "They're good folks. They've taken me in. No questions asked." The two men stepped into the barbecue place, found a booth a few minutes before the lunch rush started and ordered Cokes and thrift plates.

"How long have you been here?" Jake asked Quinn.

"Three years. Three good years."

"And how did you come to reside in this pleasant south Georgia outpost?"

"That's pretty personal. I don't share that with a lot of folks."

"I don't think your story can be much more personal than mine."

"Really? In that case, I'll make you a deal. I'll tell my story if you tell your story."

"O.K." Jake nodded. The middle-aged waitress brought them their soft drinks and both men took long gulps. "You first," Jake said to Quinn.

The chief took another long swallow, sat his glass down and thumped it with his right middle finger. "I always wanted to be a police officer. My grandfather was one and so was my Dad. I was a good cop, too, worked my way up to second in command with the Charlotte PD. But I had two faults. I worked too hard and had too much of a temper. One day I came home from work early, which happened about as often as we get snow here in Sanderson, and found my neighbor in bed with my wife. I won't give you a blow-by-blow of what happened that day. All you need to know is that I broke my wife's jaw and beat my neighbor to a pulp. I had assault charges filed against me, but the Charlotte police department was already having some public relations problems at that time, so we worked out a deal. In return for having the charges dropped, I resigned from the force, paid the medical expenses for my wife and neighbor, took anger management classes and left the state. Obviously, that was the end of my marriage. I really don't blame my wife, but to this day I'm pissed off at my neighbor. He did that to me after I had pulled some strings to make three or four of his traffic tickets disappear. After all of that, I wanted to stay in law enforcement, but even with the Charlotte department trying to hush things up, word got around. No one would hire me, except the good folks in this town. I'm still not sure why they hired me. I don't know if it was because no one else would take the job, or if they believe in giving people a second chance. When the council offered me the job, I jumped on it. I needed the work, and I figured this place would be so quiet and peaceful that nothing would ever happen that would make me lose my temper. Can you top that?"

Jake fingered his Coke glass and suggested to Quinn, "Maybe we should call this town Second Chance City. My story isn't that much different than yours." Jake stopped as the waitress returned with their lunch. "Like you, I had two faults. Gambling and the bottle. They wrecked my career and sent my wife packing. For almost four years I was an absolute mess, drunk all the time and in debt to every bookie and loan shark in Atlanta. I was a sorry excuse for a human being. I hit rock bottom on Jan. 14, a little over a year ago. In a span of two hours, I got fired from a great job as a senior reporter for one of the best newspapers in the country and my wife left me. That's when I finally decided to get help. Of course by then it was too late to salvage my job or my marriage, but I was determined to save myself. You went through anger management and I went through rehab, but I ended up like you did. No one wanted to hire me. They were afraid I wouldn't be dependable and would still be sloppy and careless with my writing. Did I mention that my newspaper had to settle a $5 million libel suit that was filed due to my careless reporting? I didn't bother to check the facts before I reported on a rumor that was going around about a state senator. I was about ready to start flipping burgers at McDonald's when Stephen House called.

I accepted his offer about as quickly as you did and to this point, I have no regrets. This place isn't bad. There's nothing to do, but it isn't bad."

Quinn swallowed a big bite of his pork sandwich and washed it down with some Coke. "Damn, Martin, I thought my story was pathetic, but you can run me a close race. I'm Irish, so I know where I get my temper. Where did your fatal flaws come from?"

"Runs in the family. You come from a family of law enforcement officers. I come from a long line of boozers and losers. My grandfather died of cirrhosis and my father went to jail for embezzling money from his employer to cover his gambling debts. When I went to work in Atlanta, I fell right into the trap. The temptations are so prevalent there. Any time you go to a social event, someone sticks a drink in your hand and then another. You've got all the college and pro sports action. You lose one bet and make another to try to cover the first. It doesn't take long for the drinking and betting to get all tied in together. It almost ruined my life. I mean I was at rock bottom, absolute rock bottom. I'm thankful to have a second chance, even if it is here in Sanderson, where the hell is it, Georgia."

"How long to do think you'll be here?"

"Who knows? It may be years before anyone else is willing to take a chance on me. Provided I don't screw up Stephen House's newspaper, I may be here a long time. I can think of fates that are a lot worse. At least, if you give me a minute, I can think of them. Maybe."

Quinn took another bite of barbecue. "How old are you?"

"Forty-five."

"You're a couple of years older than me. I don't want to work here until I retire. The worst part of being here is I get lonely. Not a lot of opportunities for female companionship. The pickings are slim. After a while, you get tired of your Friday night date being with your computer and internet porn. So, yes, I'm hoping someone will give me another shot on a bigger stage, but if they don't, so be it. I'm O.K. here. Hey, here's to second chances." Quinn offered his Coke glass for a toast and Jake tapped his against it.

"To second chances," Jake replied. "Let's make the most of them. I've got a paper to run and you've got a murder to solve."

CHAPTER SIX

"Mr. Martin, you have some visitors," Hazel announced cheerfully after a single soft knock on the door frame of his office. With his back to the door while he typed a story on his computer, Jake stopped in mid-sentence, pivoted around in his chair and was pleasantly surprised to see Maddie Hampton and two of her students. He greeted them with a smile and a polite "Hello."

"I hope I'm not disturbing you, but I had a few errands to run in town this afternoon, and I wanted to bring you some cookies my students made today. I remember how much you enjoyed our cooking competition. You remember Laura and Emily?" Maddie gently placed a plateful of assorted sweets on the corner of his desk.

"Hello ladies," Jake smiled as he stood up and offered his visitors a seat. The two students, who had accompanied their teacher to the grocery store to purchase several items for the next day's baking assignment, excused themselves to return to the school for a cheerleader meeting. Maddie, after getting Jake's reassurance that he had time to chat, sat down. She looked like a school teacher, and if she had not been introduced to Jake as one, that would have been his first guess. She was a decent-looking woman, dressed this day in typical school teacher attire of a lightweight crimson sweater, khaki pants and brown flats. She had a kind, reassuring demeanor that Jake was certain helped her connect with her students.

"May I try one?" Jake asked, even though he didn't wait for her permission to pull away the plastic wrap from the cookies and grab two chocolate chip wafers connected by a thick layer of vanilla filling. "That is good!" he mumbled with his mouth full.

"I'm glad you like them. Hazel tells me you've been busy."

"I have. Kenny and I have been putting in some hours. Kenny's great. I don't know how I would manage without him."

"That murder was awful. Things like that aren't supposed to happen here in Sanderson."

"No place is exempt," Jake warned while finishing another bite of cookie. "There are mean, evil people everywhere." He wondered what Maddie's reaction would be if she knew the full story. Per his gentleman's agreement with Quinn, Jake had not published the gruesome details of Todd Monroe's death. Instead of chronicling the severed thumbs and toes and the body tied to a tree, Jake had simply reported the victim died of multiple stab wounds. In Atlanta, Jake would have listed every gruesome detail. In Sanderson, he didn't see where doing so would serve any purpose except to upset the sedate lifestyle of these good people. And, somehow, Quinn had managed to keep the town's busy bodies and out-of-town media from learning how Todd Monroe really died, a fact that totally surprised Jake, considering how quickly gossip traveled in the little town.

"I suppose you're right. I'm sorry this is one of the first stories you had to work on in Sanderson. I don't want you to get the wrong idea about our town."

"Oh no. I'm very impressed with what I've seen. My big problem has been finding the time to meet more people and see more of the town."

Maddie smiled. Jake had given her the perfect lead-in to the purpose of her visit. "That's why I'm here. I came by to invite you to services Sunday at First Baptist. We're having a covered dish lunch afterwards. Preacher Allen can be a bit long-winded, but we have a very friendly congregation."

"I'm sure you do. I've just never been heavy into going to church."

Maddie smiled again. "You're going to find out quickly that as long as you are in Sanderson, people from all the local churches are going to keep bugging you until you start attending services somewhere. So you might as well come to First Baptist. And you don't have to worry about bringing a covered dish. There will be plenty to eat."

"So it's true what they say about you Southern Baptists?"

"What's that?"

"That you love to meet and eat."

"Absolutely. As Preacher Allen says, sometime the way to a man's soul can be through his stomach."

Jake was more inclined to say the way to a man's soul is through his testicles, but that wouldn't draw many laughs in Sanderson. "I appreciate the offer," he said, "but . . . ."

"But what? Like what else do you have to do Sunday morning?"

"Oh, I don't know. Clip my toenails. Scrub the toilet. Walk the dog."

"You have a dog?"

"No. Just fumbling for an excuse."

Maddie's green eyes twinkled. "Well, I'm not going to pester you about it, but I would love to see you there. You think about it."

"I will. There's several things I need to do, but I haven't had the time. For instance, I love to read, but haven't made it to the library yet."

Maddie's eyes twinkled again. "I can take care of that too. In fact, that's one of the errands I'm running this afternoon. I have some books to return to the library. Come with me. I'll drop you back here."

Jake glanced back at his incomplete story on the computer. He was close to finishing. "All right, but I can't stay long."

They walked down the long narrow hall to the reception area and Jake explained to Hazel where he was going and how long he would be gone. A smile crept across Hazel's face as she watched the two go out the front door.

The library was three blocks away, in a peeling white framed building on a street of forty and fifty year old houses. Inside the library, the 3,000 or so square feet were cramped but well-utilized and orderly. Jake browsed at some of the offerings on the closest shelves as Maddie handed her returns to a pleasant woman behind the front counter. "Come with me. I want to introduce you to Miss Wayne, the library manager," Maddie said to Jake. She pointed to a corner nook where a slim, blonde-haired woman who looked to be in her early or mid-thirties was bent over a teenage girl who was slowly flipping pages in a large reference book. Jake thought he recognized the girl, and after a second remembered her as Kenny's friend Sunny.

"Hello Miss Wayne," Maddie said. The library manager took a break from assisting Sunny and stood erect. She offered a weak smile to Maddie and took a quick glance at Jake before looking back at Maddie.

"Miss Wayne, this is Jake Martin, the new editor at the Sentinel."

Miss Wayne extended her hand to Jake. His hand, even though not large by a man's standards, engulfed her small, limp-feeling hand. "Nice to meet you Mr. Martin. I hope you'll visit the library frequently."

"I intend to. The library is very nice." So was Janet Wayne, Jake admitted to himself. She was easily the most attractive woman he had seen in Sanderson.

"Thank you. It's too small, though. The city has promised a new facility, but they keep on building ball fields and parks instead. Sometimes it seems like sports is all that matters around here."

"I've already found that out," Jake smiled. He glanced at Sunny who was still flipping through the book.

"Sunny?" he asked, hoping he had correctly identified her.

Surprised, she looked up at him. Her expression indicated she had no idea who Jake was.

"I'm Mr. Martin from the Sentinel. Your friend Kenny works with me."

Jake's statement evoked a fragile smile from the teenage girl whose hair was pulled back in a pony tail. "He likes you. He thinks you're cool," she said in a low library voice.

Maddie and Miss Wayne both smiled at Jake. Being cool was the ultimate compliment from a Sanderson teenager. "I'm helping Sunny with a paper for Mr. Hines' Georgia History class. She's writing about one of our former governors, Lester Maddox," Miss Wayne explained.

"A very interesting character," Jake added. "Tell you what, Sunny. You get an A on your paper and I'll publish it in the Sentinel."

That promise brought big smiles from Sunny and Miss Wayne. The librarian gently put her hands on the teenager's shoulders and said, "We'll get that A, won't we?"

"Yes ma'am," Sunny replied as she returned to her book.

"Very nice to meet you," Miss Wayne offered to Jake. "Please come back to see us."

"I will," Jake nodded. "And I'm looking forward to getting Sunny's paper."

Leaving the library, Jake could not get Sunny out of his mind. She had a somber, almost sad face, exactly opposite of the perky, flirty demeanor he expected of most teenage girls and the opposite of Kenny as well. On the quick drive back to the Sentinel, he tried to find out more about her.

"I don't know a lot," Maddie admitted. "She lives alone with her Dad. I'm not sure what happened to her mom. I don't think her Dad takes very good care of her. In fact, from what I hear, he's pretty sorry. Stays gone a lot, shacks up with a lot of women. I believe that's been difficult on Sunny emotionally. She's embarrassed about her home life, and some of the kids at school won't have anything to do with her, which is terrible. She's really a sweet, smart girl. Miss Wayne has taken a special interest in her, says she went through some of the same rejection as a teenager. That was nice, what you offered. Did you see how her face brightened?"

"I did. Now I hope she gets an A on the paper."

"She will. Miss Wayne will see to that. Well, I hope I didn't keep you away from your work for too long."

"No you didn't. Thanks for the library tour and thanks for cookies. Any time you've got extras, I'll gladly take them off your hands."

"I'll keep that in mind. There will be lots of good cookies at church Sunday."

"We'll see," is all Jake offered. They exchanged courteous goodbyes and Jake walked inside the Sentinel where Hazel immediately greeted him with "Quinn called."

Jake went back to his office and ignoring the still unfinished story on his computer, called Quinn. He was put on hold and Quinn answered a minute later.

"I've got some off the record information for you," Quinn explained after Jake had identified himself. "The crime lab found traces of semen and vaginal fluid on our man tied to the tree."

"Interesting. This takes the pleasure-pain sex session to a whole new level, huh?"

"Obviously. We couldn't find any evidence of a struggle at the site, or that more than two people were involved. Looks like the killer tried to cover their tracks and did a good job of it. We were only able to come up with two sets of partial shoeprints in the soft ground. One matched the victim. We found his clothes and shoes tossed in the woods twenty feet from the tree. The other set of prints was a woman's shoe, seven and a half, with a narrow spiked heel. So our killer is either a woman or a small man with a kinky shoe fetish."

"Hmmm. So our victim probably started this thing as a willing participant."

"He could have been drugged, but my guess is Todd readily accepted an offer for a little bondage sex, and allowed himself to be tied to the tree. I don't think a woman could have forcibly got him tied to the tree. He was small but scrappy as hell."

"Bondage sex. Consensual bondage sex. Back to the banker," Jake suggested.

"Yeah, the urge is strong to link the two deaths together. But Gregory Carson didn't have his thumbs and big toes cut off. He died of a heart attack. I think Gregory got involved in some hanky-panky, and it was more than he could handle. It wasn't a homicide"

"But what if Gregory was about to have some appendages sawed off, and when he realized what was about to happen, he panicked, went crazy and his heart gave out?"

"Maybe, but I don't think so. I'm gonna keep that in the back of my mind, but not pursue it right now. I believe the two are totally unrelated."

"Well, one good thing about the Silver Lake homicide. You can rule out all the men in town as suspects, unless as you said, the killer was a guy with a fetish for women's shoes."

"I hope to hell we can rule a man out in Gregory's case. I'd hate to find out old Gregory's buddy was a boy. Now in this little town, that *would* be tough to swallow. I would hate it for his family too."

"So, what you're saying is, we have no suspects, for Todd's murder and Gregory's non-murder."

"We got a DNA sample from the vaginal fluid on Todd, but we don't have anything to match it with. That's all we have. Both death scenes were clean. Not even a stray hair."

"Anything on what was used to saw off Todd's thumbs and big toes?"

"A serrated knife, a dull one. The boy went through some excruciating pain. I'm sure he did some screaming, but as deep in the woods as they were, he could have made as much noise as a July thunderstorm and no one would have heard him."

A chill shot down Jake's spine as he imagined the torture Todd had endured and then helplessly writhed on the tree as he bled to death. "The killer certainly was a sadistic bastard. How are you going to catch him, uh, or her?" Jake asked.

"Keep digging. Eventually, sooner or later, we'll come up with a clue, a piece of evidence that will break this case. Right now, we're at a dead end. No motive, no nothing. Confession time, Jake. It's been a long time since I worked on a case this complex and I feel a little overwhelmed. In fact, I'm flat-out scared, nervous."

"You? Nervous? I don't believe it."

"Believe it."

"Can't you bring in some help?"

"I don't want to."

"I don't understand. If you're so nervous, why not bring in some help, uh, like the Georgia Bureau of Investigation?"

"As scared as I am, as nervous as I am, I want to be the one to nail this killer's ass to the wall. I've got to prove to myself that being in this little town hasn't eroded my instincts as a cop."

Jake understood and nodded. "For what it's worth, Quinn. I've got confidence in you. You will solve this case."

"Thanks. I'm going to try my best."

"And Quinn . . ."

"Yes?"

"Why are you telling me all of this? Cops aren't usually so loose-lipped to the press with information about their unsolved cases—and their personal insecurities."

"It didn't take you long to figure out I have an ulterior motive. First, I'm asking you to still sit on all the details about this killing. Printing what really happened would just upset the folks in town. So far I've been able to keep the out-of-town reporters at bay, but those big boys, especially the TV folks, are persistent. Eventually they'll uncover what really happened."

"I know. Remember I used to be one of those big boys. Don't worry, Quinn. I won't break your confidence. I can fill up the paper with stories about the Founders' Day Festival and school news. Something's always going on over at the high school. Just promise that when the story does break, you'll time your release of information so I can get it in the Sentinel at the same time the big boys go to press and on the air and Internet."

"You got it. Thanks. And there is one other reason I'm telling you all of this."

Jake didn't reply as he waited for Quinn to continue. "I need someone to talk to. I feel more comfortable talking to you than anyone else in town. After all, we're both second chancers."

"We are," Jake agreed. He hung up and swiveled his chair back to the almost finished story on the computer. Compared to the task facing Quinn, Jake realized that finishing the story on the city council's latest disagreement over the property tax rate was terribly unimportant.

Quinn, finished with his conversation with Jake, started out of his office to deliver a report that was due at city hall, but Sam Rogers stopped him. "Mary Jane Hamilton is here to see you," Rogers whispered. "She's hysterical."

"About what?"

"She wouldn't say."

"Bring her back," Quinn said. He waited at his office door for her.

Sobbing uncontrollably, Mary Jane Hamilton entered Quinn's office. He greeted her, shut the door and asked her to be seated. Seeing that the tissue she was using was soaked, Quinn pulled a small box of facial tissue out of his desk, handed it to her, and pulled up a chair next to her. He held her trembling right hand while she used her trembling left hand to dry her face with a fresh tissue.

"What is it, Mary Jane?" he asked fatherly.

It took Mary Jane a minute to control her sobbing so she could talk. She dropped her head and started to speak but stopped. Quinn had to lean forward and softly urged her to talk. "Come on, Mary Jane. Talk to me," Quinn urged calmly.

"I . . . I . . ."

Quinn didn't rush her. He softly squeezed her hand and gave her time to wipe her face.

Mary Jane swallowed hard, took a deep breath, paused and admitted, "I was with Gregory Carson the night he died."

Quinn rose up and waited for the shapely dark-skinned brunette to continue. She sobbed again for a few seconds and wiped her face once more before trying to talk. "This is very embarrassing . . . and humiliating," she started.

"Go ahead," he urged her.

"How can I explain this?" Mary Jane bit her lip and looked down at the floor. With her head still down, she started, "Gregory loved his wife, but she's a, uh, a south Georgia Bible-thumping prude. She didn't like sex nearly as much as he did, in fact, she didn't like it at all. He loved to experiment and loved to get a little . . . a little kinky. I'm a thirty year old single mother and what I'm making as a teller at Gregory's bank doesn't go very far. Do you know how expensive providing for a six year old girl and an eight year old girl can be?" She looked up and focused her watery eyes on Quinn.

"What happened was, I could give Gregory what he needed, and he could give me what I needed."

"He was paying you for sex."

"Yes," she admitted, starting to sob again. "It wasn't an affair, because he loved Sarah and Hannah. He really did. He would never have left Sarah for another woman, but his physical needs weren't being met."

"What happened the night he died?"

"We were into heavy foreplay like usual. He liked being tied up. I was wearing long lace gloves and rubbing his body. He gasped, his eyes rolled back and he quit breathing. It all happened so fast. I panicked and left the house. The next morning I heard he was dead, but when I left his house I knew he was dead. The news made me sick, but there wasn't anything I could do for him that night. Really! There wasn't!" She started crying.

"You're right, Mary Jane. There was nothing you could have done. Gregory had a massive heart attack. He died instantly. Why didn't you come to me sooner?"

Mary Jane had to stop crying before she could answer. "Embarrassment. Humiliation. I couldn't face the people I see every day if they knew what Gregory and I had been doing, not to mention the fact that I would lose my job. I was afraid too. I was afraid I'd be arrested and my children would be sent to a foster home."

"What made you finally decide to tell me?"

"Guilt . . . and Todd Monroe's murder. I was terrified that people would start linking Gregory's death with Todd's and that I would get blamed for both of them."

"Why do you think people would link the two deaths together?"

She managed a weak smile. "This is a small town. Word gets around. I know you've tried to keep what happened to Todd under your hat, but some people know. They know Gregory was tied to his bed, and that Todd was tied to a tree."

"Is there a link between the two, Mary Jane?"

"Chief Quinn, you can call me a whore or a prostitute, but I'm not a murderer!" She started crying again, more forcefully than before.

Quinn gently patted her left leg. "I appreciate you coming to me with this. With your statement, we can close Gregory's case." He softly placed his hands on her shoulders and looked at her at arms' length. "You know we are going to have to tell his family."

"I know," she sniffed. "Are you going to arrest me?"

He squeezed her hand again and tried to make sure he was addressing her in a calm, reassuring manner. "No. Gregory died of natural causes."

"Thank you," Mary Jane said almost inaudibly.

Quinn studied the woman's face. Tears had made a mess of her makeup. "Admitting you were with Gregory was the right thing to do. But what about Todd Monroe? Are you sure you don't know anything about what happened to him?"

She didn't let him continue. "You're doing exactly what I was afraid people would do, that they would link Gregory's death with Todd's and blame me for both! I wasn't with Todd! I didn't kill him! I've dated him. We've even had sex. But I didn't kill him, Chief! I haven't talked to him in weeks! My sister will back me up! Talk to her!" Mary Jane was frightened. Quinn saw the fear in her eyes.

"I know you didn't, but I had to ask. It's my job. Everything is going to be all right."

"I'm so sorry," she said, sobbing again.

"We all make mistakes. You'll get a second chance."

She managed another weak smile. "I hope so. You know anybody's who hiring? I think I may be in the market for a new job."

"If you go into sales, just don't offer what Gregory was buying," he suggested.

CHAPTER SEVEN

J ake was having trouble staying awake. His eyes kept slowly closing and his head kept inching forward, sending his chin toward his chest. The first part of Rev. Allen's sermon on integrity from the second chapter of Titus was thought-provoking and kept Jake's attention, but the good pastor had gone on and on far too long. Jake had lost concentration and now he was losing his battle with drowsiness. The only thing keeping him awake was the fear of his head flopping on to Maddie's shoulder, or that he would begin to snore. On top of that, his stomach was growling. He knew everyone around him could hear the noises. "Why did I ever show up here today?" Jake asked himself silently. "Thank God!" Jake mumbled under his breath as Rev. Allen completed his sermon, but he started squirming again as the Minister of Music started singing *Just As I Am* for the invitation. Seven verses and three professions of faith later, an energized Rev. Allen finally dismissed the congregation to the large covered pavilion on the east side of the church for the covered dish lunch. Jake glanced at his watch—12:43. Church was supposed to end promptly at noon. Everyone knew that but the preacher.

By no means did Jake consider his appearance at First Baptist a date, but Maddie had become his escort, admitting to him that she had looked for him all morning, and had almost given up when he finally showed up at the church at 10:55, five minutes before the start of services. He sensed that everyone in the congregation was watching them, and he was convinced that anytime a couple of folks got together for whispering conversations, he and Maddie was the

Gary Watson

topic. That didn't upset Jake. People had whispered behind his back down through the years about much more serious offenses.

When Jake saw the spread of food on the long wooden table under the pavilion, he immediately decided that suffering through Rev. Allen's long-winded sermon was worthwhile. Plates of fried chicken, meatloaf and roast were surrounded by fresh south Georgia vegetables—squash, green beans and fried and boiled okra and Vidalia onions. All of that was on one end of the table. The fresh cakes, pies and cookies and homemade ice cream were on the other end. Waiting patiently in the long line while his stomach continued to growl, Jake finally was able to load up his plate. He and Maddie, whose plate looked far less intimidating, found seats at one of the picnic tables the church had set up.

Jake recognized the faces of many of the congregation from running into them in town, but he could not yet put names with most of the faces. He did recognize Robert McIntire, the local real estate agent intent on selling him a house, and Paula Miller, owner of a Main Street dress shop. He noticed Janet Wayne, the librarian, at a table not far away, and Kenny and Sunny soon took seats at the same table with Jake and Maddie. Quickly, every seat at the table was filled, and the jovial conversation turned to how life in small towns centers on schools and churches. Between munching on forkfuls of food and complimenting the residents of Sanderson for being so hospitable, Jake glanced at Sunny. She wasn't saying much, and at times it seemed as if she and Kenny were at a table by themselves. Kenny looked like he wanted to join in the adult conversation, but the bulk of his comments were directed at Sunny. With faces close together, they talked softly. Kenny giggled once or twice, but Sunny would only force a smile, and not much of one. Jake's heart went out to Kenny. He obviously had an interest in the blonde who reminded Jake of singer Taylor Swift, only cuter, and certainly appeared up-to-date in fashion styles. She just didn't want to be social, no matter how hard Kenny tried. Jake didn't know if the girl was excruciatingly shy, or if the bad home life Kenny and Maddie had mentioned had caused her to withdraw. Either way, Jake was impressed with the patience Kenny showed with her. He hoped the girl appreciated what Kenny was doing, and if nothing else, would occasionally hold his hand, or maybe even plant a kiss on his cheek.

A few minutes later Jake started getting an answer to his questions about Sunny. A polished late model red quad cab slowly rolled along the narrow road between the church and the eating area and stopped. "That's my Dad. I've got to go," Sunny said in a whisper.

"But you haven't finished eating. I'll tell your Dad I'll bring you home," Kenny said. Jake and Maddie were watching.

"No, I'd better go on," she repeated. Before she could get up from the table, the man in the truck was pumping the horn, getting the attention of the 125 people who were enjoying the afternoon. Sunny began walking toward the truck but stopped when prompted by a voice behind her.

"Let me talk to your Dad. I'll tell him I will bring you home," Miss Wayne requested. She stroked the girl's hair.

"I . . . don't know . . ." Sunny responded nervously.

Before Sunny could protest any more, Miss Wayne headed for the pickup. Interested in what was about to happen, Jake got up from the table, took a few steps and watched.

Sunny opened the passenger door to the truck and got in, but Miss Wayne grabbed the door before she could shut it. The stench of cigarette smoke permeated the cab and there was a hint of alcohol as well. "Mr. Krause, won't you join us for lunch? We have tons of food left," Miss Wayne offered.

"No! I've got to be somewhere in a few minutes," Krause replied bluntly. Sunny's Dad was tall, perhaps 6-3, and close to 225 pounds. He was ruggedly handsome, with a two-day facial scruff and buzz cut.

"We're not quite through here," Miss Wayne explained.

"Sunny told me to pick her up at 1:30, so here I am."

"Yes, but we got a late start. We were late getting out of services."

"Look lady. I need to go and Sunny's going with me. Now will you get out of the way so Sunny can shut the damn door and we can get the hell out of here!"

"Mr. Krause! This is a church!" Miss Wayne scolded him. "Please watch your language!"

"Mind your own business lady! Sunny, shut the damn door so we can go!"

Even from a distance, Jake could see Sunny's embarrassment. Kenny seemed angry rather than embarrassed.

"I'll call you later, O.K." Kenny said to Sunny as she shut the door without replying. The truck drove off, leaving Kenny and Miss Wayne angry, frustrated and hurting for Sunny. Jake walked up to Kenny and put his arm on the boy's shoulder.

"He's an asshole. A total asshole." Kenny snorted. "He treats her like that all the time."

From what he had just seen, Jake couldn't argue with the assessment.

"I'm going home," Kenny growled, anger still prevalent in the delivery of his words.

"See you tomorrow. And calm down. Things will work out," Jake replied. Kenny walked away and Jake turned his attention to Miss Wayne who had not moved from the spot where she had talked to Krause. "That was good of you to go to bat for Sunny like that," he told her.

"The man is evil!" she said bitterly.

"So he's an evil asshole?"

"Beg your pardon?"

"Never mind. Why does he treat her that way?"

She didn't answer Jake's question, instead proclaiming, "The man will pay for his sins. There comes a time when all of us are judged before God for our actions. The way he treats his daughter is a sin!"

"Well, you'll get some extra stars in your crown for being such a friend to her. You and Kenny both."

"I feel a bond with her. A deep bond. When I was her age, I needed a friend too, but no one cared. I was alone, a scared immature child having to work through some serious issues without the guidance and love of a caring adult. I refuse to allow Sunny, or any other child for that matter, to face their demons alone."

"Lady, you missed your calling," Jake offered. "Instead of managing a library, you ought to be minister, or at the least, a social worker."

"You can do God's work, no matter your occupation."

"Good luck to you," Jake replied. He went back to Maddie, who had watched the proceedings from the table.

"He's not a very pleasant person, is he?" Maddie asked rhetorically.

"That's an understatement."

Pastor Allen came to the table and sat beside Jake and offered more insight about Sunny. "Mr. Krause's wife got her fill of him several years ago. One day she just left, didn't bother to take Sunny with her and gave no explanation for leaving. Sunny hasn't heard from her since. It has been very difficult for Sunny to accept the fact that her mother simply washed her hands of her. That's a huge factor in Sunny being such an introvert."

Jake looked at the slice of lemon pie he had cut earlier, but pushed it away instead of eating it. Hearing Sunny's background caused him to lose his appetite.

"So nice to have you with us," Pastor Allen smiled at Jake. "I hope you'll be back."

"Yes we do," Maddie chimed in.

Jake returned the smile, "Thank you," he said, not wanting to make any commitment. He wanted to tell the preacher that he would give more thought to coming back if he would shorten his sermons by about twenty minutes.

"I want to give you something," the pastor said to Jake. "Here's a Bible and a guide to reading through it in a year. It's something we give to all of our first-time guests."

"Thank you, preacher," Jake replied. He wasn't going to admit he didn't have a Bible. In fact, it had been a long time since he had even opened a Bible or read a single line of scripture.

"Most people are intimidated by the thought of trying to read through the Bible, but this study guide makes it easy. All it takes is a little effort. You've done it before, haven't you Maddie?

"Yes sir, several times."

"Maddie is being humble," Rev. Allen explained. "She knows the Bible as well as many preachers. She can spout out obscure scripture verses that even I don't know."

"I'm impressed," Jake acknowledged Maddie with a smile. He turned to Rev. Allen. "Thank you," Jake said again. "I've enjoyed being here today. You have a nice church and a friendly congregation. And the food was wonderful." Glancing at his watch, Jake made a lame excuse about having another appointment and got up from the table. Maddie walked with him to his car.

"Thanks for coming. I wasn't sure if you would," she said.

"Thanks for inviting me. It took care of lunch."

"Well, if you're so worried about eating, what if I make supper for us one night this week? You name it and I'll fix it."

"Sounds great. Can I get back with you the next couple of days?"

"Sure."

Jake slipped into his Maxima, which still had the scratch from the trip to Silver Lake. Maddie folded her arms and sighed as she watched Jake drive away. He went to the extended stay lodge where packing his few belongings and settling up with the registration desk didn't take long. Following Kenny's directions, Jake drove to Stephen's place. He was impressed. The rustic log house, at least 2,000 square feet, maybe 2,200, sat on three acres covered in hardwoods and pines and was a lot of house for a bachelor like Stephen. Surveying the inside, Jake figured all he would use was the kitchen, one of the four bedrooms, the well-equipped home office and one of the three bathrooms. He found an empty closet and chest of drawers for his clothes and settled in for the afternoon. Flipping on the television that was fed by satellite dish, Jake found nothing worth watching. Tossing the remote control on the end table, he noticed the Bible and study guide Pastor Allen had given him. Feeling guilty that it had been so long, Jake opened the Bible and started looking at the first page of Genesis. Scanning the pages more than reading, he stopped when he got to the lineage of Adam in Genesis 5. "This is boring," he grumbled, placing the Bible back on the end table. He walked into Stephen's study, turned on the computer and began researching ritual killings on the Internet. Maybe he could find something to help Quinn solve the Silver Lake murder.

CHAPTER EIGHT

This was more than a typical Barber County—Eagleton game. Battling for the first time since the brawl, the teams were fired up and talking trash. The bleachers were full and the fans were jawing at each other. A lot was on the line. The winner finished first in the region and received a bye in the first round of the state playoffs, while the loser dropped into a tie for second and faced a coin toss for seeding. Security was tight. Quinn had called in a couple of off-duty state troopers and county sheriff's officers to stand around and be noticed, hopefully preventing another free-for-all. The high school association had considered cancelling the game, but chose not to at the request of administrators at both schools. The crowd was easily the largest of the season, and the gate receipts were being split 50-50. Barber County and Eagleton could make enough off this one game to pay the umpires for the season. Quinn wasn't happy about the decision to play, but once it was made, he was going to make sure nothing happened.

Joe Lambert was mouthing off at the Barber County fans and players before the first pitch was thrown. Quinn, standing along the third base line, shook his head, and ordered one of the state troopers to bring Lambert to him. Quinn crammed two sticks of Black Jack chewing gum into his mouth, and uncharacteristically for him, tossed the wrappers to the ground.

"What I'd do?" Lambert asked innocently as he arrived at Quinn.

"I'm going tell you one time, and just one time. Keep your mouth shut and behave, or I'm running your ass out of here! You got me? You do want to see the game, don't you?"

"Yes sir," Lambert replied meekly.

"Then get back in the stands and don't embarrass yourself or your son again. I want to watch the game too."

Quinn sighed and chomped on his gum, and Lambert, like a Barber County freshman who had been disciplined by the principal, went back to his seat and didn't say a word even though everyone around him was yelling, with an occasional four letter word being heard among the noise. The game started, and as usual, the teams went back and forth, the lead changing hands three times in the first four innings.

Jake was standing against the third base fence with Quinn, whose head was on a swivel as he surveyed the rowdy crowd. So far, there had been no hint of trouble, but a couple of close calls had caused several fans, including Joe Lambert, to get out of their seats and scream at the umpires. Lambert quickly returned to his seat when Quinn shot a menacing glance his way.

"It's strange," Quinn said to Jake as his eyes took a panoramic tour of the whole park, starting along the right field line into the bleachers behind the plate and then down the left field line.

"What? That everyone is so well behaved?" Jake teased.

"No. It's strange not to see Todd Monroe here. He never missed a game. Barber County and Eagleton could have played field hockey in Taiwan and Todd would have been there."

"Any progress on his case? What about the Hamilton woman?"

Jake's question caught Quinn by surprise. "Why did you ask that?"

"Because I know she came to your office with a confession."

"And how did you find that out?"

"This is a small town, Quinn. You're the best I've ever seen at keeping information under wraps, but even you can't keep secrets forever. And once word gets out, it spreads faster than a swarm of south Georgia piss ants descending on a ham sandwich that's been discarded at a picnic."

"Do you know what she confessed?"

"That she had been fooling around with Gregory Carson and that she did know Todd Monroe—intimately."

"She did come to talk to me—about Gregory's death, and I did ask her about Todd Monroe. She has an alibi, sort of. Her sister says Mary Jane hasn't had anything to do with Todd recently, but the problem is I don't trust her sister. She's been in trouble in every county in this area, and I don't put much stock in anything she says. But she did tell me Mary Jane was at her house around the time Todd was likely murdered, and I haven't been able to find anyone to tell me otherwise."

Jake replied, "I feel sorry for the girl. You know the tongues in Sanderson are wagging about her, and that any time she sets foot out of her house, every set of eyes is on her. For that matter, the same thing can probably be said about Gregory's wife and daughter."

"No doubt. I wouldn't be surprised if they all leave town eventually. I don't think I would want to stay. I'll tell you one thing this case has me doing. I look at the feet of every woman I see, trying to imagine if they belong to the killer. God, do you know how ugly some women's shoes are these days?"

"No. I don't make it a point to look down at women's feet. That's not the part of the body that attracts me."

"A boob guy, huh?"

"No. Hair and eyes."

"Sure. Whatever you say, Mr. Martin. What attracts you to Maddie Hampton?"

"Her personality, of course."

"Oh please! Give me a break, Martin. That's pure bull . . ."

The conversation was broken as Barber County's third baseman turned on a high fastball and sent it screaming over the leftfield fence, putting the Pirates ahead. Half the crowd was screaming and applauding and the other half was booing as the stocky batter trotted around the bases with a clinched fist held high above his head.

"Do you mind if I play detective?" Jake asked as the batter ended his exaggerated waltz around the bases by touching home plate and being mobbed by his teammates.

"What do you mean?"

"I started doing some research the other day on ritualistic killings. I think I found something on every imaginable type of killing except one with the thumbs and big toes cut off. But I'm going to keep trying. I thought I'd go by the library and see if Miss Wayne can help me out."

"So you think you can find something when I can't? Or are you just looking for an excuse to go by and see Miss Wayne?"

"It doesn't hurt to look, does it?"

"Look at what? The books or the librarian?"

"The books, of course."

"Of course. Sure, play detective, but watch what you say. In spite of what you say about not being able to keep secrets around here, we have managed to cloak most of the true details about Todd's death. Most everyone in town thinks Todd was stabbed to death. The funeral home and Todd's family have cooperated by keeping quiet. This little town doesn't need something like that to worry about."

"Your secret—what's left of it—is safe with me. I'll tell Miss Wayne I'm doing research for a book. I've always wanted to write a murder mystery."

"Well, I think the mystery you'd really like to solve is how to get in Miss Wayne's pants. But if you ever do get the opportunity to write a book about this killing and how I solved it, lie a little bit and make me sound more handsome than I am."

"Gosh, Quinn, I don't know if I can stretch the truth that much."

Quinn grunted and looked out on the field where the game had settled down. Barber County was still ahead in the bottom of the fifth inning. "Jake, do you ever want a drink?" Quinn asked, not taking his gaze off the players.

Quinn's out-of-nowhere question caught Jake off guard, but he answered truthfully. "Yeah. All the time. That's one reason I'm in this little south Georgia town. I know you can never totally escape the bottle, but I figured the temptations here are a heck of a lot less than they are in Atlanta."

Both men were silent and watched the teams exchange places for the top of the sixth.

"Quinn," Jake started, "do you ever feel like breaking someone's jaw?"

Quinn kept looking out on the field. "Yes. Hell yes. I'd especially like to smack some of these rednecks who don't know how to behave at high school baseball games."

"Let's make a pact," Jake suggested. "You keep me from drinking and gambling and I'll keep you from slobber-knocking somebody."

"Deal."

Conversation about drinking and punching abruptly ended when the beanpole of a pitcher from Barber County plunked the Eagleton first baseman with a fastball in the ribs. The wounded Eagleton player flung his batting helmet to the ground and took two steps toward the pitcher and both teams moved to the front of their dugouts. The crowd, which has been calm by Barber County—Eagleton standards, erupted. Exercising considerable self-control and good judgment, the Eagleton batter turned and sprinted to first, earning the cheers of his team's fans. Joe Lambert didn't exercise the same type of good judgment. Having restrained himself for so long that he'd almost given himself a hernia, Lambert hopped out of the stands and rushed to the side of the Barber County dugout where he let loose with an extensive barrage of foul language directed at the Pirate players and coaches.

Quinn was on Lambert quickly, grabbing him by the collar and dragging him away from the field. "Damn it Joe! You're an idiot! An absolute idiot! If you won't think about what an ass you're making of yourself, at least think about the lousy example you're setting for these kids."

"But Quinn, that punk kid hit our batter intentionally. He meant to do it!"

"No he didn't. He has trouble throwing strikes. Don't you read the Sentinel sports pages? The kid has trouble throwing strikes. Has all season!"

Lambert didn't answer. Quinn motioned for one of his officers. "Take Mr. Lambert to the Quinn Plaza and give him our finest room," the chief ordered.

"What do I charge him with?"

"Acting like a fool. Just keep him there long enough for the kids to finish playing this game, and long enough for me to figure out what I'm going to do to get him to act like an adult!"

The officer sat a still-mumbling Lambert into the back of the squad car and drove away. The crowd, having seen Quinn's response to Lambert's rowdiness, sat back and quietly watched Barber County finish off a 5-3 win. Quinn stayed around to make sure there were no post-game shenanigans, and Jake headed for the library.

Only a half-dozen patrons were in the library, which didn't surprise Jake, considering most of the town had been at the baseball game, and they were now all headed home for supper, or stopping at one of the few eating places Sanderson offered. The same pleasant woman who had been at the front counter during Jake's previous library visit with Maddie was working, and she seemed to be doing nothing more than busy work. Jake introduced himself and requested to see Miss Wayne. Emerging from her small office behind the front counter following her employee's summons, Miss Wayne was surprised to see Jake. He was surprised too. Miss Wayne looked fantastic, even more attractive than the previous times he had seen her. She was wearing a summer weight lilac skirt that dropped two inches below the knees and a white silk blouse. Her blonde hair was pulled back with a single clip, exposing her ears and small gold loops. She reminded him of the businesswomen he used to see in Atlanta on a daily basis.

"Nice to see you again, Mr. Martin," she smiled while extending her hand. "What can I do for you?"

"A couple of things," Jake replied as he squeezed her hand, but not as tightly as he would with a man. "First, I want to get a library card. I love to read, although I admit I haven't had much time to read since I got here."

"I'm glad to know you're a reader. As you can see, we don't have the greatest selection here, but we are tied into a statewide network of libraries. You have access to anything they have. What else can we help you with?"

Jake cleared his throat. "I need to do some research. I'm working on my first novel. It's fiction about a detective who's trying to track down a killer. Do you have any books about ritualistic killings or serial killers?"

Miss Wayne arched her eyebrows. "Well, that's a request I don't get every day here in Sanderson." She almost sounded like she was poking fun at Jake. "I'm not sure what we have on the shelves. Let's go to our reference section."

Jake followed her between two long shelves on the far side of the library. "This is what we have," she said, pointing her outstretched hand to a section of books. "If you don't find anything here, use one of the computers that has our network listing. Frankly, if you're going to find anything, that's where it will be, not on the shelves here."

"Thanks," Jake said, pulling a thick book from the top shelf.

"Tell me, Mr. Martin . . ."

"It's Jake."

"All right, Jake. If I may ask, what are you doing here?"

"Well, I hope to check out a couple of books."

"No. I mean, what are you doing here in Sanderson?"

"Stephen House needed someone to run his newspaper."

"Yes, but why you? Can this place keep you from getting bored? You have to be used to a much more hectic pace than what we offer here. And you come all the way to this quiet little town to write about killings and killers? I'm not sure that makes sense."

"Life doesn't make sense sometimes." Jake shut the book and put it back on the shelf. He thought Miss Wayne was coming on a bit strong with the questions.

"Did you end up here because you lost your ambition?" she asked.

Jake tried not to let his annoyance show. "No. I ended up here because I lost my direction—in life."

"I see," she nodded, showing the good judgment not to continue with the questioning.

"What about you?" Jake asked, turning the tables. "Are you local?"

"Oh no. I've only been here 18 months. God placed me here. This job opened up, and I felt God's calling to come here. I am here for a purpose."

Jake didn't realize God had an employment agency. "And what is your purpose here?"

"To help people, Mr. Martin. To help people. Small towns need ministering to as much as your big cities."

"I'm sure they do. It just seems like your talents may be underutilized here."

"Depends on what talents you are talking about. And I certainly could say the same thing about you."

"I guess you could. May I impose upon your talents now to apply for a library card?"

"By all means. Oh, one other thing. Did you enjoy going to church with Maddie Hampton?"

Considering her interest amusing, Jake smiled and offered, "Maddie just wants to make sure I don't starve to death. The couple of times she and I have been together, food has been involved."

"In that case, may I cook for you one night? I'm good with Italian."

Jake didn't answer immediately. Personality-wise, he wasn't sure if he and Miss Wayne was a match, but he was certainly appreciative of her physical attributes. "Sure," he finally said. "Give me a call."

He got his library card, browsed a few minutes and left without checking out anything or doing any research. Apparently Miss Wayne had accepted his line about looking for background material for a novel and had no idea he was actually trying to find something to help Quinn advance the Silver Lake investigation. However, her questioning about his personal standing had rattled Jake enough to get his mind off that, so he opted to go home, fix a sandwich and watch TV or read.

Munching on a ham and cheese sandwich and a bag of baked barbecue potato chips, Jake punched at the remote control to the TV in Stephen House's kitchen, but could not find anything worth watching on any of the 50 channels. Taking his last bite of sandwich, he walked into the den to pick through a dozen magazines for something to read while enjoying a bowl of chocolate ice cream. Glancing over at an end table, he spotted the Bible Preacher Allen had given him at First Baptist and decided to thumb through it again.

And thumbing through it was what Jake did. He skimmed over each page, stopping to read a verse or two only when a particular word caught his eye. He was about to start on Joshua 24 when the door bell rang. Jake flinched, because he wasn't expecting anyone. No one had come to see him since he had moved into Stephen's place, not even anyone from First Baptist, which had the reputation as a visiting church. Jake put a bookmark at the point he had reached and put the Bible back on the end table.

"Kenny?" Jake asked after opening the front door.

"I need a drink!" the young man announced. "Got a Bud Light?"

"No I don't. You're not of drinking age any way. What's going on?"

"It's Sunny. I've got good news and bad news."

"Tell me." They both sat down on the sofa.

"The good news is I got her to kiss me for the first time."

"Good for you!"

"I told her that I really like her, and that I want very much for us to be friends, like boyfriend and girlfriend."

"O.K. I'm with you so far."

"She wants that too, but her father has her so cowed down. He's never at home but he expects her to be. He questions her about where she's been and what she's been doing, and he's so critical of her. You can't prove it by me that he hasn't hit her a few times. To him, she can't do anything right. I hate the guy. He's a son of a bitch. Of course, I think the feeling is mutual. He doesn't like me either. Anyhow, as much as Sunny wants to be my steady, she's afraid to. She's afraid her Dad will get mad and start his ranting and raving again."

"Why's he like that?"

"He's just a redneck asshole. He's selfish and self-centered. Sunny's thought about running away several times, but she's afraid to do that because if the authorities found her and brought her back home, she would catch hell from her old man!"

"I'm sorry Kenny. What do you think needs to be done?"

"I don't know. That's why I need a drink. Are you sure you don't have a beer around here?"

"I'm sure. I don't touch the stuff. And where is someone underage like you getting beer?"

"You can't be that stupid," Kenny chided. "It's *not* that different here than from Atlanta. I've got friends, older friends."

"I see. Maybe you should talk to Quinn. Maybe he can have a talk with Sunny's Dad. He'd also like to know about the friends who are buying you beer."

"Forget that I said anything about beer, and no, I can't talk to him about Sunny's father. That would really piss her old man off!"

"How about Family and Children Services?"

"No, she doesn't want that. As much as her home life sucks, Sunny doesn't want to be a welfare child or stuck in a foster home. Heck, she's embarrassed enough as it is. That's what makes her so shy."

Jake shifted on the sofa. "Well, Kenny, I don't think I have any words of wisdom for you. I guess I have to ask you this. Is this girl worth all this stress? Is this going to end up getting you in trouble?"

Kenny stared a hole through Jake. "That's harsh, man! Yeah, she's worth it. I'm not gonna bail on her. Shoot, Miss Wayne, Mrs. Hampton and I are the only people she can count on."

"Speaking of Miss Wayne, she sort of asked me out."

"Are you serious?"

"She asked if she could cook for me one night. I said yes."

"What about you and Maddie?"

"What about us?"

"She's sweet on you, you know that?"

"She is?"

"God Jake! Maybe you *are* that dumb."

"Maybe so," Jake laughed. "Come on. Let's go to the kitchen. I don't have any beer but I've got a two-liter Mountain Dew. Maybe we can get a buzz from the caffeine."

For the next thirty minutes Jake and Kenny drank Mountain Dew on the rocks and discussed one of the real truths about life—you can't live with women and you can't live without them.

CHAPTER NINE

A steady light rain was falling on Sanderson and the wind was blowing just enough to rustle tree limbs. Jake and Quinn were sitting in a booth at Waffle House, downing their second cups of coffee and debating the merits of hash browns. Jake admitted to being a purist, wanting his hash browns plain with only a little salt and pepper, while Quinn was a gourmet, preferring his scattered, smothered, covered and chunked and coated with ketchup. The debate came to an obvious conclusion. Each ordered hash browns their favorite way, with eggs and raisin toast.

Both men were stalling. Jake had to meet with Hazel to go over the Sentinel's financial performance, his least favorite part of the job. Quinn had to work on the police department's upcoming fiscal year's budget, which was due in three days. They would eat slowly and drink at least one, perhaps two more cups of coffee. Attempting to stretch out the conversation, Quinn asked Jake if he had heard from Stephen House.

"I talked to him a couple of days ago. He's in California, exploring the Napa Valley. He sounded like he was having a good time."

"With the bundle he inherited from his father, he can have a good time for a long time. Do you think he'll ever come back to Sanderson?"

"I don't know. I know he was in a hurry to get away from here. What do you think? You've known him longer than I have."

"What reason does he have to come back? He doesn't have any family here, and if he wants to get back in the newspaper business, hell, he can buy a paper in a location that has a whole lot more to offer than this little wide spot in the road."

"But it's a nice little wide spot in the road."

"Yes it is," Quinn agreed.

"Do you ever regret coming here?"

Quinn didn't hesitate. "Do I ever regret coming here? No. Do I ever regret leaving myself with no options but to come here? Every day. I'm not a religious person. In fact, if I was to walk into a church, the ground would probably tremble, but people tell me there's a purpose to everything, that you are put in certain situations and places for a reason. I'm still trying to come up with the reason I'm here."

"It's interesting you say that. Miss Wayne, the librarian, told me that God put her here for a purpose."

Quinn took a swallow of coffee. "Good for her. As for me, I'd just as soon my purpose have been in Las Vegas or New Orleans or Chicago."

"She asked me out."

"Miss Wayne asked you out?"

"Sort of. She asked if she could cook for me one night, which I guess considering the limited options around here, is about the same as asking me out."

"What about you and the school teacher?"

"What about us? She brought me some cookies one time and invited me to church."

A mischievous grin spread across Quinn's face. "Remember Jake. This is south Georgia. Down here, that's as good as going steady."

"My God! In another week, everyone will have us married and expecting!" Jake exclaimed in mock horror.

"Maybe you should start to look at Maddie a little more seriously. Or the librarian. Like I told you before, the field is pretty limited around here."

"And maybe you should look at that ticket more seriously and pay for our breakfast. As much as I don't want to, I guess I'd better go to work."

"You mean I'm paying?"

"You're paying."

"Want to flip for it, double or nothing."

"I'm not a betting man," Jake said adamantly, even though he knew Quinn was kidding.

"Are you guys through?" the soft voice asked from behind Quinn's shoulder.

Quinn put his coffee cup down as the waitress stood at their booth. "Mary Jane?" he asked.

"Hello Chief," she responded. Quinn immediately realized Mary Jane was embarrassed for him to see her in a Waffle House uniform. "The bank fired me," she added nervously, giving Quinn an explanation even though he had not asked for one and didn't need one. "I got two kids to feed. There are not many job opportunities in

Sanderson. I know the manager here. He was kind enough to give me a job. The pay's not great, but the hours are good. I can be with my kids."

"There's nothing wrong working at Waffle House," Quinn readily told her. "These are good folks, right Jake?" Quinn asked.

"Absolutely," Jake agreed.

"It will do 'til my Prince Charming rides into town," she said, forcing a smile. "Let me get these plates off your table." Her hands were shaking enough that the plates and silverware rattled as she picked them up.

Jake and Quinn continued drinking their coffee after Mary Jane cleared the table. "She's a fine-looking woman," Jake said, shooting a quick glance her way.

"She is," Quinn nodded. "I can see where she would have gotten old Gregory's blood to boiling. I hope her Prince does show up, but it ain't gonna be anybody from here in Sanderson. All we've got is a lot of toads."

"So, she wants to trade her dead sugar Daddy in for a Prince Charming?" Jake asked, taking his last sip of coffee.

Jake could tell by Quinn's laser glare he didn't like the remark.

"Just kidding," Jake promptly replied. "Just kidding."

Quinn finished off his coffee and tossed two twenty dollar bills on the table for a tip. "Dang, Quinn," Jake said, shaking his head. "I've heard of big tippers, but that's ridiculous."

"She needs the money," is all Quinn said as they got up and walked to the cash register. Quinn took a quick glance at Mary Jane who was waiting on another booth. He complimented the cashier on the hash browns and was waiting for his change when the radio on his shoulder crackled. "Chief, where's your location?" the dispatcher asked.

"I'm headed back to the office."

"Something's going on at Joe Lambert's house. Trey called and he was screaming. I couldn't make anything of what he was saying, except that something was wrong with his Dad."

"I'll check it out," Quinn responded with a sense of urgency. "Call Sam and tell him to meet me there." Quinn glanced at Jake and asked, "Want to tag along?"

"Damn straight I do!"

They rushed out to Quinn's car and he told Jake to buckle up. Quinn backed up, pulled out of the parking lot and stomped the accelerator, shooting the car forward in the light rain like a bullet. For the next five minutes, Jake experienced a thrill ride better than anything at Disney World. Twice he thought his hash browns were going to come back up, and twice he was certain Quinn was going to wrap them around a tree and kill them both, thereby assuring them a spot on the front page of the next issue of the Sentinel.

The Lamberts lived in a nice double-wide trailer set up on three acres fifty yards inside the south city limits. Pulling into the front yard, Jake finally exhaled, thankful that he and his breakfast had survived the trip. Quinn was quickly out of the car, radioing his dispatcher that he was on the scene. Trey Lambert was sitting on the front steps, getting wet, looking straight ahead, his eyes glazed over.

"My God son, what's the matter?" Quinn asked. The boy didn't answer, didn't move.

"Trey, you've got to tell me what's going on."

Still not saying anything, Trey got up and opened the front door to the trailer. Quinn followed him and Jake was right behind. Jake took a deep breath, realizing his hash browns might revolt yet.

"Here," Quinn said to Jake. He handed him two sticks of Black Jack chewing gum which Jake quickly popped into his mouth. Sam was pulling into the yard as Quinn and Jake disappeared with Trey inside the trailer. Jake swallowed hard again. Without saying a word, Trey led them to a bedroom on the back side of the trailer. "Damn it! Damn it!" shouted Quinn as he slammed his fist against the wall. Jake had to turn his head for a moment. Trey stood in the room, in too much shock to speak. Joe Lambert's naked body was sitting in a wooden straight back chair. His hands were behind him, tied to the chair, and his ankles were laced to the legs of the chair. His legs and crotch were coated in blood, and the cream-colored carpet had a huge red puddle under the chair.

"Damn it, Joe! You dumb-ass redneck! Why did you have to go and get yourself killed? For once couldn't you have kept your pants on?" Quinn screamed at the corpse as if Joe was still alive and the tongue-lashing would keep him from making a big mistake. Quinn was about to cry.

Jake's hash browns finally revolted and came up, but he was able to make it to a trash can conveniently tucked away in a corner of the bedroom. He took a moment to compose himself and walked to Trey who was still in a trance. Jake took him by the shoulders and suggested, "Come on, son, let's get out of here." He ushered Trey away from the gruesome scene and asked Sam to keep the boy outside. "Call the coroner. And an ambulance," Jake requested of the deputy.

Back in the bedroom, Quinn had his faced buried in his hands. "Sam's calling the coroner," Jake told him.

"This is my fault," Quinn said softly. "I'm the reason Joe is dead."

"What are you talking about?" Jake asked.

"Because I withheld information from him and everyone else in town. If I had told them the whole story about how Todd Monroe died, this would not have happened. Joe wouldn't have put himself in this spot if he had known there was a psycho sex killer on the loose!"

"You can't say that," Jake argued. "People have no business under any circumstances allowing themselves to be tied to chairs, trees or whatever. It's not normal."

"No, you're wrong. Anything goes in sex between two consenting adults. I'm certain Joe didn't consent to having a knife rammed repeatedly into his stomach, and he wouldn't have put himself in that spot if he had known about Todd."

"He knew enough about Todd's death not to do this. Everyone in town knew enough about Todd not to do this."

Quinn stood motionless in the room, staring at Joe Lambert. Jake walked closer to the body and felt like throwing up again, but he had emptied his stomach the first time. He could not take his eyes off Joe's face. Jake shook his head and bit his lip as he imagined what that awful final moment must have been like for Joe. Another thought struck Jake. How horrible was it for Trey to come home and find his Dad murdered in such a wicked manner? How does anyone forget such a moment? How do you keep it from scarring you the rest of your life? Jake looked back at Quinn who was bent over, his hands resting on his knees. He was sniffling.

"Come on Quinn," Jake said, having to summon inner strength himself. "You've got a job to do. You've got a murder to solve. You've got two murders to solve, and the same son of a bitch committed them both!"

Slowly, Quinn stood up, snorted to clear his nose and throat and took a deep breath. "You're right. Let's get to work. I guarantee you I'm going to find the son of a bitch who did this! I'm going to tear this place apart until I find a clue, something that will solve this case. Every killer slips up some way. This one's no different."

"What are you going to do about Trey?"

"Call his mother. I think she lives in Savannah. She and Joe have been divorced for a couple of years. Trey refused to go with her. He didn't want to change schools. I'm also going to send him to the hospital in Callaway County. I don't think there's anything physically wrong with him, but emotionally, he's going to need some counseling. A lot of counseling."

Jake and Quinn studied the body some more and surveyed the room. Nothing was out of place. Without doubt, Joe, with his football player's physique, had readily agreed to being tied up. He had paid a terribly high price for a few minutes of sexual bliss.

"Damn, Martin," Quinn fussed. "You come to town and all hell breaks loose. You've been here a few weeks and this little town has already had more murders than it had in the past two decades. I'm beginning to think you're a bad omen or something."

"No, I've already used up my quota of bad luck. That's how I ended up in Sanderson."

"Let's just catch this son of a bitch before this happens again. Come on, let's try to talk to Trey."

Sam was sitting on the front steps with Trey. "Hasn't said a word," Sam said to Quinn who sat down on the other side of Trey. Water was dripping off the bill of Sam's cap.

"Can I talk to you?" Quinn asked calmly. Trey didn't respond. His eyes were fixed straight ahead. "Is there anything you can tell me?" After not getting a response, Quinn realized that a bomb could go off and it wouldn't shake Trey out of his trance. Quinn continued to sit next to the boy. Neither said a word until the ambulance arrived. The paramedics gingerly led Trey to the back of the ambulance for the twenty mile trip to Callaway General. "I'm going to find out who did this, Trey. I promise," Quinn said through gritted teeth. He watched the ambulance drive off and yelled to Sam, "Get my bat out of the car," which Jake thought was an unusual request.

"Do you think we need to talk to Maddie Hampton about this?" Sam asked.

Quinn wasn't expecting Sam's question, but it struck a chord with him. "Yeah. Yeah we do," Quinn agreed. Sam nodded and walked away to fulfill Quinn's order.

"What do you mean you need to talk to Maddie about this?" Jake asked.

"There's a history between Maddie and Todd and Joe," was Quinn's short reply. He looked back at the house instead of Jake.

"What kind of history?"

"It's involved. I'll tell you later."

"How about telling me now."

"Later."

Sam returned from the car with a long, thin plastic bat children use for backyard games of Whiffle baseball. Quinn took the bat, twisted his hands on the handle and walked to a pine tree a few feet from the road in the Lambert's front yard. With the rain falling heavier, Quinn whacked the bat ten times against the tree, each whack generating more force. Quinn tossed the bat back to Sam, used his handkerchief to wipe rain off his face and went back into the house with recent arrival Lawson Lockridge.

"What's the deal with the bat?" Jake asked Sam. They were both wet enough to need a change of clothes.

"Ask Quinn some time," Sam said. "It's a long story."

CHAPTER TEN

S anderson, the little town where nothing ever happens, was afraid of its shadow. That two murders had been committed was unnerving enough, but the manner in which the two men had died was what had everyone's tongues wagging. Quinn, still toting a backpack of guilt about Joe Lambert's death, had finally released more details of that murder and Todd Monroe's. The information changed the town's outlook overnight. People were scared. Smiles were fewer and less sincere when friends and neighbors met on Main Street or at the Waffle House or grocery store. Single women, particularly those known to enjoy the company of the opposite sex on a regular basis, were getting curious looks. Suddenly, wives and girlfriends had a much greater interest in the whereabouts of their husbands and boyfriends. Since the killings had occurred at night, Quinn considered implementing a curfew, but he didn't have to. Men were being given strict, not open for discussion orders by their better halves to be home early every night. Everyone had a theory, from quick no-thought finger pointing at Mary Jane Hamilton to claims that a band of sex-starved, cutthroat gypsy women had been spotted just outside town.

The news media wasn't helping. Crews from CNN, Fox News, and USA Today led the invasion of TV, radio and newspapers into the town like the swarms of beetles that occasionally threatened Sanderson's crops. Townsfolk accustomed to the Sentinel's laidback journalism and harmless questions about school activities or the occasional moronic decision by the city council were having microphones stuck in their faces for their reactions to the killings. Most residents disliked the intrusion and just wanted the outsiders to go away. Realtor Robert McIntire, for instance, was worried the negative publicity would dry up what little real estate activity still existed. A few, like service station owner and unofficial town historian Spare Tire Turner were enjoying the attention and couldn't wait to see themselves on television or read their quotes in the paper. Spare Tire got his nickname not from his inventory at the gas station, but because he appeared to be concealing one under his shirt. The only positive aspect to the onslaught? The two local motels and handful of eating places were increasing their cash flow.

Pressure was mounting on Quinn. Reporters were dogging his every move, throwing him questions he couldn't answer. He didn't have any motive or suspects for the killings and no, Sanderson had never before experienced such horrific crimes. The mayor and council were fuming, first because Quinn had allowed a second murder to be committed before he released crucial details about the first, and second, because no progress was being made in identifying a suspect. Quinn was having to give the mayor daily updates on the case, and at the council's insistence, had called a town hall meeting. Two hundred and fifty people, some angry, all on edge, filtered into the high school gym to grill Quinn and get his assurance that everything would be all right and that the killer *would* be caught. The audience's questions ranged from the appropriate "What precautions can we take?" to the preposterous "Did a witch really cast a spell on the two victims?" Unsolicited comments blurted from the bleachers included "You're a damn sorry excuse for a police chief" to "Catch this killer, quick!" By the time Quinn, sweating like a field hand under the hot south Georgia sun, was through talking and answering questions, the audience seemed more at ease, but not much, experiencing that same type of apprehension when a loved one has undergone surgery and the doctors tell you they're all right, but not yet out of danger.

Catching his breath and shaking the hands of several supporters as the mumbling crowd filed out of the gym, Quinn waited for the perfect postured, broad shouldered dark suited man he had noticed out of the corner of his eye. Quinn finished with the knot of people surrounding him, thanking them all, and turned to the suit, who immediately extended his hand. "Travis Stamps, Georgia Bureau of Investigation."

"Agent Stamps," Quinn acknowledged, completing the handshake.

"Very interesting case you have here."

"It is. Uh, I'm sorry, but I don't recall requesting GBI support."

"You didn't. Your mayor asked me to talk to you. I'm here to help any way I can."

"Oh, he did?" Quinn asked, glancing to the back of the gym where the mayor was still shaking hands, patting folks on the shoulder and gesturing with his hands. "Well, I'm sorry he called you. We've got everything under control."

"I'm sure you do. So it shouldn't take you long to wrap up this case."

Quinn wasn't sure what Stamps meant, so he replied with, "We're putting all our resources into making an arrest."

Stamps asked, "How many people are in this little town? You ought to be able to interrogate the whole town in a week. Somebody's got to know something."

Quinn didn't know if Stamps was serious or joking.

"It may take a little longer than that," Quinn suggested.

"I'm going to be in town several days. I've got several cases in surrounding counties to look at. If you don't mind, I'd like to come by your office and take a look at what you've got on this case."

"Why don't you work on the other cases? My department can handle this one."

Stamps looked to the back of the gymnasium at the mayor and cleared his throat. "Let me explain this a little more succinctly. The mayor suggested I help you."

"What if I tell you no?"

"Then I'll have to talk to the mayor. Look, Chief. I'm not here to take over the investigation. I'm here for help, for support. You tell me what you need me to do."

"Stay out of the way."

"Let's not have an adversarial relationship. That's not going to help catch the killer."

Quinn studied the agent's face. Stamps showed no anger or frustration at Quinn's hostility.

"You're right," Quinn relented. "I just don't want anyone thinking I run a country bumpkin police department that can't find the toilet paper to wipe its ass with."

Stamps offered a small smile. "Crude reference aside, we don't think that. We know your history."

"That could either be good or bad."

"I'm talking about the good."

Quinn extended his hand. "In that case, I humbly accept your offer of assistance." "Good. Some time tomorrow."

"Tomorrow," Quinn nodded.

The two men shook hands again and Quinn watched as Stamps went directly to the mayor. Their conversation was brief and they both left. Quinn muttered, "Damn it!"

While Quinn was peeved that he suddenly had help he didn't want or think he needed, one development he appreciated was Trey Lambert's improvement. Aided by counselors called in by Callaway General Hospital and the love and support of his friends, Trey had recovered enough emotionally to help his mother plan Joe's funeral. They did not belong to a church, but Pastor Allen volunteered to conpacking the service at First Baptist. On the morning after Quinn's public meeting, First Baptist's 300-seat sanctuary was standing room only, and in a heartwarming gesture brought about by two episodes of terrible misfortune, Trey Lambert and Nick Monroe sat side by side. The baseball teams from Barber County and Eagleton sat behind them, swapping, for at least a few precious moments, competitiveness for compassion. Pastor Allen urged both boys to go on with their lives, to put the tragedies behind them and make the most of every day. He told them to take comfort that their Dads were in a better place and that the killer would have to answer not only to worldly authority but the Heavenly Father as well. The punishment on earth would be mild compared to eternal judgment, the wise old preacher warned.

Quinn led the funeral procession to the city cemetery where Preacher Allen made a few final remarks at the graveside. A hundred or so people filed by under the canopy to hug Trey and his mother before somberly returning to their cars. Quinn couldn't take his eyes off the woman in a black sheath dress and black hose who was standing alone away from the crowd and seemed to be waiting for everyone to leave.

As Trey was receiving final condolences from his teammates, Quinn approached the woman in black. "I'm surprised to see you here," he said.

"I knew Joe," Mary Jane Hamilton told Quinn. "We cried on each other's shoulder after his wife left and I kicked my husband out.

I felt like I needed to be here today, but I am very uncomfortable. I feel like everyone is staring at me. Half the people here think I killed Joe and Todd." Mary Jane glanced at some of the mourners who were leaving. She was certain she could detect them shooting quick, accusatory looks back at her.

"Is that all you and Joe did, cry on each other's shoulders?"

"That's a question I don't have to answer today. It's not appropriate."

"You're right. I'm sorry." Quinn studied the woman's curvy figure. He was trying not to be obvious that he was gawking at her.

"Any leads on the murderer?" she asked. "It's awful, isn't it, that we'd have two killings in this little town."

"The investigation is coming along."

"I guess I need to go. I wanted to speak to Trey, but I've got to be at work in thirty minutes. Got to keep serving those hash browns," she smiled weakly.

"Guess so," he replied with his own weak smile.

Mary Jane began taking the last few steps to her seven year old car but stopped when Quinn called her name. She turned around and he walked toward her.

"I feel a little awkward asking this," he started, "do you need some money?" He reached for his billfold.

"No Chief," she smiled. "I'm doing O.K."

"Are you sure?"

"I'm sure," she assured him and turned to start back to her car.

"If you don't need any money . . . can I treat you to dinner one night?"

Mary Jane turned back around. By the look on her face, Quinn couldn't tell if she was pleased or sickened.

"Are you sure you want to do that, knowing what you do about me and Gregory, and that everyone in town is talking about me? What about your investigation? Am I a suspect with you? I am with everyone else."

"You can't pay attention to what other people say. To hell with them. I'd just like to have someone to talk to besides Jake Martin. I'm getting tired of looking at his ugly face."

Mary Jane smiled. "I'd love to have dinner with you." She started to walk away, but stopped and turned around again. "As long as we don't have to eat at Waffle House." She took another step toward her car, but stopped and turned around again. "Are you *sure* you want to do this?"

"I'm sure," he replied emphatically. He stood and watched as she sat down in her car and pulled her exquisite legs inside.

CHAPTER ELEVEN

The year-old sports car was moving much too fast for the narrow two lane road linking Sanderson with Thomasville. The two Barber County coeds, returning from a trip to shop for prom dresses, were rushing back for a meeting of the First Baptist Youth Council, which was scheduled to start in five minutes.

"The guys are going to love our dresses," Emily, the passenger said. "I love the long slit up the leg of yours."

"I'm showing leg and you're showing cleavage," Laura, the driver, giggled in return. Headed directly into the late afternoon sun, Laura peeked into her pocketbook, grabbed her sunglasses and slipped them on. "The guys will love them, but I'm not sure about Dad. I'm not sure what he will like the least, all the leg I'll be showing or that I charged a hundred dollars more on his credit card than he told me I could."

"When was the last time your Dad fussed at you about anything?" Emily asked. "You've got him wrapped so tight around your little finger, I'm surprised he can breathe."

"You're right," Laura replied happily. "Dad and I do get along really well."

"We're not going to make it back in time for the start of the meeting. Let's try to call the church and let them know we're running late," Emily suggested.

Laura glanced down again and rummaged through her pocketbook for her cell phone. Struggling to dial the church's number, she dropped the phone and instinctively lunged for it. Her hand jerked the steering wheel, causing the speeding car to veer off the road and go airborne over a drainage ditch in Evil Knievel fashion. Bouncing violently when hitting the ground, the out-of-control car clipped a small pine tree, rolled over twice and crashed broadside into a larger pine, the sounds blending together into a sickening, tragic symphony. The accident happened so fast, the girls never screamed.

Within seconds, other motorists were at the smoldering, twisted car to render aid. Emily had been thrown from the car, her head smacking against the tree, crushing her skull and killing her instantly. Laura, crushed, battered and bloody and still in the car, strapped in by her seatbelt, was conscious, barely. As the frantic good samaritans tried to begin rendering aid, Laura, her voice fading, begged them to help her friend. She didn't know it was too late. It was too late for anyone to help Laura too. In front of a horrified, helpless audience, she died before an ambulance could arrive.

So, as quickly as two murders had grabbed Sanderson's attention, the murders just as quickly slipped into the background following the tragedy on Thomasville Road. The news spread as quickly as a south Georgia brush fire. The town's emotional and physical resources, which had been poured out on behalf of the Monroes and Lamberts, now had to be directed toward the families of the two girls. As disturbing as the men's deaths had been, particularly the manner in which they occurred, this accident was even more devastating. The two girls were true All-Americans—honor students, cheerleaders, active in the church, friends to everyone. Every pastor in town, the high school counselor, the staff at Callaway General, even visiting professionals called in by the hospital, were put to work helping students and adults deal with their grief. The board of education considered cancelling classes for a few days, but the experts said no, the teenagers needed to be together so they could comfort each other. No one, not even the town's oldest resident, ninety-eight year old Estelle Patterson, could remember a time when Sanderson was so heart-broken, so emotionally drained.

Jake knew he was emotionally drained, and he didn't even know the people whom tragedy had befallen. He sat at his desk in his cramped office at the Sentinel feeling guilty, beginning to believe that Quinn was right, that some type of curse had accompanied his arrival in town. In a matter of weeks, Sanderson had gone from a place where nothing ever happened to a place where all hell was breaking loose. Maybe he did need to leave. If doing so would return this mourning town to its previous state of bliss, he'd depart in a second.

The sun had already gone down and Jake had work to do, but he could not get his mind off the sadness that had engulfed this decent, undeserving citizenry. He sat slumped at his chair, staring at his computer monitor. Words would not come. He wished he could write something that would make this town feel better, that would take away the hurt.

His funk was interrupted by Kenny who had been impacted as much as anyone by recent events. As a Barber County alumnus, he knew Nick, Trey and both girls well and all four had been featured in many of his articles for the Sentinel. Jake was glad to see him. They could feel miserable together.

That wasn't the purpose of Kenny's visit. "You need to go see Mrs. Hampton," he told Jake.

"I'm not in the mood."

"You need to go see her. Those girls were two of her favorite students. She was very close to them. She's hurting, a lot. She hasn't been out of her house since the wreck. You need to go see her."

Jake sat up in his chair. "I'm pretty stupid, aren't I?" Jake meekly asked Kenny.

"If you're talking about not having enough sense to realize you could make Mrs. Hampton feel better, yeah, you're pretty stupid."

"What should I get her? Flowers? Candy? A card?"

"Who says you have to get her anything? Just go see her!"

"I'm going be out awhile," Jake told Kenny as he headed out of the office. He stopped, though, and asked, "What about you Kenny? Are you all right?"

"I'm all right. You go see Mrs. Hampton."

Thirty minutes later, Jake was standing at the front door of Maddie's aging, but well-kept vinyl-siding house in what twenty years earlier had been Sanderson's nicest subdivision. Despite trying to convince himself not to be, Jake was nervous. He didn't know what to say to Maddie. He didn't know if he was there as a friend, comforter or potential suitor. His heart was definitely beating faster than normal as he rang the door bell.

Maddie was surprised to see Jake. She had been crying. Jake could tell that by her red eyes and blotchy face. After greeting him, she used tissues in both hands to wipe her eyes dry. "I know I look like a mess. I would have dressed up if I had known you were coming over," she apologized.

"You look fine," Jake assured Maddie as she led him in. She looked comfortable shoeless, in blue shorts and a white Barber County High School Beta Club t-shirt. "If this isn't a good time . . ."

"Oh no! I'm really glad to see you. Sit down, please."

Jake sat down on the sofa and handed her the video he had rented on the way over. "It's *Young Frankenstein*," he explained. "I love this movie. I've seen it a hundred times, but it always makes me laugh."

"Thanks." She forced a smile as she accepted the video. She gently dropped it on the floor and sat down in a side chair. "I could use a good laugh."

"I'm so sorry about your two students," is all Jake could think to say.

A tear trickled down Maddie's cheek and she wiped it away. "They were special girls. Since my husband died and Robbie left for school, I've sort of adopted all of my students as my children, but Laura and Emily were special. We were very close. You know they were with me when I brought the cookies to your office."

Tears started streaming down her face again. Jake, with a lump in his own throat, remembered the day Maddie and the girls visited. They were so cute, so filled with the enthusiasm of youth. He got up and handed her the box of facial tissue that was on the end table. She thanked him and wiped the tears away again.

"How are their parents doing?"

"They're devastated, as you would expect. Thankfully, both families are strong Christians. Their faith and their First Baptist family are helping them get by. I've been such a mess myself I haven't been able to give them much comfort."

Jake shifted on the sofa. "You do so much for people, Maddie. Let some other folks help them—and you. I admire them—and I admire you for your strong faith. That's something I've never had. I wish I did."

"This is testing my faith. But then I've had my faith tested before, and God always sees me through whatever crisis I'm facing."

"You make it sound so easy, like you can snap your fingers and God makes you feel better."

"It's not quite like that, but you can find peace of mind. Just pray, read the Bible and find a church. Your faith will come. And if that church happens to be First Baptist, well, that would be nice."

"I've just never made those things a priority."

"You have to make them a priority. I know how busy you have been, but try setting aside five minutes a day to start with. It will make a huge difference in your life. Now, enough of me preaching. Any new developments on the murders?"

"We don't have to talk about that."

"I'd like to. Maybe it will get my mind off the girls."

What Jake wanted to talk about was why Quinn felt compelled to quiz Maddie about the murders of Todd Monroe and Joe Lambert. What connection did she have to them? "Right now, Quinn is stumped, but he will solve the case. I'm certain of that. And no matter how busy I've been, that's not an excuse for not coming by to see you. I'm sorry."

Maddie smiled and Jake could see a little sparkle in her moist eyes. "That's so sweet of you Jake. But your timing is perfect. I needed someone to come by tonight."

"Do you want to watch the movie? I can run to the store and get some popcorn and soft drinks."

"No. I'm not really in the mood for a movie, but I do have a favor to ask of you."

"Sure."

Maddie looked down at the floor, was quite a moment and then looked up at Jake. "Will you stay with me tonight?"

Jake was totally surprised and was speechless.

"I just want someone in the house with me. I am feeling so alone and depressed."

"Sure, if that's what you want."

"That's what I want. I'm so tired. I think I might be able to get a good night's sleep if someone is here with me."

Jake looked at Maddie. He could see she was exhausted. "Come here," he requested while extending his hand. She got up and clasped his hand. "Lay your head in my lap and rest for a few minutes."

She readily accepted his offer, putting her head in Jake's lap and stretching out on the sofa. Maddie closed her eyes and Jake studied her face. Confident that she wouldn't object, Jake leaned over and kissed Maddie on the forehead. She was asleep in two minutes. He carried Maddie to her bed and he spent the night on the sofa.

CHAPTER TWELVE

Kenny stormed into Jake's office, plopped down in the nearest chair, folded his arms and mumbled "Damn it!"

Jake looked up from the Sentinel budget numbers he was struggling with, studied Kenny's face and said, "Mmmm. Must be Sunny, right?"

"How did you know?" Kenny asked, unfolding his arms and scratching the back of his head with his right hand.

"Well, with you, it's either sports or Sunny. There weren't any games last night, so it must be Sunny. Correct?"

"Correct."

"What was it this time?"

"She and her Dad had a knockdown, drag out fight. I was late getting her home. She rode over to Thomasville with me to help me pick out a tux for the prom. Her Dad was already home when we got there and he started raising hell, about her not having supper ready. He bitched about going to work early and working hard all day, and the least she could do was have supper ready for him. I mean, he went nuts over nothing. Well, that must have hit her the wrong way, because she went ballistic. She threw a frying pan at him, he called me a wormy little son of a bitch, and it was all I could do to hold my temper. Sunny told her Dad that she wished he was dead and ran out of the house. I would have killed him myself if I had had a gun, the bastard! I called him a son of a bitch back and went to see about Sunny. She was outside bawling her eyes out. Her old man came out a few minutes later and apologized. To me, it didn't sound like he really meant it, but she went back inside. I think they ended up going to Waffle House for some supper. I couldn't stay. I had to get away. I don't know how she stays."

Jake shook his head. "Sounds like a bad scene, and you got caught right smack in the middle of it."

"Yeah, and it wasn't the first time."

Jake got out of his chair and walked to within arm's length of Kenny. "I've asked you this before, but I've got to ask you again. Is she worth all this stress?"

For the first time, Jake noticed a trace of doubt with Kenny who got out of his chair and stood at the doorway to Jake's office. "She is . . . I think. But I've got to admit. All of this leaves my stomach in a knot. And I've met a girl at the community college that I'd like to ask out, but . . ."

"But what Kenny?"

"I don't know that I can do that to Sunny. If I stop seeing her, she won't have any body. Yeah, Miss Wayne and Mrs. Hampton will look after her, but she won't have any friends her own age. Do you know how hard it was to convince her to go to her own senior prom?"

"I admire what you're doing for her, but there comes a time when you have to look out for yourself. I think that time may have come for you. I'm beginning to worry about physical harm. I don't want to see her hurt, but I don't want to see you get hurt either. Maybe it's time to report some of this to Quinn or Family and Children Services."

"I'm not going to report it, I'll tell you that flat out. Besides, Sunny will be 18 in a few weeks and then she can be out on her own. I just hope she'll leave."

"But in a situation like this, a few weeks is a long time. Long enough for someone to get hurt."

Kenny sighed and propped against the door frame. "I don't know what to do, Jake. I really don't."

"Have you talked to your parents about this?"

"Of course. They don't want me seeing her and have told me that in pretty strong terms. That's why I'm talking to you. You're not as stubborn and hard-headed as my parents."

"Thanks, I think. But I believe I side with your parents on this one."

"Well, snot! You're not much help."

"Looks like you're going to have to figure out this one by yourself. Good luck. Now don't you have a story to write or some game to cover?"

"Yeah," Kenny sighed again. "There's a softball tournament over at the recreation center. See you later. And thanks for listening."

"Sure. Any time." Jake saw that Kenny's heart was telling him one thing while his head was telling him something else. Sitting down again, Jake was glad he had not had children of his own and such dilemmas to deal with, but by the time his butt hit the chair, he was struck with a wave of melancholy. He had missed out on so much in life by not having children. And now, at age 45, not only did he not have children; he didn't have a wife or a family of any kind. He was totally alone in a little piece of nowhere called Sanderson, Georgia. Jake leaned back in his chair and he wanted to cry.

His cramped office seemed smaller than usual and the air felt hot and heavy. The budget review could wait. Jake needed to get away for a few minutes. He walked toward the front to let Hazel know he was going to be out, but suddenly that wasn't necessary.

Hazel smiled at him and said, "I was just about to ring back to your office." Maddie was there to see him and deliver a batch of cookies. Fresh cookies that she, not her students, had baked.

"Now I believe in angels!" Jake admitted.

"Beg your pardon?" Hazel asked.

"Nothing." Jake took the plate of cookies and put them on Hazel's desk. "Would you like to take a walk?" he asked Maddie.

"Sure," she smiled. "That would be nice."

"Hazel . . ." Jake started.

"I know. You're going to be out awhile."

On a beautiful cloudless spring day cooled by a light breeze, Jake and Maddie walked down the street. "Are you feeling better?" he asked.

"I do, but I didn't feel like going to work. I felt like taking the day off."

"I'm glad you did. Am I glad to see you!"

Maddie stopped on the sidewalk and smiled at Jake. "I'm glad to hear you say that. I'm glad to see you too. Thank you for helping me through these last few days. They've been difficult." She squeezed his hand.

They walked to the barbecue place at the corner of Main and Church streets, bought waffle cones of vanilla ice cream and moved on to the bench at the little town park a block away. "What was that remark you made about angels back at the office?" Maddie asked before taking a lick of her ice cream.

Jake could tell he was starting to blush. "I think today you are my angel. I'd just finished a talk with Kenny. He was telling me about his problems, but listening to his problems made me realize what a mess I've made of my life. I was really feeling sorry for myself. You absolutely could not have come at a better time. Just seeing you made me feel better."

Maddie's eyes sparkled in the bright sunlight. "I'm glad I could help. Is there something you want to talk about?"

"Do you want to know how I really ended up in Sanderson?"

"If you want to tell me."

Jake didn't finish his ice cream. He walked a few feet to the trash can, tossed away the cone and sat back down. He bowed his head before facing Maddie. "To make a long story short, I'm a recovering alcoholic and a recovering gambler. Those two vices cost me my wife and my job. I was so messed up, no one in the newspaper business but Stephen House would hire me. And I'm still not sure why he did."

"I guess Stephen believes everyone deserves a second chance."

"If you don't want to . . ."

"Whoa mister. That's enough! I don't know the person you're talking about. The Jake Martin I know is a man who has come into a little south Georgia town that he could have easily made fun of, but instead, he's made friends, done a wonderful job with the Sentinel . . . and you were my angel a few nights ago when I was so low. That's the Jake Martin I know. That's the Jake Martin I enjoy being with."

"The first day I was here, I sat in my car in front of the Sentinel office and seriously thought about backing up and driving as fast as I could out of town. Want to know what stopped me? Remember Richard Gere in *An Officer and a Gentleman* when he screamed 'I don't have anywhere else to go!' at Lou Gossett, Jr.? Well, that was me. I'm not here by choice. I didn't have anywhere else to go. But from the minute I got here, everyone has been wonderful. People have treated me far better than I deserve. In fact, there have been a couple of times when I've thought that a jinx must have followed me to town. So many bad things have happened since I arrived."

"No, you didn't bring a jinx with you. God gave us free will, and people do foolish things. I'm surprised that Pastor Allen hasn't preached a sermon on that since all of this started happening."

"If he does, I bet it will be a long one. Pardon me. I don't bet on anything these days. Not even the length of the pastor's sermon."

Maddie smiled. "You're probably right. If he does and you want to go to sleep, you can lay your head on my shoulder."

"I may take you up on that. You know, you're right about one thing. I'm not the same person who fouled things up so badly in Atlanta. I'm really trying to find the faith, the sense of purpose that most of you here in Sanderson have."

"You're not the only person who makes mistakes. We all make mistakes. God forgives us, and fortunately, so do most of the people who live here. Now tell me about this conversation with Kenny that had you so down in the dumps."

Jake spent the next ten minutes rehashing Kenny's confrontation at Sunny's. Maddie's heart went out to both teenagers. She would hate to see Kenny walk away from Sunny, but could understand if that's what he needed to do. Sunny obviously needed help dealing with her father, but Maddie knew the school counselor was too overworked and too non-confrontational to give the situation the attention it needed. With Sunny in one of her classes, Maddie could create an occasion to talk to her in a relaxed, non-threatening environment. If Sunny admitted she needed help, Maddie would do everything in her power to see that she got it, either through Callaway General or private clinics or both. She was willing to pay for help for Sunny.

Jake would have readily spent the remainder of the day talking to Maddie, but he knew Hazel was waiting for the budget numbers. Reluctantly, he walked Maddie back to her red Jeep Grand Cherokee that was parked in front of the Sentinel. "I hope you like the cookies," she said as she slipped into the driver's seat.

"If Hazel hasn't already eaten all of them," he smiled. He gently reached for Maddie's door before she could shut it. "Thank you," he said softly. "You *were* my angel today."

"Don't put me on too high a pedestal. My halo gets knocked sideways on occasion."

"Do angels go on dates?"

"This one would love too."

"Saturday night? Seven o'clock?"

"See you then."

Jake helped Maddie shut her door and watched her drive away. He stood on the sidewalk another minute, trying to get motivated enough to go back inside to work on the budget. "I know. You need them in the next five minutes," he said, walking past Hazel.

"The cookies are good. I saved you a few," she smiled. He took the plate with the remaining goodies and went straight to his office. After enjoying three of the tasty oatmeal raisin cookies, Jake grudgingly started reviewing the budget numbers. While the murders and fatal auto accident had taken an emotional toll on the town, they had been good for the newspaper's bottom line. Subscriptions were up eleven percent and rack sales had increased by eighteen percent.

Hazel was going to like those numbers. So would Stephen House, if he was around. Jake liked the figures too, although he admitted it was the series of misfortunes rather than his smooth writing style that was responsible for the improvement.

Having finished his review, Jake slipped the spreadsheet back into a legal-size file folder and got up to take them back up front to Hazel. He was about to step out of his office when he stopped and went back to his desk to answer the phone.

"Jake, you old son of a gun, do you know how hard it's been for me to track you down?" the caller fussed.

The announcement startled Jake, especially since he didn't recognize the voice. After a moment to think, Jake replied, "Jack? Jack Harper?"

"Yeah, it's me. What in the world are you doing in Sanderson, Georgia?"

"I'm editor, publisher, reporter, financial advisor, circulation consultant, toilet cleaner and all-around good guy for the Sanderson Sentinel. That's what I'm doing here."

"But I mean, how did you get there? I've never heard of the place. I had to get the Atlas out, and then it took me awhile to find it. The place is a speck on the map, like a grain of salt."

"I'm here because beggars can't be choosers. After the mess I made of things in Atlanta, I wasn't exactly inundated with offers. Down here, I got an offer I couldn't refuse. By the way, how did you find me?"

"I just kept asking mutual friends. Let's see, I think it was Bruce Bodiford who told me you had gone south. Man, for awhile, it was like you dropped off the face of the earth."

"That's how I felt for awhile."

"Isn't that place boring?"

Jake laughed and kicked back in his chair. "Oh no, this place has been anything but boring. As a matter of fact, I've worked harder the last few weeks than I have in a long time. And it feels good."

"Have you heard from Kathy?"

Jake was silent. He swiveled around in his chair and looked at the bare walls of his small office. He could feel his forehead getting warm. "No." he finally replied. "Why would she want to talk to me?"

"You guys were together a long time. I just thought she might want to know how you're doing."

"Uh . . . the last thing she said to me was *good luck.* Of course, that was right after she had told me she didn't care if she ever saw my sorry ass again."

"I'm sorry the two of you couldn't work things out."

"I'm sorry I didn't treat her better. I don't blame her for anything. She put up with me working too much, drinking too much and wasting our money betting on the Dallas Cowboys a lot longer than most women would have."

"That's because she loved you."

"Yeah, well, love will only carry you so far. But enough about my wonderful life. What's going on with you? Are you such a caring humanitarian that you called solely to check up on me?"

"Actually, sort of. I did call to check up on you, and since you asked, things are going wonderfully for me. Before we get into that, I want to chew your butt out for not letting me know what you were doing. How long have we been best friends?"

"A long time."

"That's right. And you split town without telling me anything. Is that any way to treat your best friend?"

Jake shut his eyes and rubbed the back of his neck with his right hand. He didn't say anything.

"Well is it?" Jack pressed the issue.

"No, it's not. I guess I was embarrassed. Embarrassed about how low I'd let myself get and how badly I'd mistreated you and Kathy and a lot of other people. But I'm glad to report that I'm better now. A hell of a lot better. In fact, I'm doing fine."

"I'm glad to hear that. I really did want to know, Jake, and since you're doing fine, I've got a proposition for you."

"I'm listening."

"I've gotten involved with some good folks in Charleston who want to start a new lifestyle magazine. They've got a nice wad of cash to get the project started, and we're recruiting people to join the team. You're the first person I thought of. This would be perfect for you."

Jake got up from his chair and stood at the side of his desk. "I'm flattered but . . ."

"But what? Beautiful Charleston on the Atlantic coast or podunk Sanderson in that vast wasteland called south Georgia. What is there to decide?"

"It's not that easy," Jake quickly argued. "The people here have been great to me. Besides, I'm not sure I'm ready to go back into the kind of pressure you're talking about."

"It's a sweet deal Jake. The money's good and the people behind us are good. You know me. I don't go off on half-ass wild goose chases."

"No, you don't. I know the offer's legitimate and I appreciate it. I just don't know."

"You don't have to give me an answer today. You've got a little time to think it over. All I want from you today are two promises—that you are O.K., that your problems are a thing of the past, and if they are, that you'll think about coming with me to Charleston."

Jake ran his fingers through his hair. "You are a good friend Jack. You don't know how much this means to me, after the way I fouled things up so badly that you'd even consider me. I make two promises to you. One, if I do come, you'll get one heck of an effort from me. Two, I will think about it but I can't give you an answer today."

"Understood. Well, I know where you are now, and I've got your phone number. Let me give you my cell phone number and e-mail address. I'm really glad to know that you're doing so well, Jake. You deserve something good to happen to you."

Jake wrote down Jack's information and the two old friends exchanged goodbyes. He handed Hazel the budget numbers and went for a drive to ponder Jack Harper's offer.

CHAPTER THIRTEEN

Barber County High School's 12:45 bell rang, sending Maddie's students out of her classroom and to the cafeteria for lunch. "Sunny, can I see you a minute?" Maddie asked as the twenty seniors noisily walked out the door. No one gave any thought to Maddie's request because she was always talking to students individually about special projects and extra credit. That type of interest in her students had helped Maddie be honored as Teacher of the Year three times. If Barber County High ever conpackinged a popularity poll regarding its teachers, Maddie would either win or be in the top three. Sunny, her arms crossed over her books, walked up to Maddie's desk and politely said, "Yes ma'am."

"You and Kenny are going to the prom, right?"

"Yes ma'am."

"Everything going O.K.? Do you have your dress yet?"

"Yes ma'am. Kenny and I went shopping for it. It's a lavender tight fit with spaghetti straps. I got matching lavender sandals with two-inch heels."

"Very nice. It sounds pretty. Are the flowers taken care of?"

"Yes ma'am. We ordered mine and his."

"Good. Sit down a minute, Sunny."

With a bare hint of a smile, Sunny complied, choosing an extra chair a few feet to the right of Maddie's desk. She set her three textbooks and a composition notebook in her lap.

Maddie studied the girl's soft face. She could not remember ever seeing Sunny offer a cheek-to-cheek smile or laugh out loud. "I don't you want to think I'm snooping into your personal business," Maddie started kindly, "but I want to talk to you about things at home. How are you and your Dad doing?"

"All right," is all Sunny offered.

"Do you have plenty to eat? Is your Dad taking care of you?"

"I'm all right, Mrs. Hampton," Sunny responded softly. "Dad makes decent money. There's always food in the house. I have plenty of money for clothes. We've never had our power cut off or anything like that."

"That's good. I guess what I'm trying to get around to asking, and I feel a little uncomfortable doing it, is, is your Dad treating you all right?"

"I'm fine, Mrs. Hampton. I really am. I know you don't like my Dad, but everything is all right. Dad and I fuss, but don't all teenagers fuss with their parents? This isn't something I'm comfortable talking about. May I go? I won't have very long to eat lunch."

"Sure. One last thing, quickly. Are you and Kenny getting along all right?"

Sunny nodded affirmatively. "He's very nice to me. He's my best friend. But some of the girls here at school have been teasing me that Kenny has another girlfriend at the community college."

"Do you believe that?"

"No. I think they're just trying to be mean to me. They don't like me."

"Do you really believe the other girls don't like you?"

"They act like they don't like me. They won't have anything to do with me."

"Maybe you should make more of an effort to make friends with them. You take the first step."

"All I want to do now is get this school year over and graduate."

Realizing she wasn't getting through to Sunny, Maddie sighed and urged, "You're a beautiful girl, Sunny. You have so much going for you. Give yourself a chance. As for Kenny, I don't think you've got anything to worry about. Those other girls are just jealous. O.K., you go on and get some lunch."

Sunny stood up and started to walk out of the room, but stopped and turned back to Maddie. Showing her modest smile, Sunny said, "Thanks for being concerned. I appreciate it, but I'm all right." Sunny left for the cafeteria where she would likely sit by herself, and Maddie remained at her desk, not sure at all that Sunny was all right.

While Maddie's students were headed for their lunch break, Jake was returning from his, via the public library. His intention was to check out the latest James Patterson book and then stop at the police station to visit with Quinn before returning to the Sentinel to work on one story about an increase in the city's monthly trash collection fee and another on the calendar being proposed for the next school year. Jake handed his books to the personable woman who had been at the front counter every time he had visited the library, exchanged a short cordial greeting with her and was about to walk out.

"Do you like chicken and rice casserole?" the voice asked from behind him.

Jake knew the question was meant for him. He turned around to see Miss Wayne, who had come out of her office. "Yes, I like it," he replied truthfully, but then what else could he say?

"Good. That's what I'm preparing for supper tonight. Why don't you drop by around 6:30. I live on Florida Street. Five-eighty-five Florida Street."

"Sounds good. Do I need to bring anything?"

"Just your appetite. I'll see you tonight." She smiled and returned to her office. Jake noticed the woman at the front counter smiling at him. He took a quick last glance at Miss Wayne as she closed the door to her office. Jake felt a major sexual surge every time he saw her, much more intense than anything he experienced when he was with Maddie. He just wasn't sure his personality was a good fit with Miss Wayne. He reasoned he would find out a lot more about that theory in a few hours.

A few minutes later, Jake was at the police station, asking the young girl at the front lobby desk for Quinn. If the police department had a personnel chart, the girl would be listed under receptionist, information officer and secretary. In the scheme of city government in Sanderson, a lot of people did a lot of different things, sort of like Jake at the Sentinel. "Quinn's out back. Go on through," offered the girl, who knew Jake was with the newspaper. She pressed a button and a heavy steel door unlocked, allowing Jake entrance into a long corridor. The door to Quinn's office was open, but he wasn't at his desk. Hearing a muffled "Wham! Wham!" Jake determined Quinn's whereabouts and proceeded down the hallway, all the way to a back door that led to a fenced-in yard where the department kept its few pieces of emergency equipment such as a generator and an old army surplus jeep. Quinn was flailing away at a ten-foot metal pole with his plastic baseball bat.

"All right, Quinn. You've got to tell me," Jake demanded as he approached. "What is it with this baseball bat?"

Quinn took one last hard swing with the bat and clanged it against the pole, which shook and vibrated all the way to the top. Quinn, puffing from the exertion, exhaled and admitted, "Damn that felt good!" He asked Jake to sit down with him on a nearby bench.

Before he sat down, Quinn took a couple of practice swings with the bat as a major leaguer would do in the on-deck circle. He finally dropped the bat beside the bench and sat down. "Anger management," Quinn said, his breathing almost back to normal.

"Anger management?"

"Anger management. You know my history. Remember my wife and neighbor? The broken jaw?"

"Yeah, I remember."

"That landed me in anger management classes. The counselor told me I had to find some way to harness my anger. Well, I knew the counting to ten crap wouldn't do it for me and I didn't like any of his other suggestions, so I came up with my own plan. I've got it broken down to two levels. When I first start getting stressed out, when I think I'm about to start losing it, I cram some Black Jack chewing gum in my mouth. For some reason, that gum has a wonderful soothing affect on me."

Jake knew where the rest of the story was going, but he waited for Quinn to continue.

"But when things really start to get to me, that's when I pull out the baseball bat and find something I can pound on." He picked up the plastic bat and patted the barrel against his left palm. "Fifteen or twenty whacks with this bat and all the stress is gone. I haven't broken anyone's jaw since, well, since my wife's," Quinn smiled broadly.

"What's got you so riled up today that you had to pull out your bat?"

"Everything. I'm not getting anywhere with this damn murder investigation, and I've got a GBI Agent looking over my shoulder at everything I do."

"You mean the big guy in the black suit?"

"Agent Travis Stamps. You've seen him?"

"Who hasn't? He's been all over town, asking questions. Besides, he looks totally out of place around here. I thought I did at first, but this guy sticks out like a pimple on the prom queen's nose."

"All over town, huh? He told me he was here to help, not take over. Sounds to me like that's what he's trying to do. Think I'll take a few more swings," Quinn said as he stood up.

Jake stopped Quinn. "This looks interesting. Let me try it."

Quinn tossed the plastic bat to Jake who stepped over to the metal pole and swung fiercely. Even with the bat being plastic, Jake could feel the vibrations in his hands. The swing created good movement in the pole but hurt Jake's right hand. He shook his hand vigorously and flexed it several times.

"Hurt your hand, softy?" Quinn kidded Jake.

Jake opened his right hand and showed a thick scar all the way across the palm. "A souvenir from my drunken days," Jake explained.

"That should be an interesting story."

"I expect it is. The only problem is I can't remember how I got it."

"Take another swing," Quinn urged and Jake did. Several times, but not with the same force. The softer swings still hurt his hand, but not as much.

"Quinn, you're on to something. Heck, maybe you should drop out of law enforcement and start your own counseling service. You could charge fifty bucks an hour just to tell someone to get a plastic bat and knock the crap out of a tree."

"Not a bad idea. I may need another job if Agent Stamps solves this case before I do."

"Keep this thing handy. I may need to use it tomorrow. I'm going over to Miss Wayne's for dinner tonight."

"Well, well. Dinner and do her. Is that what you've got in mind?"

"I don't think so, although I do admit she gets my juices to flowing."

"What do you think Maddie will say?"

"Why do people keep asking that?"

"Because people around here want you to be a couple."

"I do have a date with her Saturday. I'm looking forward to it, although I am nervous about tonight and Saturday. It's been a long time since I've been on a date. What is this about you wanting to talk to her about the two murders?"

Both men sat back down. "You know about Maddie's son Robbie?" Quinn asked.

"I know that he went off to college, a million miles from here."

"Did Maddie tell you why Robbie went to a school so far away?"

"Not exactly. She said something about him wanting to follow his dream, sort of like Stephen House."

"There's more to the story than that," Quinn said. He twisted his hands around the bat handle again. "Robbie was out of place in Sanderson. If I had to describe him, I'd call him a sissy. Other people weren't that kind with their description, if you catch my drift."

"Uh, I think I do."

"To make things perfectly clear, he wasn't, and most people knew that. They liked Robbie. He was a good kid. He just wasn't in to the same stuff your typical Sanderson hormonal male is—deer hunting, fishing, making out with their girlfriends on Saturday night. There were, unfortunately, a few people who couldn't accept Robbie being different."

"Let me guess. Joe Lambert and Todd Monroe."

"And Regal Krause, Sunny's Dad. I called them the Three Stooges, although I think that's an insult to Moe, Larry and Curly."

"Something must have happened."

"It did. Those three wouldn't leave Robbie alone. Any time they ran into him, they harassed him. It all reached the boiling point about two years ago when Robbie left a Barber County basketball game early. The three idiots followed him out into the parking lot. Joe and Todd held him down and tried to put a pair of women's panties on him, while Regal was writing 'Faggot' on Robbie's car. The funny thing is, normally Joe and Todd couldn't stand each other, but their hatred of someone who is different was a bond they had."

"Those sons of bitches! Was Robbie hurt?"

"Not physically. Maddie came out of the gym swinging a bat, a real one, not a flimsy plastic thing like this," Quinn said, holding the bat at arm's length. "She beat the hell out of Joe and Todd. Cracked some ribs and put some knots on their heads. Drew blood. Regal, big mean Regal, ran away." Quinn swung the bat as if to show how Maddie defended her son. "People say that's as angry as they've ever seen her. It was like she was possessed. I really think she might have killed one of them if other folks had not come out of the gym and taken the bat away from her."

"Good for her," Jake said in admiration. "I guess parents can call on an inner strength when they're protecting their kids."

"She sure as hell did that night. I arrested the three buttheads. Charged them with assault. They're lucky. At first the DA wanted to charge them with a hate crime and almost called the FBI on the case, but chose not to. He decided making an example of the local boys wouldn't be good for his re-election bid. So, a plea deal was struck and the three losers ended up paying a fine, getting probation and being ordered to stay away from Robbie. Maddie wasn't real happy with the disposition of the case. In fact, she was livid. Took her a long time to settle down."

"What about Robbie?"

"He immediately transferred to a private boarding school in Atlanta and graduated last year. He told his mom he would never come back to Sanderson as long as those three losers are here, and he enrolled in college in Hawaii to prove it."

"And you've come up with the preposterous notion that Maddie may have killed these two guys because of what they did to her son? Come on Quinn. Maddie's not capable of that."

"Really? She might have killed one of them that night. All it would have taken was for Maddie to have hit one of them in just the right spot in the head, and she would have been facing a manslaughter rap."

Jake looked away. "You're the chief, Quinn. Do what you've got to do. But I'll bet—hell yes I'll bet—that you're way off base with this."

"I'm sure you're right, but I've got to talk to her. Quinn slammed the bat against the pole three more times, the loud noise echoing through the storage yard.

"Hey, go easy on the bat!" Jake suggested. "Remember, I'm probably going to need it in the morning."

CHAPTER FOURTEEN

His first glimpse at Miss Wayne's house made Jake think he was back with Kathy. Both women had the same tastes. Miss Wayne lived in an old section of town, in one house of several that artsy types would call "picturesque." Jake preferred to call them rundown and in need of considerable fixing-up. Kathy had always said she wanted an old farm house, complete with tin roof, wooden shutters and big front porch, out in the country, that she could fill with antiques and collectibles. The house on Florida Street in Sanderson didn't quite fit that description, but Jake was sure his ex-wife could be happy in it. Inside, Miss Wayne's house had a definite sixties look, with pine paneling, space heaters, window air conditioning units and hardwood floorboards that looked as if they would be better suited in an old barn. She didn't have a lot of furniture and accessories in the house, but what she did have looked like vintage yard sale and flea market pickups. Or, as Jake was prone to describe such items, "junk." The house was filled with the tantalizing smell of bread baking which made Jake realize he was hungry and ready to eat.

"I don't serve alcohol, but I can offer you some sweet tea or a soft drink," Miss Wayne offered.

"Sweet tea is fine," Jake replied. He studied Miss Wayne's figure as she disappeared into the kitchen to get the tea. Her royal blue skirt was a little too long for Jake's liking, and her white blouse could have fit a bit more snugly, but Jake couldn't deny the fact that she was attractive. He was interested in her personal past, details like had she ever been married, and if not, why, but he wasn't going to ask. Of course, if she wanted to volunteer that information, he would be more than happy to listen.

He did have one question he needed to ask. "I'm embarrassed to ask this," he admitted as his hostess handed him a large glass of tea. "I don't know your first name. I may have heard it, but I'm sorry, I don't remember."

She smiled as she sat down in a plush old velvet chair across from him. "It's Janet. Janet Marie Wayne."

"Well, Janet Marie Wayne. You have an interesting house. I can guess how you spend a lot of your time on the weekends."

"If you're talking about the antique shops and yard sales, you're right. I love doing that. As you can see, I've still got a lot of space to fill up. I haven't been in town that long, and with trying to get established at the library, I haven't had the opportunity to do that much looking around."

"How long have you been in Sanderson?" Jake asked after taking another swallow of the refreshing tea.

"About eighteen months. Not long enough to really put my stamp on the library. There's still a lot I want to do."

"Does that mean you're in Sanderson long term?"

"If that's God's will. He put me here, and if He wants me to stay, that's what will happen. Right now, I'm happy. I believe I have a purpose here. What about you? Forgive me, but you just don't seem to me to be the type who would hang around this little town very long."

"I'm like you. Right now I'm happy. And busy. There's more going on here than I ever imagined."

"You mean those horrible murders?"

"And the accident with the two high school girls."

"I hope Chief Quinn catches whoever is responsible for those murders and brings them to earthly justice. Of course, one day they will have to stand before their Heavenly Father and their punishment will be severe. We all pay for our sins."

Heaven and hell and sinning were not something Jake felt comfortable talking about, but he wanted to know how Miss Wayne had become so religious. He wasn't quite ready to classify her as *spiritual*, merely *religious* to this point. To him, there was a difference. A big difference. Maddie was spiritual. Miss Wayne seemed religious. "I'm impressed with your Christian beliefs," Jake offered as a way of expanding the conversation.

"I grew up in a very strict Church of God family in Ohio. Over the years I've tried to be a little more liberal in my beliefs—that's why I'm attending a Baptist church—but I still have my core values. I don't expect to ever lose them. I don't want to. God has to be first in your life and family is second. Nothing else matters. What about you? You've been coming to church."

"Let's just say my faith isn't anything close to yours, or that of most of the other people in this town. I'm trying, though. I've started trying to read through the Bible."

"That's good to hear. As you have no doubt noticed in your Bible readings, the early Christians liked to eat. How about you? Are you ready to eat?"

"Absolutely. The bread smells divine."

"Made from scratch," she smiled as she led Jake to the small dining room. Miss Wayne asked Jake to be seated while she brought the food to the vintage farmhouse table. Miss Wayne explained the farmer had passed away and his two sons, both having contemporary tastes, had sold most of their Dad's belongings. "Personally, I think that's a sin," she said of the boys' actions, "but we won't get into that tonight." Miss Wayne sat down and asked a blessing, which to Jake, went on much too long and covered far more territory than it should have.

The meal, including the chicken and rice casserole, tossed salad and the wonderful melt-in-your-mouth homemade bread, was delicious. Jake and Miss Wayne shared some of their experiences about adjusting to small town life in south Georgia before she started asking some of the inevitable questions about Jake's past. Knowing her zeal for following the straight and narrow, he wasn't about to share a lot of details. He was willing to let her know he had been divorced but that was as far as he was going. "All I'm going to say is that I accept full blame," Jake told her. "None of it was my wife's fault."

Miss Wayne dropped her head and started picking at the rice on her plate with her fork. "I loved someone once, many years ago," she started without looking up. "It didn't work out. It still hurts, but I believe God has something great in store for me."

"Don't give up. I'm sure you will find someone," Jake said as encouragement.

"Well, there certainly aren't many choices here in Sanderson. All the good men—and a lot of the bad—are married. And the ones who aren't married, well, you can understand why they aren't. All they are interested in is sex. Oh, please excuse me. I didn't mean to imply that you're here tonight for that reason. You're not, are you?" she asked playfully.

"Of course not," Jake smiled, although if Janet Wayne was willing to offer herself as the evening's appetizer, Jake would be a gracious guest and accept.

"Really, you strike me as someone who has learned his lesson," she said. "Whatever your mistakes were, I don't believe you will make them again. I can see you establishing roots."

"Don't bet on it." Jake immediately realized his poor choice of words, but his slip of the tongue about his old habit meant nothing to Miss Wayne.

Over a warm homemade peach cobbler dripping in butter, Jake and Miss Wayne continued to talk in generalities, coming close to revealing their deepest secrets but always pulling back at the last second. Janet Wayne was becoming an enticing paradox to Jake. She spoke of God and good and bad and rules of behavior, but there was something teasingly sensual about her as well. The evening passed quickly, with ten p.m. arriving before Jake realized it. He would have willingly stayed another hour, perhaps longer, but got interrupted by a call from Quinn to his cell phone. Normally Jake would not have answered his phone in the presence of company, but he felt obligated to when Quinn's number popped up on the caller ID.

Quinn was providing a bail out. "It's getting late. I thought I might need to rescue you. A phone call always gives you an excuse to leave," Quinn told Jake.

"What's going on?" Jake asked as if had not yet learned why Quinn was calling.

"I thought your evening might not be going so well, and that you might need an excuse to leave. Thus, the phone call."

"Thank you for letting me know," Jake said, playing along. "That is something we need to check out. Give me fifteen minutes."

Jake hung up, frustrated with himself at playing along with Quinn's call. He preferred to stay and find out if he could write a chapter in the librarian's book before the night was over, but she had heard him say he had to be somewhere in fifteen minutes. He apologized to Miss Wayne. "That was Quinn. Something about a burglary," he explained. "I'm sorry to have to rush off, but I have been here awhile. Let me help you with the dishes before I leave."

"Oh no. You go on. Please be careful. We've had enough misfortune around here recently. It has been a very enjoyable evening. Let me walk you to the door."

"Yes it has," Jake admitted.

"I'd love to do it again."

"Sure. I don't see why not."

"Great!" To Jake's surprise, Miss Wayne gave him a soft hug and he liked it, making him even angrier at himself for cutting the evening short.

At Quinn's place, Mary Jane Hamilton was sitting on her curled up legs in an overstuffed sofa in the compact living room of the breadbox house. Sipping on a margarita prepared by Quinn with ingredients he had purchased during his last trip to a town large enough and progressive enough to sell adult beverages, she asked, "Is that how you guys cover for each other, making phone calls that give you an excuse to leave?"

"Oh yeah. It's a time honored tradition."

"So, if you get a call within the next five minutes, I assume it's Jake Martin calling you back to give you an excuse to end our evening?"

"Not a chance." Quinn, holding his own margarita in one hand, leaned down and gently kissed her. "I'm not going anywhere. I'm happy right where I'm at."

"I'm glad. So am I." She kissed him back.

"I just don't think Jake and Miss Wayne are a match," Quinn said, taking another sip on his drink. "He and Maddie are a much better match."

"I know Miss Wayne can be self-righteous. She's been so hateful to me since all of this came out about Gregory. I quit taking the girls to the library because she's so hateful. I've gotten dirty looks from everyone in town, but they're not saying anything to me, at least not to my face. Miss Wayne does. She doesn't mind at all preaching about how I will have to pay for my sins. I know what I did was wrong."

"Don't pay attention to her. She's just one of those holy roller hypocrites."

Mary Jane stroked the back of his head. "I feel so fortunate . . . and unworthy," she said, burning deep into Quinn's soul with her hazel eyes. "I don't deserve to be treated the way you have treated me. The short time we have been seeing each other has been wonderful. I can't believe you would even think about going out with me."

"Why wouldn't I? You're beautiful and smart. I feel comfortable talking to you."

"But I've made so many mistakes."

Quinn kissed her again. "Look, when it comes to messing up your life, no one can hold a candle to me. I certainly don't have any room to be criticizing anyone else for their mistakes. Like Jake and I have told each other hundreds of times, life is all about second chances, looking ahead, not back."

"I try to look ahead, but I don't see much future for me here in Sanderson. I need to get away. Don't you ever want to get away from here, Quinn?"

Taking another sip of his drink, Quinn looked around the room before answering. "I think about it a lot, but I'm not sure that's possible for me right now. I don't have any other options if I want to remain a cop, and I do. Actually, I like this little town. The people are nice. They've been good to me. And since I had the good sense to finally ask you out, well, that's another reason for staying." Quinn kissed her again, this time slowly and with passion.

"Well Chief Quinn, if we're stuck in this place, perhaps we should find something to make our time here more enjoyable." She pulled his head toward hers and kissed him before running her hand down to his chest.

"An excellent idea." Quinn gently stretched Mary Jane out on the sofa and slowly pulled off her lightweight knit shirt. "With apologies to Waffle House," he said, "I believe I'll smother you and cover you."

As Quinn and Mary Jane were making out, Jake was arriving home, not the least bit sleepy, partly because of the three glasses of ice tea he had guzzled, and partly because he was still trying to decide what he missed by coming home. Would there have been more of Miss Wayne's religious babble, or could he have coaxed her out of the blue skirt and white blouse? Janet Marie Wayne was fascinating. She was attractive, intelligent and a good conversationalist, but a bit too heavy-handed with the religion. Obviously, she was carrying some baggage from some type of failed relationship, but then so was Jake. His stack of baggage was as big as anyone's.

Flipping through the cable channels, Jake quickly saw television offered nothing worth watching. He remembered what Maddie had told him about devoting five minutes a day to finding his faith, so he picked up the Bible Pastor Allen had given him and started thumbing through it. Having ended his last session at Joshua, the sliver of paper he was using as a bookmark was at Judges. Jake's method of reading the Bible was skimming, not reading. But this time, he had hardly started when his eyes quickly stopped and froze at the words on the page: Judges 1:6.

But Adonibezek fled, and they pursued after him, and caught him, and cut off his thumbs and his great toes.

He read the verse again, concentrating on the last few words: a*nd cut off his thumbs and his great toes.* "Todd Monroe," Jake muttered in disbelief, recalling the first murder. He slapped the Bible shut, not using the bookmark and nervously gave Quinn a return call.

"So how was Miss Wayne?" Quinn asked before Jake had a chance to say anything. Mary Jane had left Quinn's house just a few moments earlier.

"Forget Miss Wayne. You need to get over here now. Like in the next five minutes."

"What's the big deal? A good skin flick about to start on the Spice Channel?"

"I'm not joking, Quinn. Get over here."

Realizing Jake was serious, Quinn dressed and got to Jake's fast. Not in five minutes, but close to it. Instead of his usual khaki uniform, Quinn had on blue jeans and a tight golf shirt that showed a bit of a pooch in the stomach.

"O.K. newspaper man, what's going on?" asked Quinn, more than a hint of irritation in his voice.

Jake picked up the Bible. Without the bookmark and with little knowledge of its books, Jake had to hastily flip through the pages to find Judges. "Read this." Jake thrust the Bible at Quinn.

"Read what?"

"Judges. Chapter One. Verse Six."

Quinn's irritation was rising, but he took the Bible and found the verse. He read it, looked at Jake and read it again. "Damn!" Quinn gasped. "That's how Todd Monroe was killed!" He read the verse a third time and sat down.

"What do you think?" Jake asked. He sat down as well.

"What do I think? Hell, what I think is, that now, we've got more unanswered questions than we had before. We still don't know who killed Todd, why they killed him, and now we don't know why the sick son of a bitch patterned the murder after the killing of some guy two thousand years ago who's name I can't even pronounce."

"Technically, it would have been more than two thousand years ago, before the birth of Christ."

"Thank you Mr. Bible Scholar. Got any more tidbits for me?"

"No. You're the cop." Jake was starting to realize his revelation had done little to shed light on the case.

Quinn opened the Bible again. "We've got more than one murder. Did you find anything else interesting in here?" he asked.

"No. When I came to that verse. I stopped. Here, let me see." Jake took the Bible from Quinn and started scanning again. Nothing else in Chapter One, Chapter Two, Chapter . . .

"Here. Listen," Jake told Quinn. "Judges, Chapter Three, Verse 21."

And Ehud put forth his left hand, and took the dagger from his right thigh, and thrust it into his belly

"Damn! Death by scripture!" Quinn fumed. He took an entire pack of Black Jack gum, unwrapped the individual sticks and wadded all of them into his mouth.

"You didn't save any for me," Jake complained.

"Get your own."

"What do we do now?"

"What do you mean we? You're not a cop."

"No, but I'm neck deep in this thing. Besides, if I'm with you, you won't have to worry about where I am and what I'm writing about the investigation."

"You've got a point. I'd just as soon none of this get out. I especially don't want Agent Stamps to find out about this."

"Don't you think we should tell him?"

"Hell no! Let him come up with his own clues. This is my case to solve. This may be my ticket out of town."

"Can I make a suggestion?"

"Haven't you done enough for tonight?"

"Let's go talk to Pastor Allen. Maybe he can explain some of this to us. Maybe he can tell us what kind of person would use these scriptures as motivation."

"That's a good idea," Quinn agreed. He sighed and smacked on his Black Jack gum. "Let's don't disturb him tonight. We'll wait until morning." Quinn sighed again. "Well, I don't know about you, Martin, but I'm wide awake. I don't think I'm going to sleep any tonight."

"That's two of us."

Jake and Quinn drank Cokes and Mountain Dews long into the night and talked about a variety of subjects. As much as Quinn tried to prod him, Jake wouldn't tell him about his evening with Miss Wayne and that he actually had a good time. Quinn was more than willing to offer a few details on his intimate evening with Mary Jane Hamilton.

CHAPTER FIFTEEN

Weak-eyed and weary from no sleep, Jake and Quinn were at Sanderson First Baptist Church at 7:30 the next morning. Quinn, back in his chief's uniform, knew Pastor Allen always went to the church early Saturday morning to pray and put the finishing touches on his Sunday sermon. The casually-dressed preacher, head bowed at his desk in an unpretentious office with full bookcases against every wall, was surprised and worried when Quinn and Jake arrived. Although his congregation understood that Saturday was their shepherd's quiet time, one of the few segments of the week that he could be alone, the good reverend never locked the door behind him, just in case someone with a special problem needed to talk. His first reaction was that Quinn was bringing him bad news that one of his church members was in trouble or had been injured or killed in an accident. Quinn had broken that type of sad news to him too many times.

Preacher Allen was relieved but at the same time saddened when Quinn started explaining the purpose of the visit. After briefly recapping the killings, Quinn took the Bible from Jake and pointed out the two verses they had stumbled on. "It can't be coincidence that our two killings mirror these two scriptures," Quinn declared.

The preacher opened his own Bible and read the two verses. Jake and Quinn waited for his response, which was slow in coming. Finally, Pastor Allen looked at both men. "This is troubling, very, very troubling," he declared and paused. Continuing, he admitted

140

with great sorrow, "It saddens me that someone has used the scriptures for such an evil purpose."

"Who would do this?" Quinn asked. He was practically begging for an answer.

"This is what I fear," Pastor Allen started. "Jake, you skipped over a verse. Look at Judges 2:18." He gave Jake time to find the verse and Quinn time to look over Jake's shoulder.

"This verse, I fear, is what may be taking place:

And when the Lord raised them up judges, then the Lord was with the judge, and delivered them out of the hand of their enemies all the days of the judge.

"I'm afraid we have someone on some type of holy quest."

Jake and Quinn looked at each other. "So we have someone who is knocking off their enemies the same way those judges did thousands of years ago?" Quinn asked.

"The theology is a little warped, but yes. I think that's what we're looking at."

Quinn looked away to one of the bookcases, glanced at Jake and then at Pastor Allen. "Describe the type of person who would do this."

"Shouldn't you be asking the GBI that question?"

"Preacher, I value your input a lot more than theirs, particularly the agent they've assigned to this case."

"Please don't let this out of this room. It's not scientific, it's not factual, I'm not sure it's biblical. It's just this old man's opinion, all right?"

"All right," Quinn agreed.

Pastor Allen hesitated again before starting. "My feeling is . . . and it's just my opinion . . ."

"I know," Quinn said quickly to get him back on track.

"My feeling is that this person believes he is always right and that his causes are just and right. He believes the Lord is on his side as he defends his cause and battles his enemies. In short, this person is a zealot. He wants to be judge, jury and executioner all rolled into one. You know the pro-life activists who bomb abortion clinics? Well, multiply that by ten and you've got this person. Now that's just my opinion, mind you."

Jake and Quinn were both speechless and needed a moment to process what Pastor Allen had told them. "But why are they killing people?" Quinn finally asked.

"That's a question I can't answer. Perhaps it's something very personal, a one-on-one issue. Or, it could be that this person has decided to rid the world of sinners in general. They can have that type of mindset."

"That's so over the top," Jake offered. "Wouldn't these people stick out like a sore thumb?"

"Not necessarily. By all outward appearances they probably look and act just like we do. They're not going to walk around in long flowing robes, carrying the Ten Commandments, but they may try to recite them to you."

"Not to be disrespectful, preacher," Quinn started, "but why didn't you or some of the other church leaders in town link these scriptures with the killings earlier?"

Pastor Allen had an immediate response. "Think back. To begin with, you didn't tell us the whole story. Then, when you first started publicly revealing all the details of the two killings, it was about the time the two girls died in the car accident. When that happened, all of our focus turned to the girls and their families. Irresponsibly, we forgot about the two murder victims. I'm ashamed to admit it, but that's what happened. And now that you've brought that to my attention, I feel terrible. I need to go see the families of those two men."

Satisfied with the preacher's explanation, Quinn stood up. His frustration was beginning to show, and he popped two sticks of Black Jack gum in his mouth. "Well, how the hell do we find the killer?" Quinn blurted out angrily. He realized what he had said the second the word popped out. "I am *so* sorry, preacher. Please forgive me."

Realizing Quinn's slip of the tongue was unintentional during a moment of frustration. Pastor Allen did not take issue with it. "I wish I could help you Chief, but that's all I know. And it's just my opinion. I may be totally off base."

"Do you know anyone who fits the description you just gave us?" Jake asked.

"I know many people with great faith and conviction, but I know no one who would use the scriptures in such a violent and perverted manner."

"There's another twist to this mess," Jake admitted. "We believe the killer may be a woman."

Pastor Allen wasn't surprised. "Deborah was a judge. A strong judge," he told them.

Quinn started to speak but nothing came out. He tried to clear his throat. Surmising that Quinn was struggling to ask a question, Rev. Allen encouraged him. "Come on Quinn. Spit it out. Whatever it is you want to ask me, go ahead."

"Pastor, do you think Maddie Hampton could have had anything to do with the killings?"

Rev. Allen's bulging eyes reflected his shock at the question. "Never in a million years would have I guessed that was the question you wanted to ask! And the short, sweet, simple answer to your question is no! What in the world makes you think she might have been?"

"The incident with Robbie. Todd and Joe were involved."

"That's over. Maddie forgave them, like any true Christian would."

"She may have forgiven them, but did she forget? Remember what Robbie said? That he'd never come back home as long as those three guys are still here. Maybe Maddie's holy quest is to get rid of these guys so Robbie can come home."

"No. Robbie was destined to leave this place any way. His future was elsewhere."

"Maddie's the only lead I've got," Quinn admitted. He sounded pitiful, almost desperate.

"Keep looking. Maddie's not your killer."

"I've at least got to question her."

"I don't think that's a good move, Quinn. You will be wasting your time, and think of the unnecessary public humiliation you will be putting Maddie through. People will find out you've questioned her."

"Thank you for your time this morning pastor," was Quinn's reply. "I'm sorry to bother you. I know how you value your time alone Saturday mornings."

The preacher got out of his chair, walked in front of his desk and stood between Jake and Quinn. "There is something else I need to tell you," he admitted. Jake and Quinn looked directly at him and waited.

"Keep reading. The Book of Judges is filled with violence. The story of David and Goliath is in Judges. There are other passages past those we've looked at this morning. If I'm right, if the killer is going by the scriptures, well . . . he—or she—may not be through."

"Oh hell! I didn't need to hear that!" Quinn caught himself. "There I go again. Preacher, I apologize again. I'm getting out of here before something else filthy comes out of my mouth and God strikes me down right here for using such bad language in the church. Thanks again. You take care of yourself," Quinn said.

Pastor Allen would not allow them to leave before he led them in prayer. Quinn squirmed uncomfortably all through the prayer which to him seemed to go on forever. Finally, the reverend finished. Quinn and Jake shook his hand and left. Pastor Allen went back to his desk and started praying for his church, his people and the little town more fervently than he had in a long time.

Outside in the parking lot, Jake and Quinn propped against Quinn's car. "I don't know where to start, what to do about solving the two murders we've had already. And now the preacher says there may be more," Quinn admitted as he pounded his fist on the hood of his car, making a noise that echoed through the empty parking lot.

"Calm down, Quinn. You don't forget how to be a good cop. Chew some more gum. Take out your ball bat. You can do this. Like you said, this case could be your ticket out of town."

"If I don't hurry up and collar this killer, the mayor and council may give me a one-way ticket out of town!"

"What I want you to do is go home and get some sleep. Last night was long. In fact, stay home the rest of the weekend, and come back Monday morning refreshed and ready to tackle this mess. You don't have to do this alone. There are people to help."

"Like Agent Stamps? I don't want help. As nervous as I am, I want to solve this case on my own. It's that important to me, whether it's my ticket out of town or not."

"All right then. Go home and get some rest."

"You too."

"I'm going to. I've got to go by the office and take care of a couple of matters. Then I'm going home and take a nap before I go out with Maddie tonight."

"You're making yourself right at home in this little town, aren't you?"

"She's a nice lady. Not your typical murder suspect," Jake said jokingly.

"Nicer than Miss Wayne?"

"They're different. Very different."

"You're right about that. Maddie's not going to put out. I bet Miss Wayne will. In fact, you've probably already found that out."

"Go get some sleep, Quinn," was Jake's only response.

"Have fun. I'll talk to you Monday. And Jake . . . thanks. I can sound things off you that I wouldn't even talk to my staff about."

"I appreciate the trust. Now get to bed."

Jake didn't follow his own advice. His tasks at the Sentinel took longer than expected because he could not keep his mind on his work following the conversation with Pastor Allen and he didn't get back home until three o'clock. He was exhausted, struggling to keep his eyes open. He had to take a nap, or else he was likely to fall asleep right in the middle of his evening with Maddie. He stretched out on his bed, expecting to sleep no more than an hour, which would leave him plenty of time to get ready for his seven o'clock engagement . . .

. . . Jake's eyes slowly opened. Confused and groggy, he lay motionless on the bed, trying to sort out not only what time it was, but the day of the week as well. He turned his head to check the clock on the nightstand. "Oh crap!" he exclaimed, realizing he had overslept and had thirty minutes to shower, shave, dress and drive to Maddie's. Jake could move fast, but not that fast. He called Maddie, and without giving any details, said he would be fifteen minutes late. Maddie playfully fussed at him, saying she had to be home at ten o'clock, but when she sensed Jake wasn't sure if she was kidding or not, she told him to take his time, that she wasn't in a hurry.

Hopping into the shower, he was out in five minutes and toweled off and dried his hair in another three. Trying to set another speed record for shaving, he nicked his chin twice, having to stick small bits of bathroom tissue on the cuts to stop the bleeding. He did another rush job ironing his clothes, a short sleeve yellow cotton knit golf shirt, a navy blue pullover vest and khaki pants. With a few wrinkles still in his pants, he left the house exactly at seven o'clock, which meant he might be only ten minutes late instead of fifteen.

Pulling into Maddie's driveway twelve minutes later, he realized he still had the two bits of toilet tissue on his cheek. "Thank goodness I noticed," he mumbled to himself. "That would have made me look like a total dork."

When Maddie opened the door, Jake laughed and she did too. "This is too funny," she giggled, noticing how close her khaki pants, yellow short sleeve cotton t-shirt and sleeveless blue sweater came to matching Jake's wardrobe. "Come in while I change. Maybe I'll put on a dress," she told him.

"You're fine," he assured her.

"You don't think people will believe we're an old married couple who think so much alike that we dress the same?"

"Let them think that. That's not such a bad thing."

"If you're sure . . ."

"I'm sure."

Maddie stroked her tabby cat several times, said goodbye and left with Jake for the twenty mile drive to Polk City, not much bigger than Sanderson, but big enough to have a couple of nice restaurants, including the Italian bistro chosen by Jake. During the drive, he apologized for being tardy, admitting he had overslept after doing some work at the office. He did not mention the long night with Quinn, the disturbing talk with Pastor Allen, or Quinn's fixation on Maddie as part of the murder investigation. She told Jake he didn't have to keep apologizing. He wasn't that late, and he had called to let her know.

They only waited five minutes to be seated at the restaurant and the waitress quickly took their orders. Jake took a deep breath to try to relax. He looked at Maddie who smiled at him. She was relaxed and talkative. He wondered if she would be so relaxed if she knew that any day, Quinn was probably going to ask her flat out if she had been involved in the murders.

Maddie took a drink of water and asked Jake, "How was your evening with Miss Wayne?"

He almost choked on the garlic breadstick he was eating and did not offer a prompt response. "It's all right, Jake," she smiled.

"Uh . . . she asked me out . . . I didn't think I . . ."

"It's all right, Jake," she reassured him with another smile. "I don't have exclusive rights to you . . . yet."

The "yet" Maddie tossed in at the last moment caught Jake off guard. Maddie was smiling again, like she was playing a game with him. She seemed to be enjoying watching him squirm and turn crimson.

"She is a good cook," Jake admitted.

"Perhaps she took home economics in high school. You know, there are some wonderful home ec teachers."

That made Jake smile and the awkwardness was broken. He studied her face. She wasn't beautiful, and probably would not draw a second glance from some men, but Jake liked her demeanor. She seemed happy with who she was, not concerned with putting on airs or impressing anyone. Saying it to himself, it sounded corny, but Jake admitted Maddie's inner beauty was more important than outside appearances. To him, she was a good woman, and he suspected that she had been a very good wife.

Their meals came soon and the polite, general conversation began. "Have you heard from Stephen House lately?" Maddie asked before taking her first bite of spaghetti and meat sauce.

"Not in awhile. I figure he's either having the time of his life and doesn't care how we're doing, or he's got such confidence in us that he's not worried."

"Probably both. He knows Hazel is still around. She's almost as much an icon to the Sentinel and this town as Mr. House was. Now when she retires, that's when you may have a problem."

"What if I leave first?"

Maddie stopped in mid-chew. She didn't say anything.

"A friend—my best friend—has asked me to come to Charleston to help him start a new magazine."

She swallowed and started cutting strands of spaghetti with her fork. "Are you going?"

"I'm thinking about it. The opportunity is a good one."

"Well . . . I guess I knew you'd leave eventually. What is there to keep you here? I admit, though, this is a lot sooner than I expected."

"First, I haven't gone yet. I'm only thinking about it. Second, there's more reason to stay here than you know. Stephen has given me an awfully good incentive to stay. I've sort of grown fond of Quinn too, the old goat." He didn't mention another reason for staying was his involvement with the investigation into the murders of Joe Lambert and Todd Monroe. He wanted this case resolved as much as Quinn.

Maddie smiled at Jake's reference to Quinn. "The chief has his hands full, doesn't he?"

"He does. He's stressed out, but he's handling it well. As long as he's got a good supply of chewing gum, he'll be all right."

"Chewing gum?"

Jake nodded. "But not just any chewing gum. Black Jack chewing gum. I'll tell you about it later."

"Well if chewing gum helps Quinn to keep his stress level down, he better stock up before next weekend. He'll have his hands full."

"How so?" Jake couldn't imagine anything that would tax Quinn more than his present caseload.

"Junior-Senior Prom is a week from tonight. Quinn will have to be there to make sure everyone is on their best behavior."

"Will Quinn be wearing a tux? I'd go just to see that. Talk about looking like a chubby penguin."

"No. He always wears his uniform. How do you look in a tux?"

"It's been a long time since I wore one."

"Well Mr. Martin, may I be so forward as to ask you to be my date to the Barber County High School Junior-Senior Prom? I have to be there as a senior faculty member, and it would be very nice to have an escort."

"Oh, I don't know. I don't do the formal stuff and dances very well."

"I won't ask you to dance. All you have to do is stand around and look handsome, a job I think you can handle rather nicely."

"Where is this social event of the year held?"

"At the community college student center over in Freeburg. It's nice."

"Uh, I . . ."

"We can put a rush order in for your tux Monday."

"Can I have a few minutes to come up with an excuse not to . . ."

"No."

Jake knew he was trapped. Other than being borderline anti-social, he had no reason to turn Maddie down. "All right. Besides, I guess I can keep an eye on Kenny and make sure he behaves. I don't have to rent a limo or anything like that, do I?"

"No. Just show up at my house at 7."

"What next?" Jake kidded. "First you talk me into going to church, and now you talk me into going to the prom. Next thing you know Charles Chambers will have talked me into joining the Rotary Club."

Maddie's eyes danced. "Such is life in the booming town of Sanderson."

CHAPTER SIXTEEN

F ashion magazine handsome in his rented traditional black tuxedo, Jake was sitting with Maddie and two other Barber County High School faculty members at a table in a dark corner of the Freeburg Community College Student Center. Even though the young coeds and female faculty members were firing frequent approving glances his way, Jake felt as awkward and uncomfortable as some of the seventeen year-old pimple-faced boys who were at their first prom. He was out of his element. Jake was at ease interviewing governors and business tycoons, but having to make small talk and schmooze in an intimate setting wasn't his strong point. He tried to remember the last time he wore a tux. The only other time he could remember was at his wedding a long, long time ago and he had been just as uncomfortable then. At least no alcohol was being served at this affair, meaning no one was shoving a drink under his nose every five minutes. He would most definitely be tempted to down a few shots.

Maddie had spent the hour since their arrival dragging Jake around, introducing him to other chaperones. All of them were doing their best to make Jake feel comfortable, but that wouldn't happen until the last dance had been danced, the place cleared out and he was home and out of his monkey suit. Jake had noticed other teachers smiling and sneaking glances at him and Maddie. He was certain that he and Maddie, not the stud quarterback and his date, or Miss Barber County High and her date, were the talk of the night.

That added to his discomfort, but he could handle it. He was pleased that Maddie was getting some well-deserved attention.

The students, taking their time to eat at area restaurants, some almost fifty miles away, were slow to arrive at the prom. By 9 o'clock, an hour after the scheduled starting time, only half of the 400 expected guests had arrived. Thirty minutes later, the room was three-quarters full, and by 9:45, only a few stragglers were missing. Quinn and Sam Rogers were on duty, but had been called on to do no more than move a table away from a fire exit. Quinn looked as miserable as Jake. Conversely, Sam was having a fine time, especially since he could keep his eye on Sam, Jr., a rather handsome junior and point guard on the Barber County basketball team and a source of competition for several Barber County coeds.

The ultra loud music was rattling inside Jake's skull. His date was swaying to the music, snapping her fingers and mouthing the lyrics to the rap song that Jake had never heard. "How do the kids listen to this stuff without their heads exploding?" Jake shouted at Maddie. Not hearing him, she scooted her chair closer. He liked the scent of her perfume, which was considerably stronger than her normal wisp of fragrance, almost overpowering, but appropriate on this evening of adorning excesses.

"How do the kids listen to this stuff without their heads exploding?" Jake asked again, leaning toward Maddie.

"It's easy to see you don't have children. To them, this isn't loud. When Robbie was at home, he'd have the music so loud that the walls in his room would shake. You get used to it."

"Personally, I think the government should consider using this stuff as a secret weapon. I think you could start blaring this garbage, and even our most wicked enemies would surrender immediately."

Maddie laughed and gently put her hand on Jake's shoulder. "I hope you're having fun," she smiled.

"I am, I admit. And you?"

"Yes, but I am a little sad. It's sad not seeing Emily and Laura here. Their smiles would have lighted up this room. I know they would have been beautiful."

"It was a nice gesture for everyone to pin the snippet of white ribbon on their gowns and tuxes tonight in their memory." The music stopped, and Jake lowered his voice accordingly. "I've enjoyed seeing all the kids in their different tuxedos and dresses. Quite an assortment of styles and colors. I especially like the two dudes with the tails and top hats."

"Yes, those two are our trend setters. I'm not surprised to see them in those outfits."

"And Mrs. Hampton, may I say that you look very pretty tonight?"

"Yes you may! Why thank you, Mr. Martin. You look quite dashing yourself." Maddie's face was bright and full of life.

The disc jockey started playing music again and the rattle came back to Jake's head. He looked out to the crowded dance floor. "I haven't seen Kenny and Sunny yet," Jake said. "They should be here by now."

"They probably are. It's not easy to spot anyone in this crowd in such dim light."

"I'm going to check with Quinn. Maybe he's seen them. Would you like some more punch?"

Jake walked along the perimeter of the room to reach Quinn who was standing in an opposite corner of the large ballroom. "Isn't it against the law to play music this loud?" Jake asked.

"I wish it was. I would have arrested that disc jockey an hour ago."

"We've got to put up with this for two more hours?"

"Yeah. Time flies when you're having fun, doesn't it?"

"Have you seen Kenny and Sunny?"

"Nope. Think they skipped the dance and went somewhere for a little motel action? Wouldn't be the first time that's happened, you know?" Quinn suggested with a smirk.

"Not with those two. At least I don't think they would."

"Take it easy, Jake. If they're not here in a few minutes, I'll call dispatch and put out a lookout for them. That way, if they are doing something they shouldn't, maybe we can locate them and put a little scare in them. By the way, you look marvelous tonight. And your date really looks marvelous!"

"Thanks. You look marvelous too. Love the uniform. Police brown is in this year," Jake joked.

"This old thing? I simply pulled it out of the closet, especially for tonight. You know, I've been busy lately. Not much time for shopping."

"I halfway expected you to have a date for this shindig."

"You did?"

"Sure. Mary Jane. You know that everybody's talking about you seeing her."

"What's the big deal?" Quinn asked, not taking his gaze off the glob of teenagers dancing in the middle of the big room.

"It's not a big deal to me, but it is to some people. The girl was fooling around with a married man. A married man who died while he was having extramarital sex with her. Not exactly the kind of relationship that's going to go over very well at First Baptist."

"Screw First Baptist. The girl admits she made a mistake. Should she be crucified for it? Haven't you and I talked about second chances? Besides, old Gregory was just as much at fault as she was."

"No doubt about that. I just want to remind you this is a small town and people . . ."

"And people talk. I know that. Remember, I've been here longer than you." Quinn turned to Jake. He had to raise his voice to be heard above the music that had started back. "I think the people in this town like me. I haven't done anything to betray their trust, and I'm not doing it now with Mary Jane. She's lonely and needs a friend and so do I. If people are going to criticize us for that, to hell with them. It's not so different than you and Maddie."

"O.K." Jake replied with hesitation since he didn't share Quinn's take on the situation.

Quinn saw Jake's reluctance. "I appreciate your concern," Quinn said. "I value your opinion. But I feel comfortable seeing Mary Jane. As for the criticism, the talk behind our backs, well, I can handle that. In law enforcement, you get used to that. I'm sure the same is true in your line of work."

"It is. And I try not to put myself in compromising situations."

"There's your boy Kenny and his date," Quinn said, pointing to the entrance to the ballroom. "Too bad they showed up. I was hoping to have a little fun with them. They do make a nice looking couple."

Jake told Quinn he would talk to him at the first of the week and scooted off to intercept Kenny and Sunny. He met them at the refreshment table that was covered with three bowls of punch and a half-dozen trays of finger sandwiches and pastries. "You guys had me worried," Jake told them. "I was beginning to think you weren't going to show."

"You look good in the tux," Kenny told his boss. "We had a slight problem."

"What's going on? Grab some punch. I've got a table over in the corner." Jake didn't like Kenny's admission and his expression. Sunny was quiet as usual and would not look directly at Jake.

With the disc jockey starting another ear-splitting number, Jake and the two teenagers made their way to the table where Maddie was sitting alone, still swaying and snapping her fingers. "Sunny, you look beautiful!" Maddie exclaimed as the slender blonde sat down.

"I helped her pick out the dress," Kenny proudly proclaimed.

"And you look rather handsome as well, Mr. Richards," Maddie added while inspecting his burgundy jacket and black pants with a wide side stripe that matched the jacket.

Jake handed Maddie her punch refill. "You said you had a slight problem," Jake said to Kenny. "What happened?"

He was hesitant to answer. He looked at Sunny, started to speak and then stopped. He looked at his date once more, and she dropped her head and wouldn't look at him. "We were late . . . . we were late because Sunny's old man hit her."

"Sunny, no!" Maddie said in horror. "Where did he hit you?"

Kenny answered for her. "On the left cheek. Thank God it was a glancing blow. We went by Miss Wayne's and she helped with Sunny's makeup to cover up the welt. You can barely see it, especially in this dark room. Sunny's self-conscious about it though. Miss Wayne and I had to do a lot of talking to get her to come on to the prom."

"Let me see," Maddie said tenderly. She took Sunny's chin in her hand and turned the girl's face toward her. "You're right," Maddie said. "Miss Wayne did a good job. You can't see it. Does it hurt?"

"A little," the girl said so softly she couldn't be heard but Maddie read her lips.

"Can I talk to you a minute?" Kenny asked Jake.

"Sure. If we go out they won't let us back in, but I see a vacant spot over against that wall," Jake suggested.

Jake and Kenny got up, leaving Maddie and Sunny to talk. "I'm so sorry," Maddie said compassionately. "What happened?"

Sunny was quiet. Obviously she didn't want to talk about what had happened.

"You need to talk to me," Maddie urged. "Someone needs to know."

Reluctantly, Sunny opened up. "Dad lost his temper. I'm not sure why. All I said to him was we were leaving, and he hit the roof. I think he had been drinking. Dad hit me and was about to hit me again. Kenny stepped between us and caught Dad's hand as he was swinging. Dad lost his balance and fell and we ran out of the house. He ran after us and was yelling and cussing as we got into the car."

Maddie shook her head in disbelief. She looked around at all the other young people in the room who were dancing, laughing and having a grand time, unaware of the trauma Sunny had endured that night. "Has your Dad hit you before?"

"A few times . . . but he doesn't mean it. He's just got a bad temper. And he drinks too much."

"No, that's not an excuse," Maddie quickly told the girl. "Sunny, what he's doing is criminal. As a teacher, I'm supposed to let the authorities know if I think one of my students is being abused. It's the law. If I don't tell, I could go to jail."

"Please don't tell, Mrs. Hampton," Sunny pleaded. "Dad and I will work it out. He's the only family I have. I don't want the state to take me and put me in a foster home!"

"I don't know Sunny . . ."

"Please, Mrs. Hampton!" Sunny wiped a tear out of the corner of her eye. "I don't want to cry. It will mess up my makeup and then everyone will see the bruise."

Turning her head away to again look at the crowd, Maddie gave careful thought to Sunny's request. She looked at the welt on Sunny's cheek that Miss Wayne had so carefully covered with heavy makeup.

"O.K., I'll make you a deal," Maddie started. "I won't say anything for now on one condition. That you spend the night at my house. I don't want you going back home tonight."

"I suppose I could . . ."

"I won't take no for an answer. I want you to get some rest, and then in the morning, I'll fix you a big breakfast. And Kenny can come over and eat too."

"Thank you Mrs. Hampton. That's very nice of you."

Sighing, Maddie studied the young girl. "You really do look beautiful tonight. I'm glad you and Kenny decided to come on to the dance. For the next couple of hours, I want you to forget everything else that's happened tonight and have a great time. This is your senior prom. This should be one of the greatest nights of your life. And I think it would be appropriate if you end the night by giving Kenny a big kiss. I think he deserves it after he got you out of your house tonight."

"Yes ma'am," she smiled in weak reply.

In another area of the room, away from the dancers and food, Jake and Kenny were about to begin their conversation. Kenny had his back to the table where his date and Maddie were sitting.

"It was bad tonight, Jake. The asshole hit Sunny for no reason! I think that asshole would have really hurt Sunny if I hadn't been there. Heck, I think he was ready to hurt me."

"You're right. It is bad. You've got to tell someone, Quinn, maybe, before he hurts Sunny or you."

"But Sunny says he's all the family she has. No one knows where her mother is. She freaks out over the idea of going to a foster home."

"She's about to turn 18, right? Then she can move out on her own and not worry about being sent off. But in the meantime, we need to tell someone about this. I don't think it's safe for her to be in her house one more night."

"I don't know. I've got to talk to her. Don't tell anyone, not yet any way," Kenny pleaded.

"I'll think about it during the rest of the weekend. You did good tonight, getting her out of there Kenny. I'm proud of you."

"Thanks Jake. To tell you the truth, I was so scared I was about to piss all over this expensive tuxedo. It got hairy, man, real hairy."

"What I want you to do now is enjoy the rest of this dance. You deserve that and so does Sunny. Can you do that for me?"

"I'll try my best."

Jake slapped Kenny on the back and they walked back to their dates. Both of the guys were pleased to see Sunny with a trace of a smile. Kenny immediately took her by the hand and led her to the dance floor. Maddie and Jake looked on approvingly.

"Those two have had some night," Jake said, exhaling as he slumped into his chair.

"Something's got to be done, Jake, but I promised Sunny I wouldn't tell anyone just yet."

"I made the same promise to Kenny."

"Sunny's spending the night at my house. I insisted."

"Good. You know, I told Kenny to enjoy the rest of this evening, and I think we should too. I'm not very good at it, but I'm willing to try. This DJ is finally playing some slow music I can relate to. Would you like to dance?"

Her face lighting up like the fireworks display Barber County High has after every homecoming football game, Maddie was out of her chair before the words were out of Jake's mouth. They moved to the middle of the dance floor where everyone could see them, and Jake didn't mind if they did. "I've got a confession," he whispered softly in her ear as they pressed together during the soft love ballad. "When I was in high school a thousand years ago, I didn't go to any of the proms."

"You didn't? A handsome lad like you? I would have thought you had girls hanging all over you."

"I was shy."

"I'm glad to see you coming out of your shell."

"I owe it all to you."

"How are you enjoying this prom?"

"It's getting better by the minute."

"I will certainly go along with that."

"It would be even better if the lovely lady I'm with would allow me to kiss her. Right now."

"Sorry. School rules do not allow public displays of affection."

"I have another confession to make."

"What's that?"

"I never was very good at obeying the rules when I was in school." He moved his lips to Maddie's and offered a slow, tender romantic kiss that any of the teenage couples would have graded an A-plus. Maddie melted in his arms, feeling delightfully wicked about breaking the rules in front of the principal, guidance counselor, school board president and everyone else at the Barber County High School Junior-Senior Prom.

CHAPTER SEVENTEEN

Gesturing like a hostess on a TV game show, Hazel pointed to the deliveries that were waiting for Jake when he arrived at the Sentinel office at 10 a.m. on the Monday following Saturday's prom. "Judging from these lovely parting gifts, I'd say you had quite a weekend, Mr. Martin," she teased.

"Good morning Hazel," Jake replied, trying not to smile too obviously.

"Who's the better cook?" she asked.

"Oh, I'm not answering that question, no way," Jake replied as he studied the pecan pie and loaf of homemade bread. Hallmark cards accompanied both treats. Looking at Hazel and unable to contain his smile, Jake took the card from the pie.

I felt like a school girl at the prom. It was a wonderful, wonderful night.

Thank you. Maddie

Sliding that card back in its envelope, Jake put it down, smiled at Hazel again and opened the other.

I was thinking about how you enjoyed my homemade bread.

I hope we can sit down and break bread together again very soon

Janet Wayne

Sighing playfully, Jake shook his head and boasted, "So many women, so little time. What's a man to do?"

"My advice to you is, if you're not already, start taking a multi-vitamin. I think you're going to need the energy. Now tell me about the prom. I've already heard about it from Kenny."

"Kenny's out early today. What did he tell you about the prom?"

"That you and Maddie made a dashing couple—and that you sneaked a kiss late in the evening, right out on the dance floor in front of everyone. I'm proud of you Jake! Bring some life to this town!"

Jake started blushing. "Kenny told you that, huh? Guess it must be all over town by now."

"Probably, but that's all right. I'm glad to see Maddie happy. She deserves it. She was so devastated by her husband's death. She grieved a long time. I'm glad she's finally moving on, and I'm glad she's found someone like you. You've been good for her."

"It's just the opposite, Hazel. Maddie's been good for me."

"What about Miss Wayne?"

"She's an interesting woman, but I can't see anything happening between us. The dynamics between Miss Wayne and me are so different than between Maddie and me"

"I think what you're trying to say is you're sweet on Maddie."

His blush getting more crimson, Jake didn't answer, instead changing the subject. "What else did Kenny say about the prom?" Jake asked, wanting to know if Sunny's troubles were discussed.

"Nothing. He had to rush off to cover a story. One of Carl Flemister's cows is stuck in the creek and they're having a problem getting her out. I was going to tell you about it. I thought you might want to go take a look."

"You're right Hazel. I do want to go. I can truly say, that in all of my years in the newspaper business, I have never reported on a cow rescue."

"Head straight out Highway 47 for about two miles. Flemister's Farms is on the right. You can't miss it."

Quickly deciding that nothing on his morning's agenda was more important than the cow rescue, Jake asked Hazel, "Will you take these goodies back to my office? And yes, feel free to sample them."

"You had better hurry back. There might not be anything left."

"I'll take my chances."

As Hazel had promised, Jake easily found the Flemister Farm and steered his Maxima down a dirt road to the left of the huge two story farm house. The road parted a large grassy pasture and led to a grove of trees that ran along the banks of a narrow creek. Twenty-five or thirty head of cattle were grazing near the trees where Kenny's yellow Mustang, Quinn's car, a tow truck and a flatbed truck fitted with a burial vault crane were parked. "I'm surprised they didn't call in the National Guard to help," Jake joked to himself as he parked his car, starting to understand how seriously south Georgia cattlemen protect their livestock.

"How's it coming?" Jake asked Kenny, although he quickly saw things weren't coming so well. The cow appeared to be stuck solidly in soft mud smack in the middle of the creek, which would have been about knee high on Jake.

"They've already tried to push the old girl out by hand, but that just ain't gonna work," Kenny explained. "Right now, they're trying to decide if the tow truck or crane is the best option."

Quinn stepped away from Carl Flemister and greeted Jake. "Bet you never covered anything like this in Atlanta."

"I've written about a lot of politicians who found themselves knee deep in bullcrap, but you are absolutely right. This is my first cow story. What's next, Quinn?"

"We can't get the crane in place to lift the cow up, so we're going to use the tow truck. We're going to wrap a cable around her waist and pull her out with the tow truck's wench."

"Sounds like a plan," Jake nodded in approval. While Kenny got in place to take photos, Jake and Quinn watched while the tow truck driver and two agricultural agents waded into the creek to join Carl Flemister and the cow which had been quiet, but started mooing with authority as they wrapped the cable around her. The other cows in the field were answering her with a chorus of moos.

Cable secured, the tow truck driver put the wench in gear. Slowly, the cable tightened and groaned. The men in the creek pushed the cow from the backside as the wench pulled the cable forward. Bellowing like she was headed to the slaughterhouse, the cow slowly inched forward. Flemister slipped and fell face down in the creek, and everyone watching burst into laughter. Laughing himself, Flemister quickly got up and started pushing again. After ten minutes of tedious, inch at a time work, the muddy cow was back on the creek bank and the exhausted men plopped to the ground to catch their breath.

"Thanks for your help, Quinn," Flemister said between gasps for air as he scraped mud off his soaked jeans. He spoke in jest, and Quinn knew it.

"I'm a supervisor. I watch other people do the work."

"And you do that well," Jake said in a tone every bit as sarcastic as Flemister's.

Quinn walked away to talk to the tow truck driver while Kenny came to Jake to let him know he was headed back to the Sentinel office. Jake was chuckling at the filthy cow that had started chewing on some grass and seemed totally unconcerned about its need for a bath. "How are you going to start your story on this daring rescue?" Jake asked his young reporter.

"How about a small band of brave men risking their lives to save someone's future steak dinner?"

"That's good. This story does need a light, humorous touch. But you've got to admit, those guys did put in a lot of effort to save ole Bessie," Jake said with sincere admiration.

Kenny agreed. "Yeah, they put more effort into rescuing her than I would have with some people I know."

"Anybody in particular?"

"Sunny's Dad, for one. But comparing him to the cow is an insult to the cow."

"What happened after the prom?"

Kenny closed his reporter's notebook and slid it in his back pocket. "I took Sunny to Mrs. Hampton's to spend the night. Sunny didn't really want to, because she was afraid her Dad would come looking for her and cause some real problems. That thought crossed my mind too. He didn't, thank goodness, and Sunny got a good night's sleep. The next morning, Mrs. Hampton fixed us a big breakfast, and about mid-morning, we took Sunny back home. I didn't want her to go, and Mrs. Hampton *really* didn't want her to go, but Sunny insisted.

Her Dad wasn't home when we dropped Sunny off. I haven't heard from her. I guess—I hope—she's all right."

Jake could only shake his head in contempt at Mr. Krause's behavior and Sunny's predicament. "She's got to get away from him, Kenny, before he really hurts her."

"Believe me, I've told her that. More than once. I hope she'll listen to me once she turns eighteen in a few weeks, but I don't know. He seems to have a real strong hold on her."

"We've got to get her away from him," Jake repeated.

"Well, I don't think it's going to be my concern much longer."

Jake didn't respond, instead waiting for Kenny to continue.

Waving to the drivers of the tow truck and crane as they drove away, Kenny didn't immediately expand on his remark. He looked at the rescued cow that was now moseying back to the rest of the herd and collected his thoughts before answering. "After the prom, when I told Mom and Dad what had happened, they went nuts. They like Sunny, but like everyone else, they can't stand the way her Dad acts. They pretty much gave me an ultimatum. They don't want me seeing her any more. What they said, is if I want them to help pay my way to the University of Georgia, then I've got to stop seeing her."

Jake's first reaction was that Mr. and Mrs. Richards' demand was harsh, but he quickly started seeing their side. No matter how much they liked Sunny, they could not allow their son to be at risk. After all, far more was involved than Mr. Krause popping an occasional beer or letting fly with a barrage of foul language. The man had been violent. Jake wasn't about to be too critical of the Richards for wanting to keep their son out of harm's way. Even to someone like him, who had never had to make parental decisions, their stance seemed appropriate. He did, however, feel for Kenny.

"What do you think of their demand?" Jake asked. He was surprised by Kenny's response.

"I think it's best. I like Sunny a lot. She's pretty and she's fun to be with when she's relaxed, which is hardly ever. But I've got to tell you Jake, dealing with her Dad has taken a toll on me. I'm about ready to bail. I've just got to figure out the best way to break the news to her."

"I understand." Jake felt badly for Kenny but worse for Sunny. "The thing is, though, even if you split up with her, something's got to be done about her Dad."

"You're right, but what? As bad as he treats her, Sunny doesn't want anyone to do anything that will get her Dad in trouble."

"That does make it difficult." Jake looked at Quinn who was talking to Carl Flemister again, no doubt telling him to keep his cows out of the creek. Jake rubbed the back of his neck and scratched his head. "What if I get Quinn to talk to Sunny's Dad? Maybe he can scare the guy into acting better."

Shrugging his shoulders, Kenny replied. "It can't hurt. Maybe if Mr. Krause blows his stack at Quinn, the chief can lock him up."

"That's not likely to happen, but maybe Quinn can tone him down some. Now, go on, get back to the office. Check with Hazel. She's got some sweet treats that were left for me. You can have some, provided she hasn't eaten them all."

Kenny smiled. "Mrs. Hampton thanking you for Saturday night?"

"Something like that. Miss Wayne sent me some bread too."

"Miss Wayne? Geez Jake. You and Miss Wayne?"

"Don't worry. All I did was have supper with her one night. Is there a crime in that?"

"Nope. It's just that everyone in town is betting on you and Mrs. Hampton."

Jake threw up his hands. "Do the people in this town bet on everything?"

Kenny nodded. "Just about. What else is there to do?"

"Run a newspaper for one. Now get back to the office."

Kenny drove off, leaving only Jake and Quinn in the field. Walking toward Jake, Quinn stepped in a cow patty. "Damn it!" he fussed. "Why are you still here, Jake?"

"Because I wanted to see you step in a pile of cow manure. After the conversation I just had with Kenny, I need some comic relief."

"What's going on? He seemed fine to me. He had that camera rammed right in our faces, like he usually does when he's covering a story."

"He's got girl troubles. And his girl has Daddy troubles."

"Regal Krause? What's the son of a bitch done now?"

"For starters, he hit Sunny. At the prom, she had a good-size welt on her cheek."

"Damn it! That son of a bitch! Has anyone notified Children Services?"

"No. That's part of the problem. Sunny doesn't want anyone to tattle on her Dad."

"It's the law to tell. If we suspect something and don't tell, then we're breaking the law."

"I know, but Maddie and I promised Sunny and Kenny we won't tell anyone, at least not yet. What we were hoping is that maybe you could go talk to the guy."

"Ah damn it!" Quinn mumbled. He rubbed his chin with his hand and turned away from Jake to look at the creek. Turning back around, Quinn said, "I'll go talk to him, but it's not going to do any good. A leopard can't change its spots and Regal Krause isn't going to change. And let me tell you this. When I talk to him, if I get the feeling that's he's laid a hand on that girl, well, his ass is going to jail, regardless of what Sunny wants."

"Fair enough. I can't argue with that."

"Is this some way to start a Monday morning?" Quinn asked as he pulled out a couple of sticks of Black Jack gum and started chewing vigorously. "A stranded cow and a child abuser. The way this day has started, we'll probably have another murder before sundown."

"Don't say that, Quinn," Jake shot back in admonishment. "I know you're kidding, but don't say that."

CHAPTER EIGHTEEN

Back at the Sentinel office after the cow rescue, Jake discovered he was too late to retrieve much of his Monday morning treats. Hazel, Kenny and George Lancaster, the advertising manager, had gobbled down all but two wedges of Maddie's pecan pie and a single slice of Miss Wayne's bread. Their excuse was they were acting on Jake's behalf. Obviously having rehearsed their story, the trio said they noticed Jake was looking a little thicker around the waist since being introduced to Sanderson's good home-cooking, and they were simply trying to limit his temptations, thereby limiting his caloric intake. "What friends," Jake said in mock appreciation. Actually, he didn't mind his co-workers helping themselves. The pie and bread were much too much for him to consume by himself.

Gathering up the remnants of his bounty, Jake went to his office, where he elected to enjoy a slice of Maddie's pie before delving into the thick stack of mail on his desk. The pecan treat was tasty, and, after finishing the first slice, Jake, unable to resist the temptation, started on the final slice in the tin plate. About to spear the final bite, Jake put his fork down when the phone started ringing. He gave himself a moment to swallow the bite he had in his mouth before answering.

"Well, Jake," the caller started. "I'm in Charleston and you're not. What's going on? I thought you'd be here by now."

"Hey Jack," Jake replied to his old friend Jack Harper. "How are things going up there?"

"They're going fine, but they'd be even better if you were here. What's keeping you?"

"It's too complicated to talk about over the phone. There's several things going on that I just can't walk away from right now. To be honest, Jack, I haven't been able to give your offer the thought it requires and deserves. I'm interested, definitely, but I can't commit yet."

"What kind of time frame are we talking about, Jake? We need you here. Things are really beginning to pick up speed."

"I don't know. I honestly don't know. Not long, I hope. I know you need to know. How's the rest of the staff coming?"

"Good. We've got some great people coming on board. You may be familiar with several of them, but I don't think you really know them or have worked with them before. You're my man, though, Jake. I want you to be my senior correspondent."

Jake leaned back in his chair. "I don't want to keep you hanging. I'm ninety-nine percent certain I'm coming, but I do need to think about it and tie up a few loose ends. Can you give me a few more days, please?"

The other end of the line was quiet for a moment. "All right, Jake," Harper finally said. Jake sensed displeasure in his friend's reply. "Make it quick, all right."

"I will. I promise."

"And Jake . . ."

"Yeah?"

"Is this really an opportunity you can pass up? I mean, a lot of guys don't get a second chance like this."

"You're absolutely right and I appreciate it. I'll talk to you soon. I promise."

The conversation ended but Jake's thought process didn't. He was growing increasingly fond of the people in the little south Georgia town who had taken him under their wings, but Jack was right. The Charleston magazine was a great opportunity to get back into the mainstream. If he declined this job, it could be a long time, maybe never, before something this good came along again. And even though he had been in Sanderson a short time, he already felt a sense of loyalty to Stephen House, who had taken a chance on him when no one else would. Jake really needed to talk to someone, but who? Quinn and Maddie? They were numbers one and two on the Top Ten List of Reasons for staying.

Jake still had not tapped into his stack of mail when Hazel quietly appeared at his office door and caught him propped back in his chair, still in deep thought. He didn't move as she told him, "I thought you would like to know. Someone just called my desk and said there's something going on at the city cemetery. Apparently there's quite a commotion going on over there, but we don't know what."

Jake sat up in his chair. "I think I do," he said, standing up. "Hazel, this is a strange request, but do you happen to have a Bible with you?"

"Yes. I keep one at my desk."

"I'm going over to the cemetery. Can I take your Bible with me?"

"As long as I get it back."

"You will. I need to go." Jake followed Hazel to her desk. He got the Bible and was promptly out the door and into his car for the short trip to the city cemetery, which was actually about a mile outside the city limits just off the highway leading to Eagleton. The twelve acre site was like a history book for the town, holding the graves of the well-known and forgotten, the rich and the poor, movers and shakers and drunks and vagrants. A handful of the graves were 150 years old and one was a day old. A dozen plots were marked with elaborate monuments that cost thousands, while almost the same number were noted by small temporary markers that had become permanent due to either a lack of money or a lack of interest by family members or the community. There were graves that were continually maintained by loved ones, adorned with fresh flowers and greenery, and others that had been neglected for so long they were hardly recognizable.

Angling his car on to the narrow one-way road leading into the cemetery, Jake immediately spotted Quinn's car and coroner Lawson Lockridge's van parked near a tall obelisk monument in an old but well-kept, concrete-lined family plot that looked to be squarely in the middle of the cemetery. "Jesus!" Jake gasped as he parked directly behind Quinn, not taking his eyes off the monument, more specifically what was draped on it. "I guess this is number three," Jake said, striding up to Quinn.

"Number three," Quinn nodded immediately after filling his mouth with Black Jack chewing gum. A man's naked body was affixed to the monument by clear packing tape at the ankles, waist, chest and forehead. His white underwear was stuffed in his mouth. Single ten penny nails were hammered deep into each temple.

"He looks familiar," Jake said, trying to fight off a rising wave of nausea. "Quinn, I don't know if my stomach can handle this. Got any more gum?"

Quinn tossed two sticks of gum to Jake and added, "It's Regal Krause, Sunny's Dad."

"Jesus!" Jake said again. "That poor girl." Jake grabbed at his stomach as if that would keep the contents from coming back up.

"Poor girl?" Quinn responded. "What about this poor bastard who's got two nails driven into his head?"

"It goes without saying, I'm sorry for him. But Sunny seems so fragile. I can't imagine what this will do to her."

"She may be relieved, the way he treats her. We'll find out in a few minutes when we tell her. All right, Jake," Quinn, said noticing Hazel's Bible that Jake had brought with him. "Tell us which scripture we have to thank for this."

Remembering what Pastor Allen had warned, Jake scrambled to find the Book of Judges. Quickly running his finger down each page, Jake got to Chapter Four. "Come on, Jake. Move it," Quinn ordered impatiently.

Jake's finger stopped at Judges 4:21. "Here it is," he said looking at Quinn.

Then Jael Heber's wife took a nail of the tent, and took a hammer in her hand, and went softly unto him and smote the nail into his temples

"That's not the whole verse, but you get the idea," Jake said, slapping the Bible shut.

"Yeah I get the idea."

"Isn't this your GBI Agent showing up?" asked Jake, observing the suited, sun glassed driver getting out of the white Ford Explorer that had pulled in to the cemetery.

"Agent Stamps?" Quinn asked, looking over his shoulder.

"Yeah. He's been all over town asking questions. I've talked to him a couple of times."

"What did you tell him?"

"Not much, because I don't know much. Don't worry, Quinn. I'm not going to reveal anything to him before I talk to you, that is, if I ever have anything to reveal."

Approaching Quinn, Stamps took off his sunglasses. "I'm impressed, Quinn," the agent said. "For this to be a sleepy little town in the middle of nowhere, you have a very imaginative killer."

"Why shouldn't we have creative killings?" Quinn snapped back. "Hell, what else is there to do here but dream up obscure ways to kill people. Do you have any other revelations to share with us today?"

"Afraid not. How long has the body been here?"

"Several hours. I'd say he was killed during the night."

"The victim?"

"Regal Krause, one of our local malcontents."

"Any significance to him being tied to this particular monument?"

"I don't think so."

"I'm going to call in one of our forensics teams to go over the scene."

"Wait a minute, Agent Stamps!" Quinn protested. "My assistant chief and Deputy Landry are going to process the scene. They've had training. So has our coroner. We don't need your help."

"With all due your respect to your people, don't you think my agency might be a little more up-to-date on the latest crime scene technology and techniques?"

Jake stood between the two men, his head swiveling from one to the other as they continued their verbal volley.

"We don't need your help!" Quinn repeated.

Stamps turned his head away to hide his irritation and frustration. "I'm not the bad guy here, Quinn," he said, trying to remain civil as he made eye contact with Quinn. "You and I both have the same goal. To catch this son of a bitch before anyone else is killed."

"And we will."

"Maybe I need to talk to the mayor again."

"Help yourself. I'll tell him to stay out of my department's business too."

"Can I at least get a closer look at the body?"

Quinn nodded approval.

Stamps looked at Jake. "Do you always carry a Bible with you?"

"I'm thinking about going into preaching on the side. The newspaper business doesn't pay much, you know."

Stamps inched closer to the body and so did Jake. Quinn allowed Jake to nose around for about ninety seconds and requested that he back away so Sam Rogers, Officer Landry and Lawson Lockridge could begin their work. That was fine with Jake, who was beginning to feel the butterflies flutter in his stomach again.

"What is it with you and Stamps?" Jake asked.

"He's a young agent trying to make a name for himself at my expense. This is my case. I am going to solve it," Quinn told him.

"You don't think you could use his help?"

"Yeah, I could, but I'm not going to. I'm going to solve this damn case!"

"Please tell me you've got something to go on other than Maddie's history with these three guys."

"No, I don't. Don't you think it's a big coincidence that three men she has absolutely no use for have met their fates? I've got to talk to her and soon."

"I wish you wouldn't. There's got to be another angle."

"There is one thing different about this body than the first two."

Jake waited for Quinn to continue.

"The smell. Perfume. Strong perfume. Overpowering perfume," Quinn said while tugging at his nose.

"I didn't notice. I'm trying too hard not to throw up."

Quinn grabbed Jake by the arm and shoved him toward the body. Jake quickly pulled away and stumbled backwards, but not before getting a brief nasal-filling sniff of the potent perfume. He turned his back to Quinn and choked, expecting the puke to roll, but it didn't. With his hands on his knees, Jake rested a moment before turning back to Quinn.

"Wimp!" Quinn said, pointing his index finger at Jake.

"Weak stomach. Always had one," Jake said in defense of his gag reflex.

Quinn looked back at the body. "As strong as the fragrance is, the killer must have been coated in the stuff and crawled all over Regal. So now we know we have some sweet-smelling, Bible-thumping she devil who wears a size seven and a half shoe and teases her victims with sex before she kills them. Shouldn't be too difficult to find someone who fits that description."

"There's got to be a clue here somewhere," Jake said, trying to convince himself as much as Quinn. "This killer is bound to slip up sooner or later."

"If there is a clue here, we'll find it. My guys will find it, not Stamps. We'll stay out here to midnight if we have to. In the meantime, we've got to keep the Anderson family from finding out there's a dead man taped to their monument. They're one of the oldest families of the town—big shots, if you will—and I don't think they will take kindly to this intrusion. I suspect the old patriarch, Gerald Anderson, buried just to the right over there, is probably flipping cartwheels right now."

"I'm more concerned about the living," Jake offered. "Like Maddie and Sunny and the rest of the town who are going to be petrified when they find out there's been another killing. What are we going to do, Quinn?"

"Try to find some way to keep the rest of the horny idiotic men in town from being tied up and carved up. I may reconsider implementing a curfew. If I have to I'll shut down the streets of this town at 9 o'clock. I'm tired of people getting killed, even if they are sorry bastards like Regal Krause."

"We've got to tell Sunny. I think she's in one of Maddie's classes. Let's talk to Maddie. She can help us decide how to do this."

"That's a good idea. Give me a few minutes. I need to talk to Sam and Lockridge, and we'll go to the school." Quinn sighed. "Giving bad news to people. Now that's one part of this job I don't like a bit. Not a damn bit!" Quinn went to the trunk of his car, pulled out his plastic bat, walked to the boundary line of the cemetery, and proceeded to beat the heck out of an old oak tree.

CHAPTER NINETEEN

Classes were changing at Barber County High School. Students were swarming in the halls, getting books out of their lockers, gobbling down a candy bar or pack of crackers for a quick snack, or huddling together making plans for after school or the evening. None of the smiling, giggling faces had any notion of the devastating news that Quinn and Jake were there to deliver. Quinn wanted to stay at the cemetery longer, but choose to go with Jake to the school before classes let out for the day. School would be the easiest place to track down Sunny and break the news.

Jake and Quinn went to the administrative offices and asked that Principal Connery and Maddie be paged. In her classroom, Maddie thought nothing about the message over the intercom. She was frequently called to the principal's office, usually for nothing more important than a minor paperwork issue. This time she was shocked to see Quinn and Jake with Principal Connery. She immediately knew this was no ordinary visit. Tears started welling in her eyes before she was told what had happened.

"Sit down, Maddie," Principal Connery said in a subdued tone. "I'm afraid these gentlemen have some bad news."

Her legs suddenly feeling rubbery, Maddie unsteadily eased into one of the two oversized upholstered chairs in the room. Principal Connery shut the door to her office.

"Maddie," Quinn started. He stopped to clear his throat. "Sunny Krause's father has been killed. Apparently by the same perpetrator who killed Joe Lambert and Todd Monroe."

Maddie burst into tears, and Jake sat on the arm of her chair and put his hand on her back. Principal Connery pulled a handful of tissues from the box on her desk and gave them to her. Maddie continued to cry for several minutes before slowly beginning to regain some of her composure. No one said anything as she cried.

"How did it happen?" she was finally able to ask between sniffles.

"We found him in the city cemetery, tied to a monument, with two nails driven in his skull," Quinn said matter-of-factly.

Again, tears immediately filled her eyes. She was trying not to cry. "Does Sunny know yet?" she sobbed.

"No," Principal Connery said. "That's why these gentlemen are here. "We've paged Sunny. She's on her way."

"Damn it, Quinn!" Maddie shouted. "When is this going to stop?" Her expletive rang in Jake's ears.

Principal Connery didn't give Quinn a chance to respond, which was just as well, because he didn't have any response. "Maddie, we know Sunny likes you. We wanted you to be here when we break the news," the principal said.

Maddie nodded as she wiped her eyes. "Let me tell her. Please," she requested.

Quinn and the principal looked at each other. "Of course," Quinn said.

"Come in," Connery replied to a knock on her door. Sunny, looking meek and forlorn as usual, stepped in. The bruise on her cheek from Saturday night was still visible, despite a coat of makeup. Maddie, her face red and puffy and her eyes still wet, got out of her chair and hugged Sunny tightly for a minute. "Sweetheart," Maddie started, looking into the girl's perplexed eyes, "Chief Quinn brought us some bad news." Maddie paused in an effort to remain composed. "Your Dad has passed away."

Shock was evident in the girl's eyes but she didn't say anything. Sunny looked straight ahead at her teacher and for a moment Maddie thought the girl was about to go into a trauma-induced trance. Finally, Sunny's eyes misted and she asked simply, "What happened?"

"He was murdered," is all Maddie said. "Chief Quinn will tell you more later. The news of his death is enough for you to deal with now."

"What am I going to do?" Sunny asked as a single tear rolled down her cheek.

"Right now, you're going home with me," Maddie said maternally. "Sunny, do you have any family, anywhere?"

Sunny wiped her cheek with her hand and Maddie gave her a tissue. "No ma'am. I don't think I've got any relatives. Mom or Dad never talked about anyone else."

"Like I said," Maddie started again. "You're going home with me to get some rest. That's what is important now. We'll start dealing with everything else in the morning. Mrs. Connery, will you take care of my class?"

"Don't worry about it, Mrs. Hampton. You take care of Sunny."

Maddie looked at Jake. "Mr. Martin. I would appreciate it, and I think Sunny would too, if you would accompany us, and stay awhile."

"Absolutely. I'll be there in fifteen minutes."

Not wanting to face her students, Maddie had one of the administrative secretaries retrieve her pocketbook, and another secretary got Sunny's purse from her locker. Principal Connery escorted Maddie and Sunny to Maddie's Jeep and they left hurriedly. Jake stopped outside the offices, in the common area, to talk to Quinn before leaving for Maddie's. "If what the girl says is true," Jake said to Quinn, "and she doesn't have any family, then she's going need some help with some decisions over the next few days. Thank God, she's got Maddie to help."

"I'll make some calls to try to track down relatives. If they exist, we'll find them."

"You know the town's going to be in an uproar. I expect word's already gotten around."

Quinn snapped at Jake's comment. "You're not telling me anything I don't already know. I *am* going to find this son of a bitch, and given half-a-chance, I may kill her on the spot. To hell with any idea about a fair trial!" He slammed his fist against the wall.

Jake regretted his remark and attempted to calm down Quinn. "I'm sorry. That comment wasn't necessary. Remember the temper," he urged Quinn. "Calm down. Chew some more gum."

"I'm out of gum," Quinn fumed before taking a couple of deep breaths. That seemed to help. "All right. That's better," he responded in a calmer voice. "O.K. Martin. You get over to Maddie's. I'm going back to the cemetery."

Using his cell phone, Jake called the Sentinel to let Hazel know what was going on. Her voice trembling, Hazel said she already knew, and told Jake that Kenny knew as well. Relaying the plan to have Sunny spend the night at Maddie's, Jake asked Hazel to talk to Kenny, requesting that he not show up immediately, giving Maddie and Sunny time to settle in. Hazel dutifully agreed, but, given Kenny's frenetic state, she could not guarantee that the talk would have the desired results. She described him as a whirlwind of emotional energy, not knowing whether to sit or stand, talk or be silent, rant and rave or be calm. She explained that Kenny was suffering from a huge dose of guilt as well, having wished for Regal Krause's death the night of the prom, and now being blindsided by the news that he was.

When Jake arrived at Maddie's, Sunny was sitting trance-like in a chair in the living room, looking straight ahead and not speaking. Maddie had poured her a Diet Coke into a glass of ice, but the drink remained untouched on the side table. Afraid Sunny would go into shock, Maddie called Walter Merkerson, her long-time family physician, to make a house call and give Sunny a cursory examination and hopefully prescribe a sedative to help her get some rest. Kenny, despite Hazel's pleadings, headed straight to Maddie's, arriving before the doctor. Without saying anything, Kenny sat next to Sunny and hugged her tenderly. Sunny made no effort to reciprocate. He tried to talk to her but she wouldn't respond. Trying not to show his frustration to Sunny, Kenny excused himself from the living room and cornered Jake in the kitchen. "What's wrong with her?" Kenny pleaded with Jake.

"The girl's just found out her father was murdered. How would you react?"

"I don't know. I hope I'm never in that situation. Can I have something to drink?"

"Check the refrigerator. Maddie usually has some soft drinks."

"I don't mean a soft drink. I want a beer. Better yet, a shot of whiskey!"

"You're out of luck. What do your parents think about you being here? Aren't you supposed to be breaking up with Sunny?"

"Yeah, they want me to, but this isn't exactly a good time to drop that bomb on her. Which is worse, Jake? Having a father that hits you, or not having a father at all?"

"That's a question no one should have to answer."

"Well, all I know is I feel sick to my stomach. I could have killed him myself Saturday night, and now someone has."

"Get over it!" Jake ordered. "Mr. Krause was targeted by a serial killer. I'm sure his fate had been decided before your confrontation with him on prom night. Channel all your efforts into helping Sunny. In fact, go on home. We're going to need you more tomorrow and the next day. The doctor is going to be here shortly, and I'm sure he's going to give Sunny something to knock her out. And if you don't want to go home, then go to work. We've still got a paper to put out."

"I'm not in much of a mood to write, but I guess I can try. I sure as heck don't want to go home and sit around the rest of the day and night. Let me see Sunny for another minute and I'll go, unless she asks me to stay."

"Fair enough."

Doctor Merkerson had arrived and was in the guest bedroom examining Sunny. Kenny sat down in one of the plush living room chairs, but was too fidgety to be still and got up. He grabbed the Diet Coke intended for Sunny and finished it off in three long gulps. "God, it's taking them a long time," Kenny fussed.

"It's only been five minutes," Jake said, pointing at his watch.

Ten more minutes passed before the doctor and Maddie emerged from the guest room. "She's traumatized, but who wouldn't be," the doctor said, looking first at Jake and then Kenny. "But she'll be fine. Give her some time."

"Can I talk to her a minute?" Kenny asked.

"Let's leave her alone for the moment," the doctor said. "I've given her something to help her relax. Maddie, call me if there's a change for the worse. I mean it. Call me immediately."

"Thanks doctor. I will."

Maddie accompanied the doctor to the door, and Jake had Kenny in tow right behind. After shaking the doctor's hand and thanking him again, Maddie turned to Kenny and hugged him. "I'm sorry, Kenny. I know this is very difficult for you too."

"I'm all right," he said, but with his head buried on Maddie's shoulder, no one could see the tear on his cheek. "I'm worried about Sunny."

"We are all," Maddie said. "The next few days are going to be difficult. We'll get through it with the Good Lord's help and the support of our friends."

"Yes ma'am," Kenny replied politely. He turned to Jake. "I'm going back to the office. I promise I'll get some work done."

"Thanks," Jake told him. "And take care of Hazel."

Waiting for the doctor and Kenny to drive away, Maddie turned to Jake and started to cry again. "This is awful," she whimpered. "Just awful!"

"It is. And I'm going to give you the same advice I gave Kenny. Be strong. Let Sunny draw strength from your strength."

Maddie sighed. "I'll try, but I don't feel very strong right now." She looked at Jake with eyes that were glistening with tears. "Thank you for being here," she said as she gently rubbed her hand across his cheek.

The rest of the day soon became a blur of phone calls and visits. A Barber County High School English teacher was first to follow the grand southern tradition of providing food, delivering a plateful of fried chicken and fresh biscuits. A neighbor came by with a meatloaf and dinner rolls. Other Barber County faculty members called, offering meals, cash and their sympathy. Jake watched with fascination as Maddie went through a methodical, almost obsessive ritual with every phone call. On a small spiral-bound notepad placed conveniently next to the phone in the living room, she neatly wrote down the date and time of the call, the caller and the nature of the call. When Maddie was out of the room for a brief time, Jake sneaked a look at the pad that was full of entries from months back. She had recorded every incoming call, including telemarketers. That much attention to detail, Jake surmised, came from years of teaching.

Two deacons from Sanderson First Baptist dropped by, followed not much later by Pastor Stanley Allen who wanted to check on Maddie, and to offer his services and the church facilities for Regal Krause's funeral. Before leaving, he offered a sweet prayer, petitioning God to look after Sunny and to give her friends the proper words and actions to comfort her. He prayed for Regal Krause's soul as well, not knowing if he was saved. Pastor Allen was such a kindly, caring person, and Maddie greatly appreciated his visit. She thanked him for the offer to use the church, but could not accept until she had time to talk to Sunny about what she would like to do for her father's funeral.

Between the calls and visits, Maddie continually checked on Sunny in the guest room. The medicine had taken effect, and the girl, still in her school clothes, was stretched out on the bed, asleep. At 9:30, Maddie turned off the ringer on the phone and turned out the light on the front porch to discourage anyone else from dropping in. Without waking her up, Maddie managed to get Sunny into some night clothes. Exhausted, mentally as much as physically, Maddie joined Jake in the living room and collapsed on the sofa. She propped her head on Jake's shoulder. "Will you spend the night?" she requested softly.

"Of course. I'll sleep on the sofa." As tired as he was, Jake would have preferred to go home and get some rest in his own bed, but he couldn't refuse Maddie, not on this night.

"No. I don't want you sleeping on the sofa."

Jake's eyes bulged.

"Sleep in Robbie's bed. It will be more comfortable than the sofa."

"O.K." Jake said, embarrassed that he had misread Maddie's intentions.

With her head still on Jake's shoulder, Maddie closed her eyes. He stroked her hair. Maddie opened her eyes, smiled and closed them again, ready to fall into a gentle sleep. Startled by the door bell and a loud knock at the front door, her eyes popped open and she sat up. "I thought we were through with visitors tonight," she sighed.

"Sit here. I'll get it," Jake offered. Stretching as he stood up, Jake shuffled to the door. His legs were stiff from sitting too long. "Miss Wayne?" he said with surprise to the visitor.

"May I see Sunny?" she asked, stepping inside without being invited. She was still wearing a peach-colored dress, probably the same outfit she wore to work earlier.

"She's asleep," Maddie explained, getting up from the sofa.

"I would very much like to see her."

"I don't want to wake her up," Maddie countered.

"What's she doing here anyway?" Miss Wayne inquired bluntly. She stepped farther into the house.

"What do you mean?"

"I mean, who gave you authority to bring her here to your house."

Maddie was getting irritated. "No one gave me authority. I didn't think we had to hold an auction on eBay, with the highest bidder getting to take Sunny home. Jake and Chief Quinn came to the school to tell Sunny about her Dad. I thought the best thing to do was to get her away from the school as fast as possible. If you've got a problem with that, I'm sorry."

"I do have a problem with it. I've spent months trying to build a relationship with Sunny, and you're getting in the way. She needs to be with me, and she'll tell you that."

"Fine, but she'll tell me in the morning. I am not going to wake her up."

Jake put his hand softly on Miss Wayne's back. "It's been a long, tiring day," he patiently told her. "We can get this straightened out in the morning. We all need some rest."

"What are *you* doing here?" Miss Wayne asked Jake hatefully.

"I'm looking out for Sunny and Mrs. Hampton. I'm spending the night here . . . in Robbie's room."

"Of course you are," Miss Wayne responded in a skeptical tone. "Don't do anything else to traumatize Sunny."

"Wouldn't think of it." Pressing his hand firmly into Miss Wayne's back, Jake led her out on to the front porch. "I appreciate your interest in Sunny," he told her. I know the two of you have a special bond, but Sunny is going to need all of us. You go home and get some rest."

"I do want to discuss this some more."

"We will. Tomorrow. Maybe the day after."

"Sunny needs to be with me . . ."

"Go home, Janet," Jake said forcefully.

Reluctantly, Miss Wayne started down the walkway to her car. She stopped to say one last thing to Jake. "I hope you enjoyed the homemade bread I left at your office."

"Delicious," Jake said. He shook his head in confusion on his way back inside.

"What was that all about?" Maddie asked as Jake shut and bolted the door.

"Seems like Miss Wayne may have a jealous streak when it comes to you and Sunny."

"She shouldn't. I'm only doing for Sunny what I would for any of my other students."

"I know. Let's not worry about it. We'll get everything straightened out."

"Do you think she's jealous about you and me?"

Her question caught Jake off guard. "Should she be jealous?" he asked.

"You tell me."

Jake was so tired he simply shook his head and requested, "Let's go to bed. We can add that to our list of things to talk about tomorrow."

CHAPTER TWENTY

S unny's eyelids slowly lifted. She lay motionless on the soft bed in Maddie's guestroom, waiting for her vision and mind to clear so she could remember where she was.

"Good morning," was the pleasant greeting from Maddie, who was sitting on the edge of the bed.

"I'm groggy," Sunny admitted, still flat and motionless in the bed.

"That's understandable. Doctor Merkerson gave you something to help you rest. You've been asleep since six o'clock last night."

Sunny, fighting a wave of dizziness, shifted to sit up against the headboard of the bed. With her thumb and index finger, she softly tugged at the pink nightshirt, and looked at Maddie.

"It's mine" Maddie said of the nightshirt. "I didn't want you to have to sleep in your clothes."

"What time is it?"

"Almost 10:30. Do you want some breakfast? Or, maybe an early lunch?"

Maddie's tabby cat jumped on the bed, settled in Sunny's lap and started purring. That brought the slightest hint of a smile to the girl's face.

The smile didn't last long. "Tell me about my Dad," Sunny requested. She dropped her head, glanced briefly at the bed linen, and looked back at Maddie. "And I want details."

Maddie hesitated. "Are you sure?"

"I need to know. I want to hear it from you, before I hear it out on the streets, or see people whispering to each other, talking about that poor little girl whose father was murdered."

Rubbing her hands together, Maddie started. "Some grave diggers found him at the city cemetery. He was nude, tied to a monument. Someone had driven two big nails through his head."

Rubbing the cat, who appeared content to spend the rest of the day in her lap, Sunny sniffed once, looked at Maddie, and announced, "I guess we have a funeral to plan." She continued to pet the cat.

"The state crime lab hasn't released the body yet, so it may be a day or two before we can have a service. But we can go ahead and stop by the funeral home to make arrangements. We can go by your house and pick up some of your clothes too. I want you staying here for a few days. In fact, you can stay here as long as you want."

Sunny didn't respond to the offer, instead, keeping her gaze on the cat that was loving every second of the petting.

Inching closer to Sunny on the bed, Maddie studied the girl's face. There were no tears, no moisture in her eyes. She was numb, Maddie concluded, still in shock, still not certain that all of this was nothing more than a bad dream. The reality would hit her hard in a few days.

"Sunny, someone is here to talk to you," Maddie explained in a soft comforting voice. "It's Mrs. Nelson from Family and Children's Services. She wants to make sure that you're all right. Do you mind talking to her for a few minutes?"

"Can I take a shower first?"

"She's been waiting a good while. Why don't you wash your face, comb your hair and come on in to the living room. There's a robe in the closet. You can clean up afterwards. She shouldn't be here long."

Maddie waited for Sunny to freshen up and they walked into the living room together. Mrs. Nelson, a heavyset woman with graying hair, stood up. "Hello Sunny," she smiled. Her voice was soft and reassuring and she asked Sunny to sit down. "How are you, child?" Mrs. Nelson, a veteran case worker, asked.

"I'm all right," Sunny replied, nervously pulling on the ends of the sash to the white terrycloth robe she had chosen from the guest room closet.

"I'm so sorry about your Dad. With him gone, it's my job to make sure that you are taken care of properly."

"Mrs. Hampton is taking care of me. She has been very nice." Her remark made Maddie smile.

Mrs. Nelson sat down next to Sunny. "Miss Wayne, the librarian, came to see me this morning, early," she started. Maddie's smile quickly disappeared. "She wants you to come live with her."

First looking out into the living room at the cat that was bouncing across the floor, and then at Maddie, Sunny said, "Miss Wayne is nice, but Mrs. Hampton has already taken me in. Can I stay here?"

"How old are you, Sunny?" Mrs. Nelson asked.

"Seventeen. I'll be eighteen in two weeks."

"Other than your Dad, you don't have any family?"

"Not that I know of."

"When you turn eighteen, you're considered an adult and can make your own decisions and do what you want. I think you're capable of doing that now. I don't see any reason to go through any extended investigation or court hearing, because in two weeks, you can stay wherever you want, without it being anyone's business." Expressionless, Mrs. Nelson glanced at Maddie before asking Sunny, "Are you sure this is what you want to do? Would you like to talk to Miss Wayne before making a decision?"

"No ma'am," Sunny assured her. "I want to stay with Mrs. Hampton."

"I have no doubt that is a good decision," Mrs. Nelson said. Maddie let out a sigh of relief. "I'll draw up the papers to grant Mrs. Hampton temporary custody. You will help Sunny with the funeral arrangements and other personal matters, won't you, and you will contact me if there's any kind of problem?" she asked Maddie.

"Oh yes, in fact, we're going to start taking care of some of those things this afternoon."

"I'm satisfied." Mrs. Nelson stood up, and Maddie tugged at Sunny's arm to get her to stand as well. Mrs. Nelson hugged Sunny and told her, "God bless you, Sunny. Mrs. Hampton and I are going to take care of you."

"Go ahead and get in the shower," Maddie suggested to Sunny. "Let me see Mrs. Nelson to the door."

Sunny obeyed, giving the two women a moment to talk. "Thank you for your confidence in me," Maddie said.

Mrs. Nelson smiled. "My goodness, Maddie. Half the girls in this town would love to have you as a mother. I had to ask those questions, though, because Janet Wayne pitched a pretty good fit this morning."

"I'm sorry. I know she and Sunny are close, and it wouldn't have bothered me if Sunny had said she wanted to stay with Miss Wayne, at least I don't think it would have bothered me."

"It's a moot point now. You are going to be busy. So much has to be done over the next few days and weeks. I hope to goodness her father had some life insurance."

"That's one of the things we'll start looking into this afternoon."

The two women hugged. Maddie wiped a tear away, and so did Mrs. Nelson, whose heart had not been jaded by years of dealing with children who had been put through unspeakable instances of abuse and neglect. With Sunny's temporary custody decided, Maddie could now turn all her attention to the somber but necessary tasks associated with the loss of a loved one.

A fellow teacher volunteered to stay at the house to accept visitors, flowers and food, enabling Maddie and Sunny to start attending to matters. Their first stop was at Boyd and Sons, the lone funeral home in town that had been in business as long as the Sentinel. Benjamin Boyd and his boys, Blaine and Blair, had buried three and four generations of Sandersonians, and were well-respected for their professionalism and compassion. They had conpackinged many services on the promise of getting paid, and nine times out of ten they got paid. On occasion, they had swapped a funeral for a side of beef, a winter's supply of vegetables, or handy work around the funeral home. No one had ever considered opening another funeral home in Sanderson for two reasons. The town wasn't big enough, and the Boyd family was so engrained in the community that competing with them would be impossible.

Benjamin, a big hulking man with a grandfather's kindness, sat down with Maddie and Sunny in the funeral home's large, airy office. The soothing pale rose colored walls and soft, expensive leather furniture gave the room where sad, humbling business was conpackinged a reassuring, comfortable feel. After expressing his regrets, Benjamin started questioning Sunny about what type of service she would like for her Dad. Maddie was impressed with Sunny's calmness and clarity as she explained her preferences. Pastor Allen would lead a brief service that included Sunny's favorite hymns, *How Great Thou Art* and *Victory in Jesus*, and singer Tim McGraw's country tear-jerker, *Live Like You're Dying*. Regal Krause wasn't much into church, but he loved country music, his daughter explained. The request was fine with Benjamin. He had fulfilled much stranger wishes.

Sunny selected a mid-priced metallic gray casket and declared she would find some clothes in her Dad's closet to bury him in. "I don't know how I will pay for all of this," she admitted with no emotion. Maddie was amazed, and worried, about how calm Sunny was.

"Don't worry about that, honey," Mr. Boyd assured her. "We've got plenty of time to figure that out."

"We've got to check on her Dad's insurance," Maddie broke in. "We'll get back with you as quickly as we can on that, and on a date and time for the service."

"That's fine. You take care of our girl, Maddie," Mr. Boyd said. He hugged them both and they left for their next stop, Tri-County Pulpwood, Regal Krause's employer. The meeting was short but propackingive. After offering his condolences, the human resources manager explained that Regal Krause not only had the company's standard life insurance equivalent to a year's salary, but a substantial supplemental policy as well. Sunny was the beneficiary of $200,000, but she took that news like she did everything else, stoically, as if she didn't care one way or the other. Maddie, on the other hand, was relieved. The money would pay the funeral expenses, any other debts Mr. Krause may have had, and give Sunny a nest egg for college. Following clarification of a few other matters the company would be handling on behalf of Mr. Krause, Maddie drove Sunny to the Krause's cute clean three bedroom ranch house to pick up some clothes and choose her Dad's clothes for the funeral. Sunny said very little and went about her business quickly, not shedding a tear all afternoon. Regal Krause had one suit, a gray lightweight wool blend that he hardly ever wore. Sunny's inclination was to bury her Dad in jeans and a flannel cowboy shirt and boots, but Maddie delicately prodded her that the suit would be more appropriate.

There was one other stop to make. While visitors had brought enough food to Maddie's house to feed the Barber County High School student body, they had overlooked three essentials: milk, toilet tissue and cat food. Walking down the aisles of Super-Thrift, Maddie urged Sunny to pick up any snack food that looked good, but she declined. As they turned off the cereal aisle toward the dairy propackings, their cart almost bumped into another. "Sunny!" Janet Wayne said with relieved surprise as she pulled her cart back. She hugged Sunny and asked, "Are you all right?"

"Yes ma'am."

Miss Wayne gave Maddie a disapproving look and announced, "She should be with me."

"This isn't the place for this conversation," Maddie replied firmly. To her, this chance meeting was becoming more awkward by the second.

"Mrs. Nelson told me about her decision. I don't agree with it. Not at all!" Miss Wayne watched as Sunny walked away, headed for the milk case.

Maddie took a deep breath to compose herself. "Look," she said, trying to remain civil. "If Sunny had chosen to stay with you, that would have been fine with me. I know you have been very good to her. But Mrs. Nelson asked her what she wanted to do, and she said stay with me. Now, in a few days, after she gets over this trauma and gets her Dad buried, maybe she'll want to stay with you. I'm not doing this to spite you. I have no reason to."

"It's not right. It's just not right!" Miss Wayne was angry and she was about to cry.

"I've got to go," Maddie insisted. She did not want this confrontation to escalate. She started pushing her cart toward the milk case, but Miss Wayne grabbed it and brought it to a halt.

"You take care of that girl," she said hatefully. "If you don't, you have to answer to me."

Maddie shook her head and moved quickly toward Sunny who said nothing about what had just taken place. Wanting to give Janet Wayne plenty of time to get out of the store, Maddie bought two gallons of milk, one carton of Rocky Road ice cream, one carton of Butter Pecan, and two dozen Krispy Kreme doughnuts.

CHAPTER TWENTY-ONE

The Bible had been hidden forever under a stack of papers in one of Quinn's desk drawers. It looked liked it had never been used—no underlined scriptures, no highlighted parables, no sermon notes scribbled in the margin. Quinn couldn't remember when or how he had gotten the Bible, or the last time—if ever—he had pulled it out, but he was pulling it out now. He needed Divine Intervention. Three men had been murdered, and he was no closer to solving the case than he was the day he found Todd Monroe tied to a pine tree with his thumbs and big toes cut off. The keys to identifying the killer seemed to be buried deep in the pasts of the two individuals he was most reluctant to grill. Mary Jane Hamilton had admittedly been with the first victim, and likely the second, but how could Quinn pull her into the investigation, considering his increasing emotional and sexual interest in her? And Maddie Hampton had no use for any of the three dead men, but how could he even consider questioning the town's resident saint? Quinn had no other leads to pursue and the mayor and council were getting nasty, putting increasing pressure on him to make an arrest. Quinn was going through Black Jack chewing gum like crazy, and after a few more whacks against a metal pole or oak tree, he was going to need a new plastic bat.

Quinn held the Bible with both hands at arms' length, studied its black leather cover, placed it gently on his desk and opened it near the middle, at Psalm 69. He had no idea where to look for inspiration or words of encouragement. He didn't even know where to find the Lord's Prayer. All he could think of was the Twenty-Third Psalm, and he only knew that because he had heard it used at several funerals. Giving up, he finally closed his eyes, bowed his head and prayed, for the first time in his life. "God, I'm not worthy of it, and I'm not sure if I'm even doing this right, but if you see fit, please help me bring this killer to justice, and this town back to its peaceful, quite way of life. These are good people, and they don't deserve to have to go through this. I don't ask this selfishly for myself, but for the town. Amen."

Finishing his prayer, Quinn kept his eyes closed and head bowed. Some of his church-going friends had talked about how they immediately felt better after praying, that a huge weight was lifted from their shoulders when they turned troubles over to God. Quinn wasn't feeling that instant relief, but he knew he needed help. Not from GBI Agent Travis Stamps or the Barber County Sheriff's Office, but from a much higher source. Surely, Quinn thought, God would not let this killer to continue this evil or go unpunished.

Quinn's quiet time was interrupted by a knock on his closed office door. Before he could say anything, Mary Jane peeked inside. Quinn perked up and got out of his chair to greet her with a kiss.

"I brought you some lunch," she smiled.

"Let me guess," he smiled back. "Waffle House."

She nodded. "I'm off today, but I had to go by and pick up my paycheck. I thought it would be nice to surprise you with some lunch. Let's see, you like your hash browns scattered, smothered, covered and chunked, right?"

"Perfect. Put those down for a minute and let me admire you," he requested, surveying her outfit of thin, almost transparent white linen slacks and a white camisole and filmy burgundy shirt.

"What have you been doing this morning?" she asked.

"Sitting at this damn desk, pounding on my head, trying to come up with some inspiration to help solve these murders. So far, I haven't had any luck."

"You look stressed out. Sit down. Let me massage your shoulders."

He obliged and she began kneading his shoulders with her slender fingers. "You are so tense. Your neck and shoulders are nothing but a bundle of knots."

"That feels so good," he said, his eyes closed in a moment of relaxation. "Can you do this the rest of the afternoon?"

"I could, but I've got a better idea. The girls are spending the night at my sister's. I'm free tonight, and I can come over to your place and really help you relax. I'll even cook."

"You're on," he said willingly.

The massage was interrupted by another knock on the door. Mary Jane gave one final tug on Quinn's shoulders before she backed away and allowed him to respond to the knock. Following Quinn's acknowledgement, Sam Rogers came in with Elizabeth Fallow, the pleasant front desk clerk at the public library. "Elizabeth needs to talk to you," Sam explained.

"I'll talk to you later," Mary Jane said. Quinn nodded and she left.

Quinn asked Elizabeth to sit down. He expected to hear about the latest mess her younger, headed for trouble brother was in.

Wanting to make the woman feel a little more at ease, Quinn joked, "What is it, Elizabeth? Want to send the library police after someone? Who forgot to pay their late fee or return their book this time?"

Elizabeth didn't smile, and she seemed uneasy about being there. "It's nothing like that, Mr. Quinn."

"What is it, Elizabeth? You know you can talk to me. You've done it before. What's said in this room doesn't leave this room."

"You said in the paper you needed help finding the killer of those three men . . . that if the public noticed anything suspicious."

Elizabeth had Quinn's undivided attention. "Yes, I said that," he replied, eager to hear more.

"I feel very uncomfortable being here," she replied, squirming in her chair.

"Elizabeth, if you know something, if you saw something, you've got to tell me."

"This probably doesn't mean anything, but all three of those men . . . each of them was in the library right before they were killed."

A spark shot through Quinn as if he had stuck his finger in a live light socket. "Are you sure?"

"Yes sir," Elizabeth insisted, nodding her head emphatically while wringing her hands. "It never registered with me until that third man was killed. But Tuesday morning, after I heard they had found him dead on Monday, well, I remembered that he was in the library the Saturday morning before. I remember him, because we weren't busy and I had never seen him in the library."

"Are you sure it was Regal Krause?"

"Yes sir, because he wanted to see Miss Wayne, and I asked him if I could let her know who it was who wanted to see her. He said his name was Regal Krause."

"Did he see her?"

"Yes sir. He went in her office. They shut the door and talked for about ten minutes. When he came out, he didn't look mad or anything. But then, he didn't look happy, either. Kind of without any kind of expression."

Quinn stood up, walked to an extra chair, pulled it close to Elizabeth and sat down. "All right," he said to Elizabeth, who was more nervous than when she first came in. "So Mr. Krause came into the library and talked to Miss Wayne. What about the other two? When did they come to the library?"

"I can't remember the exact days they came in, but I know it was right before they were killed. I didn't know them either, but they were like the third man. Neither one of them had ever been in the library before that, but I remembered them when I saw their pictures in the paper after they were killed. They did the same thing. They came in and talked to Miss Wayne. I didn't think anything about all of this until that third man was killed. Then, I thought to myself, wasn't that strange, that all three of them would come in to the library, and all three of them would be dead right after that? Was it wrong for me to tell you all of this?" Perspiration was starting to bead on her forehead.

"Goodness no. You absolutely did the right thing, Elizabeth," Quinn said, patting her hand. "You don't know what they talked to Miss Wayne about?"

"No sir. It must not have been anything serious, though. None of them came out looking like they were mad or upset. I didn't hear any yelling coming from her office."

"And you're absolutely sure it was those three men?"

"Yes sir. If I wasn't, I wouldn't be here. I don't want anybody else to get killed, but I don't want Miss Wayne to get in trouble, either."

"No one's going to get in trouble," Quinn assured her. "I suspect Miss Wayne was probably talking to the men about their children's school work or something like that. I know she worked with Sunny Krause a lot. Probably the boys of the other two victims as well."

"It was just coincidence that they were in the library when they were, don't you think so?"

"I expect so, Elizabeth, but it's important for citizens like you to step forward with information like this. What you've told me may not end up helping the case, but then the next person who comes to see me may have the bit of information we need to bust this thing wide open."

"Well, I hope that comes soon. I've got a husband and brother I worry about."

"How's your brother doing?"

"He's doing real well right now. He found a job working for the county public works department, and he's bringing home a steady paycheck. Thank you Jesus!"

Quinn smiled. "I glad to hear he's doing well." He extended his hand to her as she stood up. "Thank you for coming. Tell your brother and husband I said hello."

Elizabeth started to leave the room but Quinn stopped her. "Has a young, good-looking guy who claims to be a GBI Agent been by the library to talk to anyone?" he asked.

She was surprised at his question. "No sir."

"There's an agent in town, Agent Stamps. He's checking into the murders too. I know he's talked to a lot of people, and I suspect that he'll make his way to the library."

"What should I tell him?"

"Tell him what you've told me. Tell him the truth."

"Yes sir. I sure hope you catch this person soon. Everyone is frightened. I'm not letting my Amos out of my sight. I don't want you finding him tied to some tree with an important body part cut off."

Quinn smiled and waved at the kindly woman as she left. He sat back in his chair and looked at the open Bible on his desk. Coincidence or Divine Intervention? He had the lead he had prayed for. He needed to talk to Janet Wayne.

While Quinn was plotting his strategy to talk to the town librarian, Kenny was plotting his strategy to talk to Sunny. Regal Krause had been buried and Sunny was back in school and settled in at Maddie's. With everyone back to trying to go on with their lives, Kenny's parents had given him a direct order—stop seeing Sunny. Despite the misfortune that had befallen the girl, Kenny's parents were still adamant that he end their relationship. They were convinced Sunny and her troubles were too much of an emotional albatross on Kenny, and Mr. and Mrs. Richards wanted their son's mind clear when he transferred to the University of Georgia in the fall. Kenny admitted the timing was bad, that he would be lugging around considerable guilt for abandoning a friend during such a difficult time, but he had essentially come to the same conclusion as his parents. On a May day that was overcast and a few degrees cooler than normal for the time of year, Kenny was meeting Sunny in the little town park to talk. He considered going by the barbecue joint to get ice cream, but decided not to. The best approach would be to not have any hindrances to what he needed to say. Say what he had to say and move on.

Sunny walked to the park bench where Kenny was waiting, and he immediately knew his job was not going to be easy. She looked rock star/movie star gorgeous, as scrumptious as Kenny had ever seen her. Sunny was wearing her blonde hair down, as opposed to the normal pony tail, and the tight yellow cotton t-shirt and jeans highlighted her slim figure. More than that, Sunny looked refreshed. Her face didn't have the tired sad look he was accustomed to seeing. Kenny's stomach knotted up and he had a flash of second thoughts, but he knew what he had to do. If he didn't break up with Sunny, he would be the next murder victim in town, at the hands of his parents.

"What's up?" she asked, sitting down on the park bench next to Kenny. He could feel his throat constricting and his pulse rate increasing.

"How did you do on your geometry test today?" Kenny asked, still trying to come up with a way to transition to the bad news.

"I think I did O.K. Not that it matters a lot. My grade is good enough that I could mess up on the test and still pass the course. It won't keep me from graduating."

"I was so ready to graduate this time two years ago. Even though I knew I was going to start out at the community college, I was so ready to get out of high school."

She patted him on the knee. "And now you're about to get your associate degree and move on to the university. I'm proud of you . . . and envious. I wish I knew what I was going to do."

"Come to Georgia. It's a great school."

"Too big for me. Besides, I'll probably be stuck here awhile settling Dad's affairs." She looked up at the clouds that were getting darker and more threatening.

Kenny shifted uncomfortably on the bench and looked at Sunny. "Are you all right?" he asked.

"I'm O.K." she nodded in reply. "Things get a little better every day. What about you? You've got a bad case of the fidgets today."

"No, I'm not O.K.," he admitted, looking away and then turning back.

"What's wrong?" she asked with sincere concern as she leaned closer to him.

Kenny cleared his throat and tried to talk, but no words came out. He tried again. "I can't see you anymore," he confessed softly.

His revelation caused Sunny to lose her breath. He could see the shock and hurt in her eyes. She bit her lip and lowered her head, and when she raised it, moisture was collecting in her eyes and about to run down her cheeks. "Why?" is all she said.

"Mom and Dad. It's all about school. How did they say it? They don't want me carrying any excess baggage when I go to Georgia." As soon as the words left his mouth, Kenny realized how tacky and cruel that sounded.

"I'm sorry," he tried to start apologizing. "That didn't come out right."

"No need to apologize," she replied, wiping a tear away with a finger. "I am excess baggage. I've always thought that's why my Mother left me."

Kenny felt like a total and complete jerk. How could he be doing this to someone who had already endured such hurt in her life? He tried to think of something to say, but couldn't. They were both silent.

"You've told me how your parents feel. How do you feel?"

He continued to stumble for the right words. "Ah . . . I am . . . I am going to need a clear mind. Georgia is a big step up academically from the community college. I'm going to have to work my butt off."

Sunny actually managed a fragile smile. "And, of course, there are 15,000 coeds at the University of Georgia too, and you just might make some new friends."

"That's not it, Sunny," he insisted, but that indeed was part of the reason. Mr. And Mrs. Richards wanted their son to arrive on campus unencumbered.

"It's all right," she said, again forcing a smile. "I'm not the first girl who's been dumped by a boy going off to college. And it's all right for you to want to meet other girls. In fact, some of the girls at school have been teasing me already about you wanting to see someone out at the community college."

Now he felt embarrassed and totally ashamed. "They've been saying that?"

"They have. It's O.K. Kenny. It's O.K. How can I be mad at you? You've been a great, great friend to me when no one else would. I definitely don't want to cause trouble between you and your parents. I'm envious of you. I wish I had had that type of relationship with my parents."

"I am such a jerk," Kenny mumbled. He was about to cry. A drop of water rolled down his cheek but it wasn't a tear. A few scattered rain drops were beginning to fall.

"No you're not," she assured him.

"But I'm worried about you. I'm worried about you being all right."

Sunny took his right hand and cupped it in hers. "I survived my Mom leaving and my Dad being murdered. I think I can survive being dumped by you."

"You're right," Kenny said, recognizing the barb Sunny had just stuck in him. He wasn't indispensable and Sunny had already proven she was strong.

"Let's go before the rain hits," Sunny suggested. She kissed Kenny softly on the lips and hugged him. "Thank you," she whispered before scurrying out of the increasing rain to her Dad's pickup she had started driving.

"I'm sorry," Kenny replied repentantly to himself while still sitting on the park bench. The bottom fell out and Kenny got soaked, but it didn't wash away his guilt.

CHAPTER TWENTY-TWO

Quinn arrived unannounced at the library, claiming that, on orders from the mayor, he was conpackinging a safety audit of all city government buildings. Elizabeth Fallow knew that wasn't the true purpose of Quinn's visit, but the other three staff members didn't give his announcement a second thought. Considering recent events, they considered a safety inspection totally warranted, and in fact, they appreciated the gesture. Quinn made up the excuse so he could be discreet. The library was a source of pride for the town and had a high patron count, and he did not want anyone to know the manager was being investigated as a possible link to three killings. That would only create more unrest for the little town whose nerves were already tattered. Before coming to the library, Quinn had at length pondered the information provided by Elizabeth Fallow, at one point considering not following up, but decided he had to.

Elizabeth escorted Quinn to Miss Wayne's windowless office. "Why Chief Quinn," Miss Wayne offered with a teasing smile. "I don't see you here at the library much. Did you hear the swimsuit issue of *Southern Sports* is out this week?

"I subscribe," he responded to her comment, which he correctly assumed was more critical than good-natured. "Actually I came to ask a reference question."

"A reference question? Couldn't you have asked one of my staff?"

Quinn shut the door to the office and sat down. "No ma'am," he started. "I need to ask you. Did you talk to Regal Krause a couple of days before his death?"

"Yes I did," she answered immediately. Quinn wasn't anticipating such a prompt response.

"What did you talk about?"

"I called him to the library to tell him that the way he was treating his daughter was a crime. More than that, it is a sin. I told him if he didn't start treating Sunny like a father should treat a daughter, I would see to it that something was done."

"Like what? Killing him?"

"Like calling Family and Children Services. Someone should have done that a long time ago."

"How did he take your threat?"

"He was angry at first, but I calmed him down. I'm good at that. God was with me during my talk with Mr. Krause."

"Do you and God have any idea as to who might have wanted to kill him?"

"No, but perhaps his death was punishment for his sins."

The comment irked Quinn. "Do you really believe that?"

"We all have to pay for our sins," she replied calmly and with conviction. She sat straight and motionless in her leather chair.

Pausing to collect his thoughts, Quinn continued his questioning. "Did you talk to Todd Monroe and Joe Lambert a day or two before they died?"

Again, Miss Wayne's response was prompt. "I talked to them both. I don't remember the chronology, but yes, I talked to them."

"About what?"

"The same thing I talked to Regal Krause about. They were mistreating their sons, and making a fool of themselves on silly high school sports and with their general behavior. I suggested they begin behaving better."

Quinn was ready to explode. What a sanctimonious bitch! "Did you tell them that God was going to get them too?"

Showing no emotion, Miss Wayne responded. "You are of little faith, aren't you Chief?"

"That's an accurate statement. If God's so great, why does he allow people to go around murdering other people?"

"Find you a church and a pastor, chief."

"Thanks, but no thanks. Besides, Sunday morning is when I read my copy of *Southern Sports*. Miss Wayne, don't you think it's a bit of a coincidence that these three men come to see you, and they are all dead a short time later?"

Miss Wayne remained composed despite Quinn's badgering. "Chief, are you accusing me of being involved in these killings?"

"No ma'am. All I'm doing is gathering information. I've talked to a lot of people. You just happen to be one of the people I've talked to."

"Well!" she snipped. "Be sure you talk to Maddie Hampton and Mary Jane Hamilton."

"Why? Why should I talk to them?"

"Do you really have to ask that question? No matter. I'll gladly tell you why. Because Maddie never forgave the three men for what they did to her son. She may look sweet and innocent on the outside, but she has rage boiling within. Revenge, Chief, revenge, and the opportunity to steal away Sunny from her father. That's her motive. As for Mary Jane Hamilton, she's slept with practically every man in town, including the three murder victims. Has she slept with you, Chief?"

"I'm going to pretend I didn't hear that," Quinn snapped angrily. "I don't appreciate the insinuation, and I know Mary Jane wouldn't."

"Protest all you want Chief, but I know for a fact that she slept with all three men and that they paid her."

Quinn was furious. "Just how the hell do you know that?"

"I make it my business to keep up with sinners. They have to be told they will go to hell for their transgressions. That was part of my talk with the three men. They confessed to me they had slept with her and they told me they paid her, but stopped."

"Why would they confess all of that to you?"

"Because I am very persuasive. Mary Jane had as much motive as Maddie Hampton to kill them. They cut off her income source, but you can't see that, or won't admit it, because you're too personally involved with her. You don't want to question the school teacher either, because she's your reporter friend's sweetie."

"Damn it lady, you don't know what you're talking about!"

"Are you sure about that Chief? How long do you think the mayor and council and for that matter, the people of this town are going to let you keep looking the other way about these women? It could cost you your job—and your respect. As for your lady friend, whatever she gets, she brought it on herself, just like the three

215

murder victims. You pay for your sins. Now, if you don't mind, I have a report to finish." She looked down at the papers on her desk and ignored Quinn.

His face was red and his blood pressure had skyrocketed. Quickly cramming some Black Jack chewing gum in his mouth, Quinn calmed down long enough to ask one last question on his way out. "What size shoe do you wear?"

She looked at him in disbelief. "Goodbye Chief!" was her curt reply.

"Do you use perfume?"

"Am I a woman?"

"Yes," he answered. She was most definitely a woman, an attractive one.

"Do women use perfume?"

"Yes."

"Well, then, by logical progression, I must use perfume."

"What type?"

"Goodbye Chief!"

Quinn left her office scratching his head and fussing under his breath. He stopped to speak to Elizabeth and the other three staff members, assuring them that the library was safe, and his officers would be patrolling the premises more often. His head was spinning from all the religious mumbo-jumbo Miss Wayne had spouted. He had a knot in his stomach as well, caused by the sickening realization that Miss Wayne's accusations, particularly about his reluctance to question Maddie and Mary Jane, were on target.

An hour later, Quinn was back at his office and Maddie was at the Sentinel. She had slipped away from school during her lunch break to bring Jake and Hazel some chicken salad sandwiches made by her students. The three were at Hazel's desk, making small talk, much of the conversation centering around the upcoming end of school and senior graduation, when Miss Wayne, her face drawn like she had been sucking on a lemon, walked in, pushing the door open with unnecessary force. Not bothering with any kind of phony greeting, she glared at Jake and ordered, "Tell your friend Quinn to leave me alone!"

Her demand befuddled him. "Run that by me one more time," he requested.

"Talk to Quinn. You get him to stay away from me and my library!" She turned away from Jake, stared at Maddie with contempt and walked out in a huff.

"What was that about?" Hazel asked in amazement.

"I don't know, but I'm sure going to find out," Jake replied.

"Well, it's a good thing looks can't kill," Hazel continued, "because if they could, Maddie would be a goner. Did you see the evil eye Miss Wayne shot her?"

Miss Wayne's brief performance had unnerved Maddie. She could feel her hands trembling. "Hazel, I think Miss Wayne is mad because Sunny Krause came to live with me instead of her," Maddie explained. "But it's not like I'm forcing myself on Sunny. She made the decision to stay with me. And I'm not holding her captive in my basement. She's free to come and go as she pleases. She can see Miss Wayne any time she wants."

"Yeah, that's why she's angry at you. Sunny picked you over Miss Wayne," Jake said to Maddie. "What I want to know is what's going on between her and Quinn. I think I'm going to walk over to his office for a little chat."

Jake asked Hazel to put his sandwich in the office refrigerator. He walked Maddie to her Jeep on his way to the police station. He knew she was upset about what had just taken place. "Don't let her get to you," he urged her. "You haven't done anything wrong. You've known Sunny a lot longer than she has. The fact of the matter is Miss Wayne is strange. That's the bottom line."

"I just don't want any big showdowns, any confrontations. I don't want that, and it's not what Sunny needs either."

Jake hugged her. "Everything is going to be fine. We'll get it straightened out." He could feel her trembling. She suggested, "I've got school meetings the next couple of nights, but why don't you plan on coming over later in the week. I'll make supper for us."

"Sounds good," he smiled. Jake kissed her and helped her get into the Jeep. He watched her drive away and then walked briskly to the police station to find out what Quinn had done to punch Miss Wayne's button.

Jake had become so familiar at the station that he walked back to Quinn's office without anyone saying anything. "I think I need some of your Black Jack chewing gum," Jake said to Quinn who was hanging up his phone.

"What's bugging you?"

"I just had a visit from Janet Wayne." Jake didn't wait for an invitation. He plopped down in a chair in front of Quinn's desk.

"Is that a fact?"

"What did you do to her? She was carrying on like you had sexually assaulted her, or worse, torn the cover off one of her precious library books."

"I went to talk to her, but I'm the one who ended up getting an earful."

"I'm listening," Jake said, rocking back in the chair until the two front legs left the floor.

"How's this for coincidence?" Quinn started. "Todd Monroe, Joe Lambert and Regal Krause. They all went to the library to talk to Miss Wayne a couple of days before they were killed."

"Interesting," Jake said, nodding his head. "Go on. You obviously have more to tell."

"She as much as admitted that she didn't like the three guys, because they were treating their children so badly, and they needed to be punished, by her, God, or somebody."

"Hmmm. A pretty big coincidence."

"She mentioned something else that I've got to follow up on."

"What?"

"She all but accused Mary Jane of committing the murders. Did the same thing with Maddie."

"What?"

"She said Mary Jane had been sleeping with all three men—for money—and they quit paying her. That, supposedly, is her motive for killing them. Maddie's motivation was the incident with Robbie."

"God, Quinn. You don't believe her, do you?"

Quinn sighed and looked down at the floor. "No, I don't believe her. At least right now I don't believe her. I don't think Mary Jane had anything to do with the killings, but I've got to ask her. Maddie too. I can't let my personal feelings get in the way of my duties as police chief."

"All of that is a crock, Quinn. A damn crock!"

"Probably, but I've got to talk to them. I'm not forgetting Janet Wayne, either, and the fact she saw the three men right before they were murdered. I'm going to be checking up on her. The mayor's administrative assistant who handles personnel is on her way over here now with Miss Wayne's file. We'll see if there's anything in the file that can help."

"Miss Wayne is throwing Maddie's name around because of Sunny. You know that as well as I do."

"The librarian will just have to keep on bitching about that. I would have done the same thing Sunny did—stay with Maddie."

Administrative Assistant Glenda Chapman arrived, and Jake started to leave but Quinn asked him to stay. "I feel uncomfortable sharing information from a city employee's file with a reporter," Glenda protested when Quinn asked Jake to stay.

"Don't worry about Jake," Quinn assured her. "What you tell us stays in this room. Jake knows not to blab. He knows if he does, I'll wring his neck." Jake playfully rubbed the back of his neck.

"What can you tell us about Miss Wayne?" Quinn asked.

"May I ask why you want to know?"

"Family and Children Services asked us to check. It's all about Sunny Krause and legal guardianship, something like that," Quinn lied with a straight-face.

Without opening the folder, Glenda explained, "Well, around City Hall we call her our miracle employee."

"Explain," Quinn requested.

"Our former librarian, Clarissa Hunt, was elderly and didn't get around too well and had really stayed on the job several years too long. She was found dead in her backyard one morning. Apparently she had slipped on the steps on her back porch, fell, and broke her neck. Two days later, Miss Wayne showed up at City Hall to apply for the job. She said she was on her way to Florida, taking back roads instead of the interstate, and stopped in Sanderson for lunch. She heard about what had happened to Mrs. Hunt, and without calling, without making an appointment, came to see us. She told us she was on a personal journey to find God's will for her life, and felt like it was divine intervention that led her here and to this job. We needed someone with experience to run the library, so we hired her temporarily while we started advertising the job. Turned out she was the best applicant, so we hired her permanently. Besides, she was on a mission from God. How could we go against that?" Glenda asked, tongue-in-cheek.

"I'm assuming you checked her references before you handed her and God the job," Quinn said.

"Of course. She was assistant manager at the library in Gentry, Ohio. Her ex-boss said she was a good worker who always showed up on time and took pride in her work. Apparently, she doesn't have much of a family, but we did talk to an aunt who spoke fondly of her. Her criminal background check was clear. So, you see, she *was* our miracle. We needed her and we were apparently what she was looking for."

"Quite a coincidence, huh Quinn?" Jake asked.

"Yeah, quite. O.K. Glenda," Quinn resumed. "What kind of employee has Miss Wayne been?"

"Exemplary. She hasn't been here two years, but she's made a lot of positive changes at the library. Circulation numbers are higher than they've ever been."

"So you don't have any dirt on her at all?"

"No. As clean as a white shirt fresh out of the washing machine. A model employee."

"O.K. Thanks. I appreciate the input. Thanks for coming over so quickly."

She looked over at Jake. "You're not to tell any of this," she insisted.

"I won't, but shoot, none of it is bad. I couldn't exactly smudge her reputation by telling anyone what you've told us."

"Goodbye Glenda," Quinn waved as she left the room. Quinn rocked back in his chair and locked his fingers behind his head. "So, what do you think, Mr. Martin?"

Mimicking Quinn, Jake rocked back in his chair and locked his fingers behind his head. "Well, Chief Quinn, model employee and mission from God aside, there's a lot of coincidence for me to stomach. She just happens to show up two days after the old librarian dies in an accident, and she talks to three guys a couple of days before they are murdered. You couldn't get odds in Las Vegas on all that happening."

"I agree. I'm beginning to see a little mystery in Miss Wayne. Make that a lot of mystery."

"More mystery to her than there is to Mary Jane and Maddie. Where do we go from here?"

"Where do we go from here? I think I'm going to make a trip to Gentry, Ohio. Want to come along?"

"Want to make a side trip to Charleston, South Carolina?"

"Sure we can do that. We'll leave in the morning."

Jake hesitated. "On second thought, I'd better stay here. I forgot how small the Sentinel staff is. I should hang around to help with the next issue."

"Are you sure you don't want to come?"

"I'm sure."

"All right, but promise me one thing."

"I'll try. What?"

"Don't let anyone else get killed while I'm out of town."

CHAPTER TWENTY-THREE

An unbecoming scowl spread across Quinn's face as Agent Stamps stepped into his office. Quinn was ready for this pain in the butt to leave town. He was tired of every other person he met on the street complaining to him about being questioned—several folks had used the word pestered—by this GBI know-it-all.

"You're holding out on me," Stamps snapped accusingly as his pants leg brushed against the corner of Quinn's desk.

"Would you like to explain that charge?" Quinn asked, rocking back in his chair, the scowl still prevalent.

"You're withholding information. Damn it, Quinn. How do you expect to solve this case if we can't work together and share what we've learned!"

"What is it that I'm supposedly holding back?"

Stamps was pacing in front of Quinn's desk. "Where do I start? How about the school teacher who attacked the victims with a baseball bat? Or the librarian who saw all three men right before they were killed. Or," he paused, "what about your girlfriend who was getting cash from the three men for sex?"

The agent's reference to Mary Jane infuriated Quinn. "Get out of here!" Quinn bellowed, pointing his finger at Agent Stamps.

"Me leave?" Agent Stamps shot back. "Me leave? You're the one not doing your job! The killer is right under your nose, Quinn, and you're too damn mousey to go after her!"

Quinn rocketed out of his chair and came chest to chest with Stamps. "You don't know anything about the job I'm doing!"

"There's some truth to that, because you won't tell me!"

"Well, here's the scoop, big boy. I'm already on to the librarian. I'll know more in a few days. You follow up on the school teacher. She's yours."

"What about Hamilton?"

Quinn turned his back to Stamps, folded his arms across his chest and lowered his head. Turning back around after ten full seconds of silence, Quinn announced, "I'll handle her too."

"Are you sure? You've got a big time conflict of interest with her."

"I'll handle it, damn it!"

"If you don't, I'll have to . . ."

"I said I'll handle it, damn it!"

"All right. Can we start having some coordination, making sure we're on the same page?"

"Yeah," Quinn reluctantly agreed with a sigh. "I'm going out of town for a few days. We'll talk when I get back."

"Good. I appreciate that." Stamps' taut facial muscles began to relax, and he turned to walk out the room.

"Stamps," Quinn blurted out and the agent stopped. "Stamps, I'm sorry. This case is driving me crazy! I want to solve this case so bad I can taste it, and I want to solve it by myself. But I don't want anyone else to get killed because of my selfishness. I appreciate your help."

"Not a problem," Stamps nodded. As the GBI Agent left, Quinn reached into his pocket for some Black Jack gum. He was out.

Several hours later, Mary Jane sensed that Quinn was pre-occupied, that something was on his mind. Sitting at the small oval table in his cramped kitchen, Quinn had hardly touched his baked pork chop, which was unusual considering his normally voracious appetite, and Mary Jane's attempts at jovial, meaningless dinner banter were met with silence. Even her not-so-subtle hint at some time between the sheets later in the evening was met with indifference. She had not seen Quinn in such a mood in the time they had been seeing each other, and his coolness made her nervous, frightened her.

She finally gathered the nerve to ask, "What's the matter Quinn? What's got you in such a mood?"

He didn't reply, instead continuing to look down into his plate, picking at an asparagus spear with his fork.

"Come on Quinn. Talk to me," she pleaded.

He finally looked up at her. The harshness on his face frightened her even more.

"I had a talk with Janet Wayne," he said in a volume much lower than usual.

Mary Jane felt a bit of relief. "Having to talk to her would put anyone in a foul mood," she said.

"I'm going to ask you a question, and I want a truthful answer."

"All right," she replied, a wave of nervousness surging through her. What was Quinn going to ask that it required a prelude demanding a truthful answer?

He grabbed his fork and squeezed it hard in his right fist, which started turning white. "Tell me what your relationship was with Todd Monroe, Joe Lambert and Regal Krause."

His question unnerved her even more. "Did this come from your visit to Miss Wayne?"

"Answer the question."

Tears quickly welled in Mary Jane's eyes and began streaming down her cheeks. She put her hand over her mouth.

"Answer the question," he repeated.

"I knew them. I knew all of them," she answered, wiping away tears with her napkin. "Why are you asking me this? I had already told you I knew Todd and Joe."

"Did you sleep with them, for money?"

She put her hand over her mouth again, as if that would prevent her from having to answer.

"Well?"

"Yes. Yes I did," she said wiping tears again.

"Damn it Mary Jane!" Quinn shouted as he hurled the fork he had been holding across the room. His outburst surprised and frightened her. She wanted to say something but couldn't. The words were lodged in her throat.

"Damn it Mary Jane! Why didn't you tell me?"

"I told you about Gregory and I told you I had slept with Todd. I thought that was enough."

He stormed out of his chair, knocking it down and barked, "Well, it's not enough!"

She stood up as well and was trying not to match Quinn's fury. "I needed the money. Raising two children is so expensive, and I'm always having to bail my sister out of some jam."

"You could have gotten a second job."

"Doing what? Making seven-fifty an hour as a cashier at Super-Thrift? Being with those men didn't mean anything to me. With them, it wasn't like what you and I have. What we have is real. I want to commit myself to you. I really do."

Quinn tried to laugh but couldn't. "You don't understand, do you?" he asked. "This isn't about the two of us at this moment. The fact that you had sex with those guys is something I can get over." He stopped and looked at her. She couldn't decide if his expression was one of anger or hurt. "What you don't understand," he started, "is that all of a sudden, you are a prime suspect in three murders."

Mary Jane was astonished. "You can't be serious!"

"Believe me, I'm serious. You're one of the few common threads linking all three men. The fact that you slept with them, they paid you, and they stopped paying you. Damn it, Mary Jane, that's enough to indict you!"

"Don't say that, Quinn. Please don't say that!" She tried to wrap her arms around him but he wouldn't let her.

Quinn glared at her. "You know what I'd really like to do?" he asked. "What I'd really like to do is slap the hell out of you for lying to me." He raised his hand back, but put it down.

"Don't you dare hit me!" she screamed back. "That's the reason I'm not still with that sorry husband I had!"

Quinn's thoughts quickly flashed back to the day he caught his wife in bed with another man and the damage his loss of self-control had caused that day. "I'm sorry. There's no way I would hurt you, but I'm angry and sad." His attempt at an apology sounded hollow.

"What does this do to us?" she asked with her head lowered.

"What size shoe do you wear?"

Mary Jane stared at Quinn. "What kind of question is that?" she asked in disbelief. "I'm spilling my guts to you, telling you my deepest secrets and you ask about my shoe size?"

"Just answer the damn question."

"Seven-and-a-half. Medium. Does that make you happy? Jesus, Quinn. What does that have to do with anything? You got a foot fetish I don't know about?"

"It's got everything to do with what we're talking about. And I need a DNA sample from you."

"In that case, you might as well arrest me!" Mary Jane couldn't wipe her face quickly enough to keep the tears from streaming down.

"Are you confessing?"

"I'm confessing that I had sex with Todd the day he died. I didn't kill him, I swear, but if I give you a sample, you're probably going to come up with a match. I can deny killing him until I'm blue in the face, but if you find my fluids on his body, I'm dead meat. I've got no chance, especially with a public defender handling my case. Yes, I may have gotten paid for sex, but it wasn't enough for me to hire a $200 an hour lawyer. I told the men to stop paying me. It wasn't their idea to stop. In fact, I told them they couldn't call on me for sex any more. I do have a conscience, Quinn, and it was getting to me. That last time I was with Todd, it was a freebie, and I told him that was it. I don't know what happened to him after I left his house. I'm sure you don't believe me, so let's get it over with Quinn. Go ahead and arrest me. Haul me off to jail. Just give me time to make arrangements for my girls."

Quinn swallowed hard, ran his fingers through his hair and looked at the sad, tear-streaked face of the woman whose company he had enjoyed so much in recent days. Their eyes locked. Each knew how much the other was hurting.

"Here's what I'm going to do," Quinn started after several moments of silent meditation while Mary Jane continued to wipe her face. "I've got to be out of town a few days. While I'm gone, you think long and hard about what you need to tell me. I'm going to wait until I get back to get a court order for the DNA sample."

"Why wait? It's not going to matter. You believe I killed those three men, don't you? You're going to take the word of that damn self-serving witch at the library over me, aren't you?"

"I'm just looking for the truth."

"How's this for the truth? I love you. Do you believe that?"

"You need to go home, Mary Jane," is all Quinn could say. A tear trickled down the tough cop's cheek as he watched her walk away.

CHAPTER TWENTY-FOUR

The sun was setting on Gentry, Ohio, the northern equivalent of Sanderson. Located in the south central part of the state, Gentry wasn't as isolated as Sanderson, but its population was comparable and had the same small town look and feel. Quinn recognized the most significant difference the instant he stepped into the Hillside Motel to rent a room. The people weren't as friendly. They weren't rude, but they didn't have that "Hi ya'll" perkiness Quinn had embraced in Sanderson.

Quinn's journey north had taken most of three days, in part due to the distance—750 miles along a weaving, out-of-the-way route—and in part because of the three stops he had made to visit with friends and former law enforcement colleagues. Each of the three stops had taken longer than anticipated. The old buddies were glad to learn of Quinn's whereabouts and that he was doing well, and wanted to know when he was going to get back into the law enforcement major leagues. Quinn quickly explained that wasn't totally up to him. Someone had to want to hire him. Everyone Quinn visited with promised him they would let him know of any positions that became vacant in departments in larger jurisdictions. Quinn didn't mention his investigation of the three murders in Sanderson. It only came up once, and Quinn quickly found a reason to change the conversation. He didn't want to talk about a case whose prime suspect was the woman he had been sleeping with.

Quinn checked into his room, used the restroom and was about to leave to begin scouting the quaint town when his cell phone rang. Sam Rogers had some disturbing news. "Mary Jane's gone," Rogers told his boss.

"What do you mean gone?"

"She hasn't been at work for two days. When she didn't show up the second day, her boss at the Waffle House called us. We checked with her sister in Polk City. Mary Jane dropped off her girls there in the middle of the night without saying a word. Her sister has no idea where she is."

"Damn it! Damn it!"

"What do you want me to do Chief?"

"Damn it! Issue a lookout for her car. Describe her as a person of interest in a triple murder investigation, and that she's wanted in Sanderson for questioning."

"Are you sure about this?"

"Yeah, I'm sure."

"I'm sorry about this Chief."

"Don't be. Just do your job."

"How are things coming up there?"

"I'm just getting started. I'll let you know." Quinn hung up, muttered "Damn it!" again and started jawing on his last two sticks of Black Jack chewing gum. He had to psyche himself into doing what he had just told Sam Rogers—do his job.

A couple of deep breaths later, Quinn was on his tour of the town. The courthouse was in the center of town, with streets traditionally laid out in increasingly large squares around it. Out of professional courtesy, Quinn's first stop was at the Gentry Police Department. The chief was out of town, but Quinn let his assistant chief know he would be in town a day or two asking questions and trying to find people who knew Janet Wayne. He provided a brief summary of what had taken place in Sanderson, and requested that local police not make a big propackingion about him being in town. The assistant chief readily agreed, but intrigued by the case, offered the department's assistance.

Leaving the police department, Quinn easily found the library two blocks from the courthouse. Tired and not wanting to bother the library staff so late, Quinn drove by and headed to the main highway leading out of town where most of the new commercial growth, including several chain restaurants, was occurring.

About the time Quinn was pulling into the Big Texas Steakhouse for supper, Maddie and Jake were finishing theirs in Sanderson. Sunny had eaten with them and was now in her room completing homework. Finished with the cleanup, Maddie and Jake finally had a few minutes to relax after busy days. Maddie stretched out on the sofa and rested her head in Jake's lap so she could look up at him. "If I close my eyes, I may go right on to sleep," she admitted.

"Need some help getting into your night clothes?" he asked naughtily.

"You wouldn't find anything very sexy," she admitted. "I sleep in pajamas, flannel in the winter and cotton shorties in the summer."

"I couldn't talk you into sleeping in panties and a cropped t-shirt?"

"Not this old, out-of-shape body. But I appreciate the thought."

"I wish you would let me be the judge in how you look in something scanty. I also wish you would consider letting me spend the night."

"You can use Robbie's bed again."

Jake looked across the room and cleared his throat. "That's not exactly what I was thinking . . ."

Jake's admission hit Maddie in the face like a bucket of cold water. She sat up, looked at him tenderly and rubbed his cheek with her hand.

"I'm sorry," Jake said, starting to blush. "I shouldn't . . ."

"No, don't apologize. I've got to be honest with you. The thought has crossed my mind."

"So, if you've thought about it, and I've thought about it . . ."

"You are a special, special person to me, Jake. You've filled a hole in my life that I wasn't sure could ever be filled, and I hope our relationship continues to grow. I really do. I'm just not ready to take the step you're talking about."

Jake felt so foolish. "I guess, in such a small town, word would get out that we'd slept together, probably before we got out of bed the next morning."

"It's far more than that. It's my kids, my students. I love them. I take my job as a teacher . . . and role model . . . very seriously. They look up to me, look to me for guidance, and I can't give them that if . . ."

"If you sleep with me."

She nodded, giving him the same reassuring look her students got when they brought her their problems and heartaches.

"I understand, and I'm trying to be patient. You've filled a hole in my life too, one I wasn't sure could be filled after my marriage ended so badly. The problem is I'm having trouble controlling my basic instincts. What can I say? I'm a man. A man who hasn't had sex in . . . well, it's been so long I can't remember."

Jake's confession generated a wide smile from Maddie. "Since it's confession time, I admit I would very much like to sleep with you. It's been a long time for me as well. But for now, I have to ask you to go slow and let time take care of things."

Jake sighed. "You're right, of course." He looked at his watch. "Well, time to go, Henrietta is waiting for me."

His comment blindsided Maddie, the shock obviously visible on her face. "Henrietta?" she asked, her voice cracking. "Do you have another lady friend? I don't know any Henrietta who lives around here."

"Oh, she's not from around here. In fact, she's from China."

"China? Tell me about her." Jake thought he detected a twinge of jealousy in Maddie's curiosity.

"She's great. Does everything I ask, and never talks back."

"Gosh Jake. It's going to be hard for me to compete with that."

"She's one of a kind."

"Why haven't I seen her before?"

"She doesn't like to be seen in public. In fact, I keep her locked in my closet."

Maddie had no words for a response. All she could do was look at Jake and wait for his reply.

"Henrietta is my life-size inflatable, anatomically correct doll."

Maddie playfully slapped him on the shoulder. "Jake, you're awful," she laughed in relief. He hugged her and she put her head on his shoulder.

"Well, I wonder how Quinn's doing on his out-of-town trip," Jake said to himself as much as to Maddie.

"What's Quinn doing out of town?"

"Seeing some old buddies. Looking for a job."

Maddie sat up. "I didn't know Quinn was looking for another job. I thought he was happy here."

"He is, but he's got this gnawing at his gut too. Once upon a time he was a big-time cop. I think he wants to prove to himself he still is." Not wanting to share any more of Quinn's deep personal secrets or let slip with the real purpose of Quinn's trek north, Jake quickly changed the subject. "By the way, have you caught any more grief from Miss Wayne?"

"Haven't seen her. But I have caught some grief from that GBI Agent Stamps. He came to the school and bombarded me with questions. He embarrassed me in front of my students and the faculty and staff. I didn't appreciate that, not at all."

"What kind of questions did he ask?" Jake inquired, even though he already had a good idea.

"The three murders. Judging from his questions, he was trying to insinuate that I had something to do with them. Can you believe that?"

"I assume he brought up the incident with your son."

"How did you know about that?"

"Quinn told me. I'm sorry all of that happened, Maddie. That was awful for Robbie—and you—to have to endure. Any parent would have reacted the same way you did."

"Agent Stamps believes I still carry a grudge. He's trying his best to get me to confess to something I didn't do. He made me mad. I lost my cool a little bit with him. I tried to get in touch with Quinn, to tell him to make this guy stop hounding me. I didn't realize he was out of town."

"Don't talk to Stamps anymore."

"I don't intend to, but I don't have anything to hide. I've told the man the truth. I don't, make that didn't, like Todd, Joe or Regal. I readily admit that, but I would never kill them or anyone else. I can't tell you how much it hurts that anyone would think I could kill another human being."

"Try not to let all of this bother you. Quinn will be back in a day or two. He'll make Stamps back off," Jake promised, although he didn't know if Quinn would or not, especially if his trip to Ohio was fruitless. That would move Maddie and Mary Jane to the top of the list of suspects.

Jake left Maddie's at 9:30, and watched the 10 o'clock television news before retiring. He got a good night's sleep, and so did Quinn, who was up, dressed and ready to go by eight o'clock the next morning. He ate a breakfast of sausage and scrambled eggs at a local diner and was at the library shortly after it opened at nine.

The library was an old brick building, several hundred square feet larger than Sanderson's, with an aura that seemed dark and depressing to Quinn. The middle-aged woman at the front desk didn't smile, and acted as if it was a pain to respond to Quinn's request to see the manager. He had only been in the Sanderson library three, maybe four times, but the staff was always cheerful and accommodating, totally different than the reception he was getting now. He wondered that perhaps his reception was so chilly because the staff was worried he was hiding a bomb in the big paper shopping bag he was carrying.

Becky Hatchett, manager of the Gentry library, was only slightly more pleasant in her greeting to Quinn, who immediately determined she was not setting a very good example for her workers. She looked old enough to retire, and Quinn had also determined, on first impression, that it might not be a bad idea if she go ahead and do that. But for the moment, all he wanted her to do was answer the few questions he had about Janet Wayne so he could be on his way.

"Mrs. Hatchett, thank you for seeing me," Quinn started in his nicest southern gentlemanly tone as he was escorted into her small office. "I'm Chief Quinn from Sanderson, Georgia. Do you know a lady named Janet Wayne?"

From her expression, Quinn could tell that was one question she was not expecting that day. "Yes . . . I do," she replied slowly.

"Miss Wayne is our librarian down in Sanderson. I'm on my way to a police chief's convention in Cleveland, and she asked if I would go out of the way a bit to deliver a gift to an old friend." He pulled a two pound gift basket of south Georgia pecans out of the shopping bag.

"How nice," Mrs. Hatchett said, finally cracking a smile. "Sit down Chief Quinn. Tell me, how is Miss Wayne doing?" Quinn smiled back at her. The old pecan gift trick always helped him break the ice.

"She's doing well. She's made some positive changes at our library that everyone is happy with."

"I'm glad that she has settled down somewhere. When she left here, I was worried about her."

"How so?"

"For the last few months she was here, she was restless. It didn't affect her work, but you could sense something was on her mind."

"Did she ever tell you what was bothering her?"

"Not really. She kept on talking about how God was leading her somewhere else, that He was sending her on a mission. When she left here, she had no idea about where she was going or what she was going to do. I asked her if she was sure God was going to put gas in her car and pay her bills during her sabbatical, and she said she wasn't worried, that God always provided. Turns out, I guess He did."

"Did she leave here on good terms?"

"Oh yes. Like I mentioned, there was nothing wrong with her work. She's a good librarian. She was just determined to follow her heart."

"When was her last day here?"

"It hasn't been two years. Let's see." She opened the right upper left drawer in her desk and pulled out a personnel file. "August 25, year before last. She worked a two week notice and left August 25. Tell me, has she met any gentlemen friends in . . . I'm sorry, where did you say you were from?"

Quinn finished scribbling Miss Wayne's termination date on a small pad he had taken out of his shirt pocket. He laughed at Mrs. Hatchett's question as he stuffed the pad back in his pocket. "There are not a lot of eligible men in Sanderson," he smiled. "I think she'd like to be sweet on a reporter friend of mine, but he's got eyes for someone else. Did she have a lot of boyfriends here?"

"No. I always told her she set her standards far too high. No man could live up to what she was looking for."

"The Jesus complex, huh?"

"Something like that. Forgive me, Chief Quinn, but you seem to be asking a lot of questions for someone just delivering a gift."

"I'm sorry, but Miss Wayne is relatively new to our little town, and she really hasn't opened up to anyone. She's an attractive woman. She's interesting, you might even say mysterious."

Mrs. Hatchett managed another smile. "That sounds like Janet. And it sounds to me, Chief Quinn, that you might have some interest in her."

Quinn emphatically denied that with a quick shake of his head. "No ma'am. She's way out of my league. So you don't know of any men she's ever had serious relationships with, or any trouble she's been in?"

"Are you sure that all you are doing is delivering pecans?"

"Yes ma'am."

"Well, to answer your question, no, but she was with me only five years. Before that, I don't know. We did our standard background and reference check and everything was fine."

"Thanks for your time. I've got one more delivery to make. Miss Wayne's aunt, an Annabelle Bitterman in Trantham, Ohio."

"I'm not familiar with her aunt, but Trantham is only about thirty miles from here, out Highway 73."

Quinn thanked Mrs. Hatchett and left the library. Before getting into his car, he filled his mouth with Black Jack chewing gum that he had purchased at a local convenience store. Mrs. Hatchett had not told him much more than he already knew. If the upcoming talk with Miss Wayne's aunt didn't provide any more insight, he would be returning to Sanderson, with no choice but to turn the heat up on Mary Jane and Maddie.

The drive to Trantham, through beautiful wooded stretches and open fields that were occasionally dotted with commercial development didn't take long. Again, as a courtesy, Quinn stopped at the police department to let them know he was in town and they might see him asking a few people some questions. He got directions to Annabelle Bitterman's house and was there in ten minutes. She was slow to respond to Quinn's knock on the door of the frame house in a deteriorating neighborhood, and once she was at the door, Quinn could see why it took her awhile. Fragile, stoop-shouldered Mrs. Bitterman had to have a walker to get around. Quinn quickly learned that while Mrs. Bitterman's body suffered from the wear and tear of her eighty years, her mind was as clear as the bottle of spring water he had been sipping during the drive over.

Her face lit up when Quinn said he had a gift from Miss Wayne, and she was equally thrilled that the gift was fresh pecans. Inviting him inside, Mrs. Bitterman insisted he have a cup of coffee, and she and her walker shuffled off to the kitchen while Quinn looked at the room full of photos and other mementos of the woman's good life. He couldn't sit down and let the kindly old lady struggle by herself in the kitchen, so he went to help.

"Please tell me about Janet," she requested in a strong voice. "I have not heard from her in ages." Mrs. Bitterman started pouring coffee into two cups.

"She is doing fine. She's our librarian in Sanderson, a very small town in south Georgia. She's been there, oh, about eighteen months."

"And she's all right?"

"Yes ma'am. She's fine."

"That's so good to know. I have not heard from her since she left the library in Gentry. I was worried that she might be about to have a mental breakdown. I think she really needed to get away from this area."

"You probably know this as well as anyone, but Miss Wayne doesn't say a lot. She hasn't told us much about her past."

"Considering everything the girl has been through, I think she has done well. Graduated from college, got a good job. I don't guess I ever thought she'd end up in Georgia, of all places. Where did you say?"

"Sanderson, way down in south Georgia. Tell me about Miss Wayne. If we know more about her background, maybe it will help us to be better friends."

"I blame her parents for so much of this. Can I get you to help me with this coffee?"

Quinn obliged, doctoring Mrs. Bitterman's coffee with cream and sugar and taking his black. He brought the cups back to the table and asked her to continue.

"Her parents were so strict. I never had much use for that church they were in. They were much too extreme with their religion for my taste. I think what they called discipline bordered on abuse. And when she had the baby . . ."

Quinn interrupted her. "Miss Wayne had a baby?"

Mrs. Bitterman paused to take a sip of coffee. "You fixed it just right," she smiled. "Yes. Janet had a baby when she was seventeen. She really loved the baby's father, but her parents ran him out of town. No one's heard from him since. As for the baby, well, Janet's parents went crazy. They ranted on and on about how she had sinned, how she had disgraced them, and that a bastard baby would not be part of their family. It was a little girl. Poor Janet never even got to see her or hold her. Janet's parents put the baby up for adoption. Between you and me, I don't think they did it legally. I know they got a lot of money for the baby, and Janet didn't see any of that either. Not being allowed to marry the baby's father, and then being forced to give up the baby devastated her. I don't think she ever got over it."

"I didn't know any of that," Quinn said apologetically. "I feel badly for her."

"Not many people do know. It was kept very quiet."

"What kind of relationship do you have with Miss Wayne?"

"I'd say it's good, or it used to be. I'm Janet's mother's older sister. Janet would stay with me sometimes when she wanted to get away from her parents. She stayed with me briefly after the accident that killed her parents."

"What happened?"

"Janet was almost eighteen when it happened. Not long after she had the baby. It was a terrible, terrible accident. There was a fire during the middle of the night. Janet managed to get out, but her parents didn't. The police said the fire was of suspicious origin, but they never made any arrests. She came to stay with me for a month or two and then went off to college. I don't know how in the world she managed to keep her mind on her studies."

"You're right about that," Quinn agreed, overwhelmed with the information Mrs. Bitterman had provided. "Would you like some more coffee?"

Mrs. Bitterman nodded yes and Quinn refilled their cups and sat back down. "So, do you think Miss Wayne is all right now, emotionally, that is?" he asked.

"I hope so. You can answer that better than me. From what you say, she seems to be doing all right, but I do know she was awfully, awfully restless when she left Gentry."

"And you're not sure why she was restless?"

"I think she just needed to get away from here. She spent her whole life around here, even the little private college she went to isn't far from here. I think she finally realized it was time to break away."

Quinn was amazed at the clarity with which Mrs. Bitterman had been able to recall the details about Miss Wayne. He could tell Mrs. Bitterman cared deeply about Janet and was hurting for all she had endured. He felt some sympathy for Miss Wayne as well, but he couldn't forget the reason he had made this journey north.

"I have some old photos of Janet. Not many. Would you like to see them?" Mrs. Bitterman asked before finishing off her coffee.

"Yes, please," Quinn replied, even though he did not actually care to see the photos.

"They're on the top shelf in the living room coat closet. In a plastic tub. Would you mind getting them?"

Quinn returned with the four inch deep, legal pad-sized tub, and Mrs. Bitterman popped off the top with her frail, thin fingers. She picked up several of the photos and smiled as she started flipping through them. "There are some photos of Janet and her family, and I have a lot of Janet's photos all through school." After she looked at each picture, she handed it to Quinn. Janet's parents were average-looking people, and he immediately noticed one thing about them. They didn't smile, not in a single photo.

The progression of Miss Wayne's school photos from first grade and up were typical. Missing teeth, different hairstyles, an occasional pimple. The pictures brought a smile to Quinn. He was thankful no one was around to show his childhood mugs to Jake or anyone else in Sanderson. As ugly and gawky as he was growing up, he'd have a hard time living down the reflections of his past.

Mrs. Bitterman continued handing him pictures of Miss Wayne and Quinn looked at them for a second and carefully set them aside.

She handed him another. He glanced at it, started to go to the next and then stopped. He looked at the photo again. Carefully. "Oh my God!" he gasped.

Startled, Mrs. Bitterman asked, "What is it?"

Stumbling, Quinn answered, "Uh . . . nothing . . . uh . . . she was a beautiful girl. I mean, she's attractive now, but golly, she was a beautiful girl. How old was she when this picture was taken?"

Mrs. Bitterman took the snapshot and studied it. "This looks like one of her high school senior portraits. I'd say she was seventeen, almost eighteen. After her parents died but before she graduated high school."

Quinn took the photo back and studied it. "Mrs. Bitterman," he started. "I think the folks in Sanderson would get a big kick out of seeing this. Would you mind if I run to the nearest Wal-Mart and have a quick copy of this made?"

"No. Not at all, if you promise you'll bring it right back and if you don't mind driving ten more miles. And you promise that you'll get Janet to call me."

"I will and she will. I promise." Quinn helped Mrs. Bitterman into the living room and left the house with the photo. He was back in an hour. He hugged the kindly old woman, and using his powers as police chief, made her an honorary Southerner for her hospitality, and was on the road for the long drive back to Sanderson.

Chapter Twenty-Five

Main Street was overflowing with browsers, funnel cake connoisseurs and artisans as Sanderson hosted its biggest entertainment and social event of the year. Organized to pay tribute to Bodine Sanders and his family who established the town on a pig trail between Eagleton and Polk City in 1887, Founders' Day was a fascinating hodgepodge of arts and crafts exhibits and performances by Miss Lillie's eight-year-old Dixie Darlin' Dancers and Fred Ford and his Banjo Boys. The biggest draw, though, had to be the food. Lots of scrumptious food, from the deliciously juicy candy apples to the tantalizingly aromatic roasted pecans and almonds. Every year, on the third Saturday in May, the city closed off Main Street for the vendors, exhibitors and townsfolk, who made a day of watching snippets of the various performances and indulging in as many of the tasty treats as their stomachs would allow. The Main Street merchants always offered specials, and some reported as much as ten to fifteen percent of their annual sales volume on this one day.

Jake and Maddie were among the hundreds of wanderers along Main Street. She was a festival pro, stopping every two minutes to talk to a friend and meticulously studying the homemade jewelry, quilts and wooden accent pieces carefully prepared by the craftsmen. Jake, in typical male manner, wanted to keep moving. He felt like a shark. If he didn't keep circulating, he would suffocate. Wanting to take a break, Jake offered to walk across the street to the Future Farmers booth that was offering hand-squeezed lemonade while Maddie tried to decide which embroidered lace t-shirt she wanted to buy from Sylvia Hardeman.

She had narrowed her choice to two, an off-white and a light blue, and was clutching both, wanting Jake's opinion. She turned around to look for him, and faced-off with Janet Wayne, whose icy North Pole glare indicated she wasn't happy with Maddie or her t-shirt choices.

"Having fun?" Miss Wayne asked tersely.

"Yes. That is, I was," Maddie answered truthfully, caught off guard by Miss Wayne's sudden appearance. "Which one do you like?" she asked Miss Wayne, not trying to be friendly, but hoping to thwart any type of unpleasant continuance.

"Neither one. I don't wear that kind of trashy stuff."

"Oh. Well, I think they're kind of cute. I was waiting to see which one Jake likes the best." Maddie felt threatened and dropped Jake's name, hoping it would chase Miss Wayne away, not realizing the net effect could be making her even more belligerent. Maddie put the t-shirts down and walked a few feet away from the vendor. Miss Wayne followed her. The crowd was too busy to be paying attention to what was about to take place.

"You've got it all, don't you?" Miss Wayne snarled with contempt. "Jake. Sunny. Do you want to manage the library in your spare time?"

Maddie wanted to be angry, but she was too nervous. "Look," she tried to say firmly, but her voice broke. "I'm not holding a gun to either of their heads. They're both free to do what they want to do and see who they want to see. I will, however, say that I'm very glad that they both have chosen to spend their time with me," she said, managing to land a blow in this sparring match of words.

"How I can compete against you?" Miss Wayne yelled, loud enough for startled browsers nearby to hear. "You're the home team. You've been in this town forever. You're the little sweetheart who everyone thinks walks on water."

"This conversation is over," Maddie responded, trying not to tremble. She turned to walk away, but Miss Wayne grabbed her by the arm and spun her around. A few people in the crowd were beginning to watch, some with amusement, others with shock.

"Let me go!" Maddie demanded.

"You little bitch!" Miss Wayne snarled. Still holding Maddie by one arm, she cocked her other arm, getting ready to slap Maddie.

"Uh, let's don't do that," Jake suggested as he grabbed Miss Wayne's free arm. "That's not very ladylike." He came close to spilling the two lemonades he was juggling with one hand. Miss Wayne pulled loose of Jake and Maddie pulled loose of her.

"What's going on?" Jake requested as the crowd that had stopped to watch moved on to the other food and craft vendors. He handed Maddie one of the lemonades.

"We were having a, uh, a conversation," Maddie said. Miss Wayne was silent, and still looked angry rather than embarrassed.

"An animated conversation, I would say," Jake, said. "Hello, Janet," he added.

She did not respond to Jake, instead peering at Maddie and promising, "I'll see you later!"

"Looking forward to it," Maddie replied with false bravado. She swallowed hard as Miss Wayne walked off to quickly disappear in the big crowd.

"I can't leave you alone for a minute without you getting into mischief, can I?" Jake kidded.

"Thanks for rescuing me," she sighed with relief. "That was about to get ugly."

"What was that all about?"

"Same thing. She's got it in her head that I took Sunny from her. And you."

"She's right. You did. On both counts."

Maddie responded to Jake's comment with a smile. "I just let things run their course," she said.

"What would you have done if she had slapped you?"

"I have no idea. The Bible says turn the other cheek. I don't know if I would have done that or tried to fight back. I do think I'm a bit old to be having a cat fight. That's something I would expect out of my freshmen girls."

"Maybe you could have out-scriptured her, although I think Miss Wayne can spout verses pretty good."

"I just want her to leave me alone. I'd hate to get a restraining order against her, but I'm not going to let her get in my face again."

"It won't come to that. She'll settle down. Did you find a t-shirt?"

"I did. Two. I want you to help me pick one."

"I don't feel like making a decision. Buy 'em both."

"Sounds good to me," she nodded. They bought both shirts and resumed their browsing and eating, trying not to think about Janet Wayne's tantrum.

On the opposite end of Main Street, a couple of blocks from Jake and Maddie, Kenny and his new girlfriend were admiring a collection of model airplanes made out of soft drink cans. Callan was one hundred and eighty degrees from Sunny. Perky and talkative, she was a brown hair, brown eye dynamo who cheered for the community college basketball team and, like Kenny, was headed to the University of Georgia. Kenny didn't know if they would have any type of long-term, serious relationship, but he readily admitted this girl had breathed life back into him. Weeks of trying to get Sunny through her dark, trying times had left Kenny emotionally exhausted.

They were zigzagging through the big crowd, munching on ears of roasted corn, stopping to study one vendor's wares but walking past the next. They stopped at a trash can to toss away their stripped ears of corn. Turning to resume their walk, Kenny saw Sunny, ten feet away, coming toward them. There was no way to avoid her.

"Hi Sunny," Kenny greeted her uncomfortably. She looked appealing in a tight pair of jeans and a white Barber County High School "Seniors" jersey.

"Hey," she said back, not looking at him, but rather his date.

"This is Callan. She's in some of my classes at the community college."

Callan offered a hello, but Sunny didn't. Her eyes were fixed on Kenny.

"Where are your purchases?" he asked, squirming, noticing how Sunny was looking at him.

"I haven't bought anything. I'm just walking around. By myself." Callan felt uneasy about the way Sunny was looking at them and reached for and clutched Kenny's hand.

"Are you ready to graduate?" Kenny asked, trying to initiate some type of cordial conversation.

"I guess."

"What are you going to do after graduation?"

"I don't know."

"You think you might go to school somewhere? Or get a job?"

"I don't know."

Callan tugged at Kenny's hand. "There's some tapestry kitty pillows I want to look at. Can we go?" she asked, pulling at his hand again.

"O.K." Kenny said, thankful to have an excuse to leave. This meeting had been terribly awkward.

"Maybe I'll see you at graduation," he said to Sunny.

"Maybe."

Kenny smiled nervously and walked with Callan to the collection of kitty pillows. Sunny stood in the middle of crowded Main Street, watching the couple walk away and dissolve into the multitude.

The day wore on and the Founders' Day crowd began to dwindle. Vendors started breaking down their exhibits and began their journey home or to the next festival on the south Georgia circuit. Maddie finally tired of browsing and shopping, much to Jake's relief, and he drove her home. She needed to look over the Sunday School lesson she would be presenting the next morning to eleventh and twelfth grade girls, and he wanted to go by the Sentinel to check messages and glance at two reports Hazel had prepared, so they kissed and said goodbye for the day.

At his office, Jake chose to check his e-mails first. He quickly deleted the first ten, none of which required a reply. The eleventh caught his attention. He read it, slapped his right hand on the corner of the desk and slammed back in his chair, almost tipping over. "Damn it!" he fussed while rubbing and flexing the scarred hand he had pounded on the desk. Jake returned his chair to an appropriate position and read the message again. Jack Harper wanted him in Charleston the day after the Fourth of July, less than six weeks away.

For two minutes, Jake stared at Harper's message and contemplated a reply. He settled his fingers on the keyboard twice but pulled them away. He used one hand to crack the knuckles of the other. On the third try, he started typing. "O.K. I'll see you . . ." That's as far as Jake got. He deleted his reply and logged off the computer, not bothering with the eight remaining messages. He forgot about Hazel's reports as well, opting for a long ride that would give him time to think. On his way out of the office, Jake noticed Quinn's car parked across the street at the police station. He postponed his drive to visit Quinn to get the details on his trip to Ohio.

Quinn's office had the smell of the Founders' Day festival. The chief, sitting at his desk, swallowed a big bite of a Philly cheese steak sandwich, took a gulp from a can of Diet Coke and laughed at Jake. "Son, you've got the look of a whipped puppy. What's the matter? Maddie drag you around the Founders' Day bash all day long?"

"Yep," Jake replied, plopping into an uncomfortable side chair a few feet in front of Quinn's desk. "She finally gave out mid-afternoon. Me, I was dead by noon. By then I really needed a stiff drink. I settled on lemonade."

"Too bad the ladies from the Bridge Club didn't have their booth this year. They've been known to doctor their lemonade. They always sell out."

"I wish they had been selling. I've been sober for months, but today I could have fallen off the wagon," Jake joked about his day at the festival.

"I call this annual event the Idiot's Heartburn Festival," Quinn said, sounding completely serious. Jake looked at the remaining chunk of cheese steak sandwich on Quinn's desk. Quinn looked at it as well. "That's right," Quinn said, pointing to the sandwich. "Even though we know we're going to get a terrible case of heartburn, idiots like me go ahead and buy this garbage . . . and eat it." Quinn picked up the sandwich, put it to his mouth, and thought better. "You can have the rest," he told Jake as he tossed the sandwich remnant back on the desk. A shred of sautéed onion fell to the floor.

"No thanks. I'm still feeling the effects of the Polish sausage. Maybe next year I'll be a vendor at Founders' Day. I'll sell antacid."

Quinn nodded. "Not a bad idea. I guess this year's festival had its usual excitement—Fred the banjo player and the mayor in the dunking tank."

"Yeah, all that and more. There was an added attraction this year. Maddie and Janet Wayne almost got into a fight."

Quinn's eyebrows arched. He got up from his desk. "Tell me more."

"It happened fast. I had gone to get lemonade and Maddie was standing alone looking at t-shirts. Miss Wayne shows up and starts mouthing off—about Sunny—and me, apparently. She raises her hand and is about to slap Maddie when I get back just in time to stop her."

"Spoil sport!" Quinn interrupted in put-on disappointment. "You should have let them go at it. What better way to solve their differences?"

"Uh, if I recall, you're a law enforcement officer, not a wrestling promoter."

"Probably wouldn't have been much of a fight any way. My money would have been on Miss Wayne."

"Well, I don't place wagers on sporting events, at least I don't now, but I think Maddie could have held her own. Speaking of Miss Wayne, tell me about your trip."

"Interesting. Very interesting. Let me tell you a story." Quinn paused long enough to sit in another side chair a few feet away from Jake and rub the palms of his hands together like he was washing them. "Once upon a time there was this teenage girl in Ohio. Let's say she was 17. She had a baby out of wedlock. Her strict, holy-roller parents made her give up the baby, sight unseen."

"Go on," Jake urged.

"Not long after the time she is forced give up her baby, there is a terrible fire at the girl's house. She manages to escape, but her parents don't. Shortly thereafter, the girl is 18 and considered an adult, free to do what she wants. Well, she goes off to school and learns how to be a . . . librarian."

"I'm with you so far," Jake said while Quinn got out of his seat to take a sip out of the can of Diet Coke on his desk.

"She quits her job at a library in Ohio just days before our librarian here in Sanderson is found dead in her backyard, the victim of what seemed to be a tragic accident. Then, three days after our librarian is buried, this lady from Ohio shows up at Sanderson City Hall to apply for the job of running our library. She showed up to apply, even though the job had not been advertised. She said a vision from God drew her to Sanderson."

"A vision from God, huh?" Jake asked. "I don't think I've ever had one of those."

"Me neither." Quinn took another swallow of his drink and burped. "My belly feels better now," he said in relief. "The Coke helped. Now, for the rest of the story. The lady gets the job at the Sanderson library and settles down in our quiet little town where nothing ever happens. That is, until a few weeks ago when men suddenly started showing up dead, tied to trees, chairs and grave markers. The interesting thing is, each of those three guys had been by the library to see our lady a day or so before they end up dead. What do you think about all of that?"

"Got any chewing gum?"

"Yeah, as a matter of fact I do. I could use some too." Quinn tossed Jake two sticks and then popped two into his own mouth.

Jake unwrapped the gum, took several chews and reflected on Quinn's story. "Two things immediately come to mind," Jake started. "First, being around this girl can be hazardous to your health. People die. Second, I've never heard of such a long string of coincidences."

"Coincidence my ass!" Quinn growled. "It's no coincidence that the sun comes up, and it's no coincidence with what's going on with this woman. Take a look at this." Quinn opened the middle drawer in his desk, took out a 5 by 7 photo and handed it to Jake, who took a quick glance.

"This is Sunny. What does it have to do with your story?" Jake held on to the photo.

"That's not Sunny," Quinn responded. Surprised, Jake looked at the photo again.

"That's not Sunny," Quinn repeated. "That's Janet Wayne when she was 17 years old. I got the photo from her aunt."

"My God!" Jake exclaimed as he took a more careful look at the photo. "You can't tell the difference! Janet Wayne at 17 looks exactly like Sunny Krause at 17!"

Quinn nodded in agreement, giving Jake time to continue studying the photo.

"Is Janet Wayne Sunny's mother? Is that what you're trying to tell me?"

"You're holding the picture. What do you think?"

"I'd say if she's not, it's one hell of a coincidence that they look so much alike, but since you've already told me there's no coincidence in this story, I'd say yeah, Janet Wayne is her mother. God, I had no idea Sunny was adopted!"

"Apparently no one knew. There was never any reason for anyone to think she was adopted. But to me, it explains why Mrs. Krause was able to walk out on Sunny several years ago without even bothering to say goodbye. Sunny isn't her biological child."

"Still, it was cruel and heartless for her to do that," Jake said, shaking his head.

"I agree, but it makes sense. It doesn't say much for Mrs. Krause as a human being, but it does help explain her actions."

Jake got out of his chair and sat on the corner of Quinn's desk opposite the cheese steak sandwich that was getting cold and still smelled. "O.K. Quinn. I confess. I'm confused. Help me put all of this together."

"From talking to people in Ohio, Janet got pregnant and her Bible-thumping parents went crazy. They didn't want anyone to know about the baby. I can't find any record of the adoption, and I have no idea how the Krauses ended up with Sunny, who was an infant when they moved here. I think Janet hated her parents for making her give up the baby, and I suspect she had something to do with the fire that killed them and I suspect she had something to do with our librarian's so-called accident. It's one of those things that you are ninety-nine percent sure of, but you can't prove. Anyway, after a few years of going to school, working and growing up, Miss Wayne started looking for her child, and she finally tracked Sunny down here in Sanderson. Hell, she's a librarian. She knows how to do research. By then, Mrs. Krause was out of the picture, but Sunny still had a father. I believe Miss Wayne wanted her baby back so badly, and she didn't want to have to share her with anyone, so she killed Regal. That would clear the way for Miss Wayne to build a relationship with Sunny, and eventually let her know she was her mother."

"But why wouldn't Miss Wayne just go ahead and tell Sunny?"

"When Mrs. Krause walked out on her family, from everything I've seen and been told, that had a devastating emotional impact on Sunny. Miss Wayne probably thought Sunny would hate her for having put her up for adoption."

"O.K. I can buy that. I can even buy the notion of Miss Wayne wanting to get rid of Regal. What you've told me also explains why Miss Wayne is so pissed off about the relationship Maddie has with Sunny. But why the ritualistic stuff? And if Miss Wayne killed Regal, did she kill Todd and Joe?"

"I believe she killed Todd and Joe to help cover Regal's murder. By having three killings, she could divert us from looking at Regal's death alone. As for the way the guys were murdered, think about the scriptures. Miss Wayne was raised in a strict, strict, religious home. Maybe she felt empowered by the scriptures to be judge and jury for these three guys who she believed were mistreating their children. On the other hand, maybe she used the scriptures just to throw us off."

"But you can't prove any of this, can you?"

"No, I can't. I know each man talked to Miss Wayne shortly before they died, but in her job, she talks to all sorts of people every day. As of this moment, the only decent clues I've got are the size seven-and-a-half shoe imprint and the vaginal fluid from the first killing. The shoe's a stretch at best. A million women wear seven-and-a-half. What I need is a DNA sample I can match to the vaginal fluid. There's a problem, though."

"What?"

"Mary Jane admitted she had sex with Todd the day he died. What if Janet Wayne didn't have sex with Todd that day? What if she promised him they could have sex *after* she tied him to the tree, but killed him before they actually had sex? That means Mary Jane's DNA could match the fluid sample we have, which is more compelling evidence than Miss Wayne talking to the guys. We could have that evidence against Mary Jane. That wouldn't be conclusive evidence, but the D.A. would be more likely to prosecute and the people in this town more likely to convict someone having sex than someone merely talking. Plus, there's another complication."

"Which is?"

"Mary Jane has split. Left town. No one knows where she is. She dropped her girls off at her sister's and hightailed it out of town. She did that after I asked her if she had any involvement in all of this. Her running away sure as hell isn't doing anything to help eliminate her as a suspect."

"Quinn, I'm sorry."

"Yeah, me too."

Jake was silent as he processed this new information. "Have you got a DNA sample from Mary Jane?" he asked after a few seconds.

"Not yet."

"Hold off. Let me get you a sample from Miss Wayne first. Let's see if she matches."

"And how do you propose to do this?"

"I don't know yet, but I'll get it."

"It won't be admissible in court."

"I'll let you worry about that."

"I don't know about this, Jake."

"One thing I learned a long time ago in the newspaper business. When you're working on a big story, and you seem to be hitting dead ends everywhere, you have to be creative. You can't always play by the book when you're digging for information."

"As I recall, you being creative got you and your newspaper sued."

Quinn's barb stuck deeply in Jake. "That wasn't being creative," he responded to Quinn. "That was being stupid."

Quinn walked to the front of his desk and looked at Jake. "Why are you so eager to help me with this, so eager to go after the librarian? I've seen you and Miss Wayne together, and I think there may be a bit of a spark. I know you and Maddie are close and getting closer, but I think you and the librarian could hit it off too."

"Janet and Maddie are totally different."

"Maybe that's what draws you to Miss Wayne. With Maddie, what you see is what you get. She's just a good ole girl, and that's all she will ever be. But with the librarian, there's so much you don't know. There's something enticing, exciting about her. And, despite her holy roller facade, I bet she's really good in bed."

Realizing Quinn was more on the money than he wanted him to be, Jake walked in a small circle before coming back to face Quinn. "I'm not going to lie to you. There's an attraction, mostly physical. Just looking at the woman elevates my pulse rate. But let's be real, Quinn. We're pointing at three women as our murderer. Mary Jane Hamilton, Janet Wayne and Maddie Hampton. Of those three, which one would you prefer to arrest and have convicted?"

"I think you know the answer to that question. But we don't have enough evidence to charge any of them now, and I'm not going to fabricate something just to make an arrest. We've got to let the chips fall where they may, Jake. We just need more chips."

Jake paused and looked out a window. "You've told me how much solving these murders means to you and that you've got to prove to yourself that being in a small town hasn't eroded your law enforcement skills. Well, I'm the same way. As much as I've come to like Sanderson, I need to prove to myself that I've still got what it takes to get the big story, that I won't let anything or anyone get in my way. That may sound heartless, but that's how it is. With so many reporters going after the same story, it's survival of the fittest. You do whatever it takes to get the job done. Part of me hopes that we're wrong about Janet Wayne. But if we determine that she's not the killer, where does that leave us?"

"With Maddie and Mary Jane," Quinn replied.

"Right, and if we learn Miss Wayne isn't guilty? We go after Maddie and Mary Jane, which neither of us want to do. So first, we put absolutely all of our efforts into either identifying Janet Wayne as the killer or absolving her."

Quinn swallowed hard. "Sounds like a plan." Quinn popped his right balled fist into the palm of his left hand. "Damn Jake! Underneath that Mr. Nice Guy shell, you are a heartless son of a bitch, aren't you?"

Jake sighed deeply. "No, I'm not heartless," he rebutted. "I'm a reporter. A good one who does what he has to do to get a story. Unfortunately, I am also a good reporter who is way too personally involved in this story who is going to be sick if *any* of these three women turn out to be our killer."

"Well, Mr. Big Time Reporter, I understand your dilemma. I feel the same way. All right, you do whatever to get the DNA sample from Janet Wayne. Be careful. Remember we're dealing with a sick, mean psycho. Don't let your reporter's ego or your need to get laid get you killed. I don't want to find you tied to a tree somewhere with your dick cut off."

"Ouch!" Jake grimaced. "I'm not going to let that happen. I've decided I ain't taking my pants off for any woman in this town until we find the killer."

CHAPTER TWENTY-SIX

"**I** was shocked, very shocked, that you called," Janet Wayne admitted to Jake as she ushered him into her living room. Two glasses of sweet tea were waiting on the end table next to the sofa, and Miss Wayne handed one to Jake as he sat down. Even though he had rehearsed a dozen times what he was going to say, Jake took a long swallow of tea to give himself a moment to put his thoughts together one last time.

He held the glass with both hands. "It seems that you and I have not been able to get to know each other as much as we would like due to the interference of others," he started calmly. "I'm sorry about that. I came to apologize and ask if we can start over."

Doubt crept across her face. "Really?" she asked while setting down her glass of tea on the small table next to her chair.

"Yes, really. I feel badly about what's happened."

Sitting on the edge of her chair, Miss Wayne was candid with Jake. "Being very honest, from the moment you called, I've been skeptical about you coming here. I've been haunted by the feeling that you've been sent here, either by Maddie Hampton or Chief Quinn or both. And if that's the case, I'd prefer that you leave." Shifting in her chair, she slipped her stocking-covered right foot out of the black pump with a two-inch heel. That immediately caught

Jake's attention. Her foot was a nice size, not too small or too big. Perhaps a seven-and-a-half.

"Oh no. I'm here on my own. Trust me. It's not my nature to let people tell me what to do." Jake was beginning to get nervous. Miss Wayne was seeing through his charade. He took another swallow of tea and put the glass down.

"If you are here on your own, let me ask you a question. A personal question."

"Go ahead."

"Just what is your relationship with Maddie?"

Jake tried not to change facial expressions. He hoped Miss Wayne would not detect his nervousness. "We're friends. That's all. She feeds me a lot."

"You certainly rushed to her side when I was about to let her have it at Founders' Day."

"I would have done that for any lady. If the roles had been reversed, I would have come to your aid. At the risk of sounding sexist, I know how catty women can be. I just didn't want the two of your to make a big public scene because of some little difference of opinion."

"Oh, Mr. Martin, it's far more than a little difference of opinion."

"Maddie says that's all it is."

"Well, Maddie's wrong. She's a goodie two shoes who thinks she's the pied piper for all the teenage girls in this town."

"I think she is. She's seen most of the girls in this town grow up, and has been a big influence in their lives. This is all about Sunny, isn't it?"

Miss Wayne didn't reply. She looked directly at Jake.

"She's just trying to help Sunny. She feels sorry for her," he explained on Maddie's behalf.

"I'm trying to help Sunny too, but I can't. Maddie keeps getting in the way, and I'm tired of it. She deserves to be slapped. I regret that you stopped me."

Jake studied Miss Wayne's face, which was wrinkled with irritation. "Something tells me you were a lot like Sunny when you were a teenager," he said, eager to hear her response.

"I guess I was. I was shy and a loner like she is. I understand how she feels. I lost my parents when I was young, like she did. That's what made me so angry about Quinn questioning me about the deaths of the three men. I'm infuriated that he thinks I could have had anything to do with Mr. Krause's death. I know how devastating it can be to lose your parents."

"He wasn't singling you out. He talked to everyone who had contact with the men before they died."

Miss Wayne wouldn't settle for Jake's explanation. "Well, I did take it personally. And why didn't he talk to Maddie? She had motive to kill all three."

"You can't be serious," Jake quickly responded. "The only thing lethal about Maddie is the food some of her students cook up in home economics."

"To just be friends, you certainly are quick to her defense."

Jake sensed this was a conversation that needed to end. "Like I said earlier, I came to apologize to you and see if you and I can start over. I want to say I'm sorry, and I would very much like to take you out to dinner."

Miss Wayne hesitated for a second before responding. "Apology accepted," she replied unconvincingly. "But I don't want to go out. I'm cooking. It's ready. Come talk to me while I set the table."

"Sure, but I need to use the restroom first." She directed him down a short hallway.

Jake locked himself in the old house's small, outdated restroom. With his heart rate increasing, he immediately located the item needed to provide the sample that had been promised to Quinn. Reaching into a small wicker basket next to the sink that had a dripping hot water faucet, Jake pulled out a hair brush and gingerly pulled away three long strands of blonde hair. Putting the brush back, Jake slipped the hair samples into a zip sandwich bag he pulled from his pants pocket. He took a deep breath, paused a moment, and then flushed the toilet to give his trip to the john a touch of authenticity. The hair sample went into his pocket.

Walking through the house to the dining room, Jake raked his hand across his forehead and could feel moisture. As he reached the door to the dining room, he stopped. His heart almost stopped as well. Janet Wayne was sprawled naked on the dining room table.

"Dinner is served," she cooed.

Frozen to the spot, Jake admiringly surveyed Miss Wayne from head to toe. Eventually he walked to the table and hovered over her, getting a tantalizing close-up look at her blemish-free skin. "Is this what you call having dessert first?" he asked.

"I guarantee that this will be the sweetest thing you've ever put in your mouth," she answered with a wicked smile.

He lowered his hand to her flat stomach and slowly began moving it up to her breasts. Jake couldn't remember the last time he had touched a woman. It felt good. Miss Wayne contracted with pleasure as Jake made circles with his index finger around her nipples.

She reached for his belt and pulled herself up so she was sitting on the edge of the table. She began rubbing the front of his shirt. "You said Maddie doesn't mean anything to you, that you're just friends," she started. "Prove it to me. Prove it to me that she doesn't mean anything to you. Make love to me." She slid off the table and softly took his hand. "Let's go to the bedroom," she suggested.

Jake went willingly. His basic instincts were overriding his good judgment. Miss Wayne carefully unbuttoned Jake's shirt and laid him down on his back on her bed. Sitting on her knees, one on each side of his waist, she put her hands on his chest and began to slide them down over his pants pockets where the hair sample was hidden. He grabbed her wrists and put her hands on her breasts which caused her to moan. She leaned down and began to kiss Jake. He had been without a woman so long that the foreplay couldn't last long.

Sliding her hand under the pillow, Miss Wayne pulled out a red silk scarf, tied one end around Jake's wrist and started to tie the other end to the slatted headboard. "I like to be in control," she said teasingly.

A wave of panic engulfed Jake and he pulled his wrist away. Grabbing her at the arm pits, he unromantically tossed her to the foot of the bed and she clumsily bounced once as if she was on a trampoline. She looked back at him in total surprise.

"I'm not ready for this," Jake admitted as he hopped off the bed and started buttoning his shirt.

"That lump in your pants tells me otherwise," Miss Wayne noted. Confused and frustrated, she ran her hand through her hair.

"Oh, you don't know how much I want to," he said truthfully. "I just . . ." He wasn't about to tell her he quit because the thought of being tied up and split open with a knife didn't appeal to him.

She didn't let him continue. "That damn Maddie Hampton!" she barked. "Go to the little bitch! Go on! Get out of my house!"

Jake didn't take the time to tuck in his shirt. He started to hurry out of the bedroom, but stopped, and hit by a sudden urge to be a smart ass, asked, "I guess this means dinner is out?"

He ducked to avoid the lamp she threw at him and sprinted out to his car.

CHAPTER TWENTY-SEVEN

 J ake had a hangover. Not the alcohol induced type of his past, but one of conscience. He felt guilty and embarrassed about his behavior and everything that had happened at Janet Wayne's house the night before. Yes, he had managed to get the sample Quinn needed for a DNA comparison, but Jake was not happy with himself about the way he procured it. Going to Miss Wayne's house under false pretenses, fibbing about how he felt about Maddie, allowing Miss Wayne to seduce him, and then running out on her at the zenith of passion kept playing over and over in his mind. Foremost in his thoughts was the realization he wanted to have sex with Miss Wayne, and would have, had she not pulled out the scarf. Everything about the night had been a mistake. He had not been fair to Maddie, to Miss Wayne, and most of all, to himself. Jake had done a lot of soul searching during a restless, sleepless night. Now, he was sitting in the Waffle House, his head about to burst, as he continued to agonize over the previous night's events while waiting for Quinn.

Two cups of coffee later, Quinn arrived. "You don't look so good," was the first thing he said to Jake.

Jake didn't immediately respond, waiting for the waitress who was pouring Quinn's coffee to leave. "Any word on Mary Jane?" he asked Quinn.

"Nothing. She hasn't called her sister, talked to her kids, nothing. It's my fault. I came down on her hard. I overreacted with her after

Agent Stamps accused me of being soft. We've issued a lookout for her, but there have been no leads. She's pulled a great disappearing act."

"She's bound to show up. I can't imagine her totally abandoning her girls."

"I hope you're right. Now tell me about your night."

"It was a long one." Jake pulled the zip bag containing the hair sample out of his pocket and tossed it to Quinn who immediately put it in his pocket.

"I want to hear all the details about how you got this."

Jake looked down into his half empty cup. "To begin with, last night I saw a side of Miss Wayne that I've never seen before. In fact, I saw *a lot* of her that I've never seen before, and it was nice! But I saw a side of me that I've never seen before and it wasn't so nice."

"Son, you've got me totally confused," Quinn said, leaning back and folding his arms across his chest.

"I went into her bathroom and got the hair out of one of her brushes. When I came out, she was sprawled out butt-naked on the dining room table. I tell you Quinn, she's got a fantastic body!"

"I hope you're going to tell me the two of you got it on. By the way, what was it you told me about not taking your pants off for any woman in this town?"

"I didn't take my pants off. My shirt, almost, yes. And yes, I wanted to take my pants off. You don't know how much I wanted to. And I would have, but she wanted to tie me to the bed."

Quinn almost choked on the coffee in his mouth. "Given the fact that we think she might have killed three other guys the same way, I don't blame you. If it had been me, I would have run screaming out of her house—minus my pants. You did have your pants on, didn't you?"

"I had my pants on. I'm not proud of what I did last night, Quinn. It wasn't right."

"All right, Jake. You're getting me more confused. A few days ago you were telling me it was important for you to do this, that you had to find out if you still had the balls to do whatever it takes to get a story. Sounds to me like you got your answer. You've still got the balls. You got me the sample for DNA, and found out an extra tidbit. The girl likes bondage. That bit of information could be important."

"Finding out that I've still got the balls is the problem." Jake stopped when the waitress came to take their order.

"Explain," Quinn requested after the waitress left.

"If that's how I'm going to operate, I can't do it in a small town, especially this small town. You get too close to people. You have to do things that hurt your friends. I didn't sleep at all last night. All I could think about was how devious and underhanded it was for me to go to Janet Wayne's house last night and string her along. Tossing and turning in my bed, I could not picture her as a killer, no matter how hard I tried. All I could see is her as the town librarian, sitting at a table and helping Sunny and other kids. I'm not accustomed to having that type of attachment to the people I'm writing about."

"I wouldn't worry too much about all of that, Jake. Heck, we don't have a series of ritualistic murders here in Sanderson every week. I doubt that you'll ever have to do anything like you did last night again."

"I didn't say I didn't want to do it. I said I don't want to do it here."

Quinn rubbed the back of his neck. "Come on Jake. Spit it out. Tell me what you're really trying to say."

"I'm going to take the job in Charleston. I know to begin with I'll be writing fluff, but it's a move I've got to make if I'm ever going to get back into the mainstream. And I don't consider writing about the guest speaker at the Sanderson Rotary Club meeting mainstream hard news."

"Are you sure this is what you want to do?"

"After last night? Yeah. First, I've got to get in touch with Stephen House."

"When are you going to tell Maddie?"

"This morning. She's got a planning period."

"Do you think that's wise? She's going to be upset, you know. Do you expect her to go back into class after you tell her?"

"I don't know. I guess I'm being selfish, but I don't want to have to carry this around all day. I want to tell her and get it over."

"There's nothing I can do to get you to stay? I kind of like having you around."

"Nope. Besides, I suspect that one of these days, you'll be moving on too. You're too good to be stuck here."

"Maybe, but I'm not going anywhere until I solve these murders," Quinn said, patting his pants pocket that contained the hair sample.

Jake glanced at his watch. "Maddie's free in thirty minutes. That gives me time to drop by my office and then head to the school." He took a deep breath.

"Take this," Quinn offered. He reached into his shirt pocket and got two sticks of Black Jack gum for Jake.

"Thanks," Jake smiled. "Hope I can find this stuff in Charleston."

After making an unnecessary stop at the Sentinel office where the morning had gotten off to a boringly routine start, Jake drove to the high school, where the front office staff greeted him with friendly waves. He had been at the school so often that like Kenny, he no longer bothered to check in for a visitor's pass. Jake's mouth was getting dry as he walked down the corridor. He felt the sweat on his hands as he reached for the handle on the door to Maddie's classroom.

"Good morning," he smiled. She was at her desk grading a stack of papers.

"You don't need to be here. I've got work to do," she responded tersely, not bothering to look up.

Her cold response surprised Jake. "How's your day going?" he asked, trying to lighten her mood.

"I've had better. I'm busy."

This wasn't like Maddie. Jake thought about leaving, but he wanted to let her know about his decision. He also wanted to know what was bothering her, if it was something at work, or if she had heard bad news from Robbie.

"I've got something to tell you. It won't take but a minute and you can get back to work," he said nervously.

Maddie looked up from the papers and glared at Jake. "What do you want to talk to me about, Jake? Last night?" She continued to stare at him.

"Last night?" Her question sent a cold chill down his spine.

"Last night." She took a brown envelope out of the oversized tote bag she used to take papers to and from home. "At some point this morning, this was put in my box in the front office." She pulled a pair of black French cut panties from the envelope and held them in her hand. "There was a note from Janet Wayne with these. She said you might want them as a memento from last night." She tossed the panties at Jake and he caught them, but quickly dropped them back on Maddie's desk.

"I'm sorry she did that to you," Jake apologized. "What she did was classless."

Maddie looked at Jake in disbelief. "Classless? You're calling what she did classless? What about what you did, Jake? Wasn't what you did, sleeping with her, classless?"

"I didn't sleep with her!" Jake shot back in rebuttal. "Let me explain."

"I think the panties explain everything. I guess in a way I don't blame you. I know that you've wanted the two of us to be intimate, but I'm not at that point in our relationship yet, so you went to someone who was. Well, I hope it was good, because you and I are finished!"

Jake pulled a chair close to Maddie, sat down and tried to hold her hand but she wouldn't let him. "I didn't see her in those panties," Jake started. "She wasn't wearing anything."

"That's supposed to make me feel better about this mess?"

"The point is, she tried to seduce me, and she almost did. I was weak, Maddie. I admit it. It's been a long time. But I didn't sleep with her."

"You expect me to believe that?"

"It's the truth."

"Why were you there?"

"I can't tell you, but it wasn't to have sex."

"That's real good Jake. You admit you were there but can't tell me why. You admit you saw her naked, but you swear you didn't have sex. Do you think I'm that stupid?"

Jake got out of the chair, turned his back to Maddie and collected his thoughts. "You'll find out what's going on eventually."

"So, what's your excuse going to be? That you were working on a story?"

"As a matter of fact, I was."

Maddie threw up her hands as she got out of her chair. "Oh, get out of here, Jake. My students will be arriving in a few minutes and I don't want them to see me strangling you." She took the panties, put them back in the envelope and stuffed it back into her tote.

The last thing Jake wanted to do was create a scene at school, and he realized this conversation was nowhere close to a conclusion, so he honored her request for him to leave. Stopping at the door, he told her, "Janet Wayne is furious at me and she can't stand you. That's why she sent you the panties, to break us up."

"Well, she accomplished her mission." The bell signaling the next class period rang, and as students flooded out of the classrooms, Jake walked out of Barber County High School sick to his stomach.

CHAPTER TWENTY-EIGHT

J ake considered ignoring the 6:30 a.m. phone call. He rolled over in his bed, buried his head under the covers and let the phone ring five times. Then, his reporter mentality took over and he answered, and he was glad he did. Kenny had news that intruders were inside Barber County High School and the police were having difficulty removing them. Jake's adrenaline took over. He quickly slipped into the clothes he wore the previous day, ran his fingers through his hair instead of using a brush and rushed off to the school, far exceeding the speed limit. He didn't worry a second about being ticketed, because all the police would be at the school. Besides, he knew the chief.

The school's front parking lot was filled with police cars, an ambulance, a fire truck and the cars of nearby residents who had heard about the standoff. Jake had hardly stepped out of the car when Kenny came running to meet him.

"What's going on?" Jake asked, continuing to walk toward the school building.

"I don't know for sure. I told you all I know over the phone. Quinn's here. We can ask him."

They found Quinn propped against his car, arms folded and his jaws working over a mouthful of Black Jack chewing gum.

"This must be serious, they way you're going at that gum," Jake said.

"What is it?" Kenny asked his eyes wide with anticipation. "Burglars? Terrorists? Is someone holding the principal hostage?"

"Pigs."

"Did you say pigs?" Jake asked.

"Yeah, pigs. A damn Senior Week prank. Somebody stole five of George Howell's pigs, greased them up and let them loose in the senior hallway."

Jake burst out laughing while Kenny seemed disappointed that he was going to miss out on a big story.

"We've called George to come get his pigs, but it's not going to be easy to catch those sons of bitches," Quinn said. He was still leaning on his car.

"Maybe you should call the football coach," Jake suggested. "Let him send his guys inside for tackling practice."

"You obviously didn't see us play last year," Kenny interrupted. "We couldn't tackle. Our defense couldn't stop a corpse from Boyd and Sons, much less those pigs."

George Howell arrived, meaning the football team's services weren't needed, and Quinn's instructions were to the point—get the porkers out of the hallway before students and teachers started arriving in less than an hour. Jake directed Kenny to get some photos of the extraction.

"Got any idea who's responsible?" Jake asked as he propped up against the car next to Quinn.

"Not now, but I'll find out. And when I do, I'm going to abuse them with my plastic bat. Take my frustrations out on them rather than some poor tree."

"These Senior Week tricks. An annual thing?"

"Oh yeah. Last year two senior boys dumped a load of cow manure in the lunchroom. They said it was their statement on the quality of the food. The bad thing is, I've eaten in the lunchroom, and I couldn't disagree with them."

"I guess that explains why no one here looks terribly distraught. They're used to these pranks."

"They are. I can't believe Kenny didn't realize what was going on. I'd bet my bottom dollar he was one of the ring leaders for his senior class. If I remember correctly, his class chained the assistant principal's car to a tree."

"Back then, Kenny was probably a bit more focused. Right now, I think his mind is running in several different directions. He's thinking about school next fall, he's got a new girlfriend, and I think Sunny is still on his mind. I can empathize with him. My mind's still going in several different directions too. Any news on Miss Wayne's hair sample?"

"Haven't got the results back yet."

"Well, thanks to Miss Wayne, I'm knee deep in that lunchroom pile of cow manure with Maddie."

Quinn moved away from the car and faced Jake. "I can't wait to hear about this," Quinn admitted, but he turned toward the school building when cheering and applause erupted. Burly George Howell was walking out with a squealing pig cradled in his arms.

"Miss Wayne sent Maddie a pair of her panties and told her to give them to me, as a souvenir of the night we spent together. Maddie's convinced I slept with Miss Wayne."

"What are you going to do?"

"Try to talk to Maddie, but she's furious with me now. She kicked me out of her classroom. I didn't even get to tell her that I'm going to Charleston."

To more applause and cheering, George Howell's brother exited the school with another pig. Quinn, before walking away to confer with Principal Connery, offered some encouragement to Jake. "Maddie's a reasonable woman. She'll come around. Give her a little time." He patted Jake on the arm.

"I hope, because a little time is all I've got left here. I've talked to Stephen House. He's making arrangements to come back for a few days to take care of the Sentinel."

As Quinn left, Kenny returned. "You're not mad at me, are you, about getting you out of bed for a bunch of pigs?" Kenny asked meekly.

Jake laughed. "Heck no! This story is exactly what I need. The way things have been going, I need some comic relief. Come on. Let's go to Waffle House. I'll buy breakfast. I have this sudden hankering for some bacon."

Walking to their cars, Jake and Kenny met Maddie and Sunny who were arriving for the start of the school day. "What's going on?" Maddie asked, unaware of the pig fiasco.

"A Senior Week prank," Jake replied. "Quinn will fill you in. How are you Maddie?" Jake asked, not knowing what type of response he'd get.

"Busy. The last week of school you know," was her polite response. Jake sensed she was as uncomfortable as he was with the chance meeting.

"Have a good day," he told her and resumed the walk to his car.

"Good morning Kenny," Maddie smiled before heading for her classroom.

Kenny awkwardly tried to start a conversation with Sunny. "Two days from now you'll be a high school graduate. How does it feel?" he asked, hoping she didn't notice his shaking voice.

"It's no big deal," she said, looking down at the pavement. "I won't have any family there, so as far as I'm concerned, I'd be happy just to pick up my diploma in the office and be done with it."

"Don't be that way. Be happy. Enjoy it. Maddie and Miss Wayne will be there to see you. I'll be there to see you. In fact, I'm going to get a graduation gift for you."

"You don't have to do that."

"I want to." Kenny's body language gave away how uncomfortable he was. "I'm really sorry things turned out the way they did."

"Don't apologize. It's time for us to get on with our lives. You've got a new school and Callan to look forward to and I . . ."

"What are you going to do after graduation?" Kenny asked, sincerely wanting to know.

"Who knows? I've got to hang around here a few days. The insurance company is about to issue me the check from Dad's policy. I'll probably tie up a few loose ends around here and then find a spot a million miles away."

Kenny looked into her expressionless eyes. "Where ever you go, I hope you find some happiness. I really do. You deserve it."

She smiled weakly at him. Kenny kissed her softly on the cheek and left to join Jake at the Waffle House. Rubbing the spot Kenny had kissed, Sunny walked to a bench in front of the school and sat alone, waiting for the homeroom bell.

Maddie's entrance into the building was halted by Quinn, who explained that janitors were cleaning up after the pigs. "Next year's seniors will really have to go a ways to top this," he told her as they watched two bucket brigades coming in and out of the building.

"Trust me, they will. I wish they spent as much time and energy on their real school work as they do this type of foolishness."

"Jake was here a few minutes ago. He thought all of this was funny. He would have thought it was even funnier if it hadn't been so early in the morning."

"I saw him in the parking lot."

"Jake told you the truth, Maddie."

"Taking up for him, huh? Why am I not surprised?"

"The other night, when he was at Miss Wayne's, he *was* working on a story. He was helping me. And he didn't sleep with her."

"You're just covering for him."

"No, I'm not. I've got too much respect for you to do that. Jake needs to talk to you. Surely you can listen for a few minutes."

"This is such a busy week. Tests, graduation . . ." She looked at the janitors emptying their buckets of dirty water. ". . . pigs," she mumbled, shaking her head.

"Make the time. Do it as a favor to me." One of the janitors waved at Quinn and held up five fingers. "Give the floor five minutes to dry and you can go in," Quinn told Maddie. "And give Jake five minutes of your time."

"All right," she agreed reluctantly. "I'll be glad when this week is over."

CHAPTER TWENTY-NINE

E very seat in the Barber County High School football stadium, capacity 2,200, was filled and another two hundred relatives, friends and well-wishers were lined along the chain link fence that circled the field. One hundred and nine seniors were about to end their high school careers. Some like Amanda Lake, class president and cheerleader captain, were already sad about missing their friends and all their extracurricular activities, while the misfits and loners, Sunny Krause in particular, were relieved to be escaping the hell of jokes and rejection. Valedictorian Palmer Prince and the high academic achievers were looking forward to Southeastern Conference schools and great dreams, while the uninspired, represented by Chuck Williams, got to report to work at the peanut processing plant Monday.

Everyone at the ceremony, graduates and spectators alike, had something in common this night. They were roasting. Even though the sun was going down, the temperature was still in the low eighties, and the hand fans, courtesy of Boyd and Sons Funeral Home, weren't helping. The crowd was drenched in sweat, and much to their relief, Principal Connery moved the ceremony along quickly. As the graduates stepped on stage to receive their diplomas, some got rousing ovations and cheers from family and friends. When Sunny stepped forward, Jake grimaced. All she got was an almost inaudible smattering of applause from a half-dozen people.

Finally, Stephanie Zabrinskie was awarded her diploma and another school year was over at Barber County High. The crowed poured out of the stands to mingle with the graduates. As Kenny was running around taking photos for the next issue of the Sentinel, Jake stood on the fifty yard line watching the hugging, back slapping and happy conversations. He kept an eye on Sunny, who received hugs from Maddie and Miss Wayne—at different moments, of course—as well as a few teachers and fellow students.

Jake was watching the football team's graduating All-Region offensive tackle all but break his cheerleader girlfriend's back in a bear hug when he felt a tap on his shoulder. "Hi," Maddie said as he turned around.

"Hi," he replied, wiping sweat away from his forehead.

"Every year at graduation, I feel like I'm saying goodbye to my own children," she sighed. "I can't watch over them anymore. They're on their own."

"You've taught them well. They'll do fine."

"I hope so . . ." Maddie was interrupted by a short overweight girl who was still in her robe. She hugged Maddie and said, "I love you."

"I love you too," Maddie responded as the girl walked a few feet away to a gaggle of friends. "She's been accepted at Emory University," Maddie explained as a tear rolled down her cheek. "She wants to be a doctor."

"I understand why you've never left Sanderson. This whole town *is* your family. These students *are* your kids. All I've got for my efforts in life are bylines on a few thousand newspaper articles that, in the grand scheme of things, don't mean a hill of beans. I envy you, Maddie. I really do."

Maddie smiled and waved at another graduate who was walking by a few feet away. She smiled at Jake and twisted the graduation program she was holding. "I talked to Quinn. He set me straight about your visit to Miss Wayne's house."

Jake scratched his head. "He did?"

"Yes. He said that you were working with him on a case—he didn't go into details and I didn't ask—and that nothing went on between the two of you. I believe him. I owe you an apology."

"No you don't. I shouldn't have gone there in the first place. I owe you the apology."

"Let's forget it. Quinn said you needed to talk to me."

"I do, but not here."

"Well, I'm going to be here for a few minutes helping to get things cleaned up. After that I'm going home. Sunny won't be there. A couple of my senior home ec girls asked her to go eat with them. That was so sweet of them, and I know Sunny will enjoy it. Why don't you give me ninety minutes or so and come over. We can talk all night."

"Sounds good. That will give me time to run home, get out of these sweaty clothes and take a shower. Want me to bring something to eat?"

"No. I've got things at the house."

"Thank you, Maddie," Jake said gratefully. At that moment, reflecting on how much she loved her students and in turn, how much they loved her, Jake was struck by how good a woman she was. She had truly made a positive impact on hundreds of young lives.

"See you in a little while," she smiled.

Maddie was at the school another 45 minutes and home fifteen minutes after that. She plopped down on her sofa, kicked off her shoes and was going to rest for a few minutes before taking a quick shower. She closed her eyes and was about to nod off when the phone rang. Maddie picked up a pen so she could record the nature of the call as she always did. The voice on the other end was frantic. "Maddie! This is Janet Wayne! Sunny's been in an accident! She's asking for you. Please come in a hurry!"

Cold chills shot down Maddie's back. "Oh no!" she screamed, as she jotted down "Sunny/accident" on the pad next to the phone. "Where? What happened?" She wanted to cry but she was too shocked.

"The girls she went out with played a horrible trick on her. Instead of going to eat, they took her to the old Kingman manufacturing plant. Sunny fell. She's hurt badly. They tried to call you, but couldn't get you, so they called me. I've called 911. Please hurry! Come to the back loading entrance!"

Maddie finished scribbling down "Kingman plant" and tossed the phone and pen to the floor where they both bounced softly on the carpet. She was so jittery she had difficulty wriggling her feet back into her shoes. Maddie rushed out the front door, not caring that it was left half-open. The tires of her Jeep squealed as Maddie peeled out of the driveway and again when she floored the gas to shoot out of the subdivision. Maddie was so focused on getting to Sunny that she did not notice the white Explorer of GBI Agent Travis Stamps fall in behind and follow her out of the subdivision.

Normally ultra-cautious behind the wheel, Maddie sped to the Kingman plant like a south Georgia dirt track racer, arriving in eight minutes. The plant had been abandoned for years and was dark and dirty and creepy. Slowly turning the corner to the back of the giant concrete block building, Maddie noticed a single car. "Why aren't the paramedics here?" she screamed out loud. She bolted out of her Jeep and carefully made her way up the steps leading to a large double door. Maddie wished she had taken time to grab a flashlight at her house. Had the clear sky not been full of stars, the area would have been as dark as blindness.

Agent Stamps turned off the lights of his vehicle and slowly pulled behind Maddie's Jeep in the back lot of the plant. "Well, this is interesting," Stamps said out loud. "That's the librarian's car. Wonder what they're cooking up tonight?" He drummed his fingers on the steering wheel, pondering if he should wait for the two women to come out, or go ahead and bust up their rendezvous inside the plant. He chose to wait.

Unaware that she had been followed, Maddie approached the back loading door of the plant, wondering if she was at the right location. Terrified that a badly injured Sunny may have been abandoned at the desolate location, Maddie pushed at the door. She grunted because opening the heavy door took all her strength. The large room was damp, musty and shadowy, illuminated only by three small kerosene camping lanterns. Her heart racing, Maddie took several steps inside and called for Sunny. She stood motionless waiting for a reply. Maddie gasped as an arm wrapped around her waist and a sharp object touched her throat. "Hello Maddie," was the haughty greeting.

"Miss Wayne?" Maddie asked in shock. She tried to step away, but the arm around her waist tightened and the sharp object pressed tighter against her throat.

"That's right."

"Where's Sunny? Is she all right?"

"Oh, she's fine. She's out with her friends, hopefully having a wonderful time."

Fear and the hot stagnant air inside the building were making breathing difficult for Maddie. She gasped for a breath as she asked, "What kind of game are you playing? Where is Sunny?" Maddie's heart was racing. She could hear it in her ears.

"You and I have some unfinished business. Step this way, please."

Miss Wayne started pushing Maddie toward the center of the big room. With a knife to her throat, Maddie didn't offer any resistance. "I don't understand . . ." Maddie said, her voice trembling.

"I'm going to fill you in on all the details . . . in just a minute." Miss Wayne pulled the knife away, but Maddie was too horrified to move. Acting quickly, Miss Wayne pushed Maddie's wrists through slip knots on the end of rope strands that were tied to iron poles holding up the roof. Maddie's legs were quickly secured in the same manner, leaving her standing spread-eagled and helpless.

"It's hot in here. You must be hot," Miss Wayne suggested. "Let's cool you off. She took the knife that had been at Maddie's throat and starting at the neck line, began to cut away Maddie's sun dress. After removing Maddie's dress, she sliced her bra in front and pulled it away and followed with her panties. "Nice figure, especially for an old woman," Miss Wayne offered as she viewed Maddie in the dim light.

"Why are you doing this? Why did you have to rip my clothes off?"

"Because I want to embarrass you, humiliate you, like you've done to me in front of Jake and Sunny."

Maddie wriggled frantically to get loose, but the motions only made the ropes tighter. "I've done nothing to embarrass you. That's crazy! You're crazy!"

"Because of you, Jake won't have anything to do with me, and you've turned my own daughter against me. When Regal Krause died, my own daughter wouldn't come live with me. You convinced her to stay with you."

Stunned, Maddie stopped her wiggling. "Sunny's your daughter? What about the Krauses?"

"They adopted Sunny. I had to give up the child when she was born and I've been searching for her ever since. I haven't searched this long and this hard for some sanctimonious high school home economics teacher to take her way from me."

"I . . . I didn't know. How could I have known? Does Sunny know?"

"No, because since she's always with you, I haven't had the chance to tell her about my life and why I had to give her up. But after tonight, you won't be a hindrance."

"Janet, I don't know what to say . . . I'm glad you finally found your daughter. If I had known, I certainly . . ."

"Your whinny little apology is not going to cut it. Let's talk about other things. Let's talk about how much I'm going to enjoy making love to Jake. Let's talk about your nice body." Miss Wayne moved closer to Maddie and ran the point of the knife down her right arm. "You really do have a nice body . . ."

"Don't do this, please! Please untie me. Let's talk. I'm thrilled that you have found your daughter. I'll do everything I can to get Sunny to you."

"Oh, zip it up, Maddie. You did come alone, didn't you?"

"Jake's on his way." Maddie hoped she could bluff her way out of the predicament.

"Well, let's see." Miss Wayne started walking toward the heavy loading door. "Don't go anywhere," she said over her shoulder to Maddie.

Miss Wayne looked out the small opening through which Maddie had entered the building. The starry sky provided enough light for her to make out the outline of three vehicles.

"We do have a guest. It's not Jake. The GBI Agent, perhaps? I need to go greet him," Miss Wayne said, still looking outside. "Hmmm," she said as she stepped back to think. "What can I do to get his attention?" Miss Wayne ripped open her own blouse, mussed her hair, clenched the knife and approached Maddie. Smiling, Miss Wayne opened a shallow two inch cut on Maddie's right arm. Maddie was too frightened to scream. All she could do was cry. Miss Wayne squeezed the cut and coated her fingers in the blood that was oozing out. Smearing the blood on her face, Miss Wayne nodded in approval. "This should be enough to convince Mr. GBI that you attacked me, don't you think?"

"You won't get away with this," Maddie said sobbing.

"Oh yes I will. Watch me." Miss Wayne picked up a ten-inch piece of discarded metal pipe from the floor and slid it down the back of her pants. She pushed the door open a few more inches and began screaming and running directly toward Stamps. Her screams got his attention. Stamps hopped out of his seat and met her a few feet in front of his vehicle.

"Help me!" she pleaded. "Maddie Hampton! She attacked me!" Miss Wayne grabbed the agent by both arms.

"What's going on? What are the two of you doing this late at night at this creepy place?" Stamps asked. Seeing Miss Wayne bolting out of the building and begging for help was not what he had anticipated.

"She called me here to pay me off. She was going to pay me to leave Jake Martin alone, so she could have him. But she started attacking me. She attacked me just like those three men she killed! I managed to stun her with a slap to the head. Thank goodness you are here!" Miss Wayne eased her hand behind her, as if to massage her back that had been twisted in the scuffle with Maddie.

Stamps pulled his gun. "Stay here!" he ordered. Turning his back to Miss Wayne, he took a step toward the dark building. Swiftly pulling out the pipe, Miss Wayne popped Stamps in the back of the head, causing him to flop unconscious to the pavement. Grunting, she pounded him again and again, on the shoulder and in the ribs. "Now, let's go inside and finish what we started," she said, tossing the pipe which bounced off Stamps and fell to the pavement.

As Miss Wayne marched back to the Kingman plant, Jake was arriving at Maddie's house, concerned that her Jeep wasn't in its usual spot in the driveway. Suspecting that she was running a few minutes late or had stopped by the convenience store, Jake decided he would sit on the front porch and wait. Stepping on the porch, he noticed the front door was ajar and immediately said aloud, "Something's not right." Using his cell phone, he called Quinn, expressing concern that Maddie's house had been burglarized. Quinn said he was on his way home from the high school but would stop by Maddie's so they could go inside and check.

Jake fought the urge to go in the house, but he waited on Quinn, who arrived in less than five minutes. Quinn drew his sidearm from its holster and carefully pushed open the door. "Stay behind me," he told Jake. All the lights were on and upon first glance nothing seemed out of place. Then Jake noticed the phone and pen on the floor. "Maddie always jots down her calls. Hopefully she did this time." Going straight to the notepad, Jake ignored the phone and pen that were still in the floor. "Look at this," he said to Quinn. "Something about Sunny and an accident . . . at the Kingman plant."

"The Kingman plant? That's been shut down for years. Come on, let's go," Quinn turned and headed out the door in mid-sentence.

Quinn squealed his car out of Maddie's driveway and called 911 on his radio to ask if they had received a request for assistance at the old plant. He grew more concerned when the dispatcher answered "no."

"This isn't adding up," Jake said. "Sunny was supposed to be out with some girls from home economics. Maddie seemed to trust them. I'm having a tough time believing they would do something foolish."

"It is graduation night," Quinn reminded Jake. "We'll soon find out. We're less than ten minutes from the plant."

While Quinn and Jake made their way on the narrow, potholed road leading to the old plant, Miss Wayne resumed ridiculing Maddie, waving the knife in her face and touching her with the sharp point, but not enough to break the skin. In the shadowy, dim light, with her hair uncombed and blood on her face, Miss Wayne was a frightening, blood-chilling apparition. "Everyone in this town thinks you're an angel," she pronounced hatefully, "but I think you're the devil! You're one of those First Baptist hypocrites. You try to be so pious in front of everyone, but behind closed doors you bed down with Jake. You're a sinner like everyone else and you do evil things. You claim you want to help people, but all you've caused me is grief!"

"You don't know what you're talking about! I haven't slept with Jake! We've only kissed a few times. And I'm sorry if I've hurt you. I certainly didn't mean to." Maddie had given up trying to escape from the ropes. She was trying to stay calm and not cry, but tears were rolling down her face, which seemed to please Miss Wayne.

"Maddie, Maddie," Miss Wayne sneered. "No use being untruthful any more. Just take your punishment like a big girl. Are you prepared to be judged?"

"You are crazy!" Maddie shouted. "Absolutely crazy! Damn you!"

"Oh my!" Miss Wayne smirked. "Adding cursing to your list of transgressions? I think it's time to get this over with."

"You'll never get away with this!"

"Of course I will! The people in this town don't have a clue!" Miss Wayne placed the point of the knife on Maddie's breast bone and broke the skin just enough to draw blood from an inch-long cut. Maddie gasped and blood started dripping toward her stomach. "I know how well you know the Bible, Maddie. Do you recall Judges 19:29?"

Maddie didn't reply. Her lip was trembling and she glared at Miss Wayne in contempt.

"Let me refresh your memory . . . *he took a knife and laid hold on his concubine and divided her, together with her bones, into twelve pieces, and sent her into all the coasts of Israel.*"

"You're perverted! You twist the scriptures to serve your needs. May God strike you dead!"

Miss Wayne slapped her hand across Maddie's mouth. "I'm going to enjoy this," Miss Wayne smiled wickedly. She raised the knife back, ready to plunge it into Maddie, but stopped, startled by the sound of the heavy door opening.

"I wouldn't do that if I were you," Quinn suggested as he drew his gun. Miss Wayne still had the knife aimed at Maddie.

"Maddie, are you all right?" Jake asked. He started toward her and she burst into tears.

"Don't move!" Miss Wayne ordered.

"You really need to think about what you're doing," Quinn suggested forcefully.

"Oh, I have. A great deal."

Jake wanted Quinn to shoot Miss Wayne, but she was too close to Maddie.

"Come on, Janet. It's over," Quinn said.

Miss Wayne was silent. She looked at Quinn, at Maddie and then back at Quinn. "You're right," she smiled. "It is over." She screamed and raised the knife above her head for more leverage to drive it deep into Maddie's chest.

On instinct, Quinn fired, hitting Miss Wayne's hand, which caused the knife to fly away. Quinn rushed to Miss Wayne, grabbed her by the arm, twirled her around and belted her in the jaw with his fist. Jake could hear the pop as her jawbone broke. She crumpled to the floor.

"What is it with you and jawbones?" Jake barked at Quinn. "You act like you enjoy breaking them."

"I certainly enjoyed this one," Quinn admitted, shaking the hand that had struck the blow. While Quinn was handcuffing the unconscious Miss Wayne, Jake stood in a trance, his deer-in-the-headlights eyes riveted on Maddie.

"Jake," Maddie started with a calmness admirable for someone in her unenviable position. "I'm glad you like what you see . . ." Suddenly her voice boomed. ". . . but get me untied! And get me some clothes!"

Jake took a step toward her and mentioned, "I don't guess this is a very good time for me to tell you I'm leaving for Charleston."

"You are? When?"

"For God's sake, Jake! Get the woman down!" Quinn bellowed.

Jake started to pick up Miss Wayne's knife, but Quinn stopped him by proclaiming, "That's evidence, stupid. Use this." Quinn took a small knife out of his pocket and tossed it to Jake. He quickly cut Maddie loose and wrapped his arms around her quivering body while Quinn went to his car to get her a blanket out of the trunk. Ten minutes later Miss Wayne was in a squad car on her way to jail and Travis Stamps, clinging to life, was being rushed to Callaway General Hospital.

CHAPTER THIRTY

J ake was propped against the back wall of the filled to capacity twenty-five seat municipal courtroom at the Sanderson Police Department, watching Quinn wrap up a press conference about the arrest of Janet Wayne. Fifteen representatives from Georgia media outlets, plus reporters for Newsweek, USA Today, CNN, Fox News and a couple of Ohio television stations had traveled to south Georgia to learn more about the scripture spouting librarian who was charged with three murders, and dozens more had called to request phone interviews with Quinn. Jake was impressed with the way Quinn was handling the attention. He was calm and poised, not once getting rattled, as he answered questions and faced the television cameras and the accompanying bright lights. The thought occurred to Jake that Quinn belonged somewhere else. Nothing against Sanderson, but Quinn deserved a larger city, a more sophisticated department and a job with more responsibility and more challenges.

Quinn explained to the cramped gathering that Janet Wayne had been charged with the murders of Todd Monroe, Joe Lambert and Regal Krause, kidnapping, assault and attempted murder for luring Maddie to the Kingman plant, and attempted murder and assault for the attack on GBI Agent Travis Stamps, who was still hospitalized with severe injuries but was expected to recover. Motive was still being considered, according to Quinn, because he had yet to completely put together why Miss Wayne had gone on the killing spree. He mentioned nothing about Miss Wayne being Sunny's mother. Sunny had not been told, and Quinn was still trying to decide how much of a factor Sunny was in her mother's rampage. Eventually, Sunny would be told Miss Wayne was her mother, but for now, there were too many other details to tend to, and emotionally, Sunny was struggling with the developments involving the two women closest to her. She was blaming herself for what had taken place.

Jake hung around while several reporters individually went up to Quinn and asked additional questions, most of which he could not, or would not answer. Even though he couldn't provide the information they wanted, Quinn was gracious and patient with each reporter. He was good at this part of the job, very good.

The final reporter left, and Quinn, pleased with how the news conference had gone, walked back to Jake. "How does it feel to be famous?" Jake asked.

Quinn took a deep breath. "I love it. Makes me realize how much I miss all of this. More than that, though, I've gotten the feeling back. The feeling you get when you solve a big case, when you nail someone who has done something terrible."

"Has Miss Wayne confessed yet?"

"She hasn't said a word, so we've got some blanks to fill in, but we will. The knife she used on Maddie doesn't match the knife wounds on Todd and Joe and we've got to find the hammer or whatever was used to drive the nails into Regal's head, but we'll find all of that and we'll come up with enough other evidence to convict the bitch. In this town, this county, this case is a slam dunk. We know that the three guys who were murdered were assholes, but they did have a lot of friends who will end up on the jury. And as for Miss Wayne attacking Maddie, well, in this town by god, that's like someone attacking a saint. Add all of that together, and Janet Wayne doesn't have a chance. When her case goes to trial, I bet the jury won't deliberate an hour before returning a guilty verdict. If the girl is smart, she should do some heavy plea bargaining to avoid the death penalty."

"I don't know, Quinn. It sounds like she's guilty, but it also sounds like you're missing some key physical evidence. You don't have the murder weapon. Have you matched any of Miss Wayne's shoes with the partial print? What about a DNA match?"

"The knife and shoe, we'll eventually find. The DNA? The sample we took off Todd Monroe was damaged. We couldn't match it with the sample we got from Miss Wayne. But I've talked to the District Attorney. He thinks our case is solid."

"I don't know, Quinn. If Miss Wayne gets a good lawyer . . ."

"You're worried about nothing," Quinn assured Jake. "Perry Mason couldn't get her cleared of these charges."

"So, what do you really think? Why did she kill those three guys, and try to kill Maddie?"

"Obviously, she killed Regal and tried to kill Maddie because they stood in her way of getting Sunny. As for Todd and Joe, I've got two theories. First, maybe she really thought she was punishing them for their sins, conveniently overlooking the fact that she was the biggest sinner of all. Second, she may have killed Todd and Joe to create the illusion of a serial killer to deflect attention away from Regal Krause's murder, because we know he was her main target all along. We may never know for certain, but it doesn't matter. She'll be convicted for all three deaths, and I guarantee you she killed her parents and Clarissa Hunt, our previous librarian, as well. She wasn't going to let anyone get in the way of what she wanted. She won't hurt anyone else."

"It's sad. Three kids are without parents now, and this town has been turned upside down. How do you think people are going to feel every time they walk into the library?"

"The library will probably have to expand its collection of murder mysteries. Plus, I think our little town is just starting its time in the spotlight. You know some producer is going to make a TV movie of the week about all of this." Quinn glanced teasingly at Jake. "And Jake, if you write a book about all of this, remember what I said before. Make me sound better looking than I really am."

"Can't do that," Jake shot back. "This is a true story, not fiction."

"You can take a few creative liberties on my behalf. How's Maddie?"

"She's getting better. She wants to get out of the house a little now. Her hands don't tremble quite as much as they did. She's starting to be able to sleep without medication."

"Have the two of you talked about you going to Charleston?"

"Yeah, some. She understands, sort of. I talked to her about how your talents are being wasted here, and she admitted that mine probably are as well. I admit it, Quinn. I'm like you. This whole mess, as gruesome as it has been, has got my heart pumping a little faster. I miss being where the action is."

"When are you leaving?"

"It shouldn't be long. Stephen House is back in town. I'm meeting with him in fifteen minutes."

"Good luck to you Jake. I'll always remember how you put it on the line for me. That was gutsy going to Miss Wayne's house to get that hair sample. Turns out we didn't need it, since we were able to get one through the courts after her arrest, but the fact you were willing to do that means a lot to me."

Jake shook Quinn's hand and smiled. "Just send me some Black Jack chewing gum occasionally and we'll call it even."

Their moment was broken by a voice from the entrance to the room. "Does the famous chief have time to sign an autograph for his biggest fan?"

Quinn's face lit up. "Mary Jane?" He walked to her. They both smiled and looked at each other, each seemingly afraid to make the next move. Finally, Mary Jane offered an awkward, clumsy embrace. Quinn held to her tightly.

"See you later, Quinn," Jake said, knowing it was time for him to leave.

Quinn nodded and looked again at Mary Jane. "You look great, but where in the hell have you been?"

"Hiding. Horrified that I was going to be arrested for murders I didn't commit."

"I'm sorry," Quinn started. "I'm sorry for putting you through what I did. I'm sorry I didn't believe you. I'm sorry I took you away from your girls."

She took his hand. "Don't apologize. You were only doing your job. With my past, you had to consider me. I'm sorry that I put you in such an awkward position to begin with."

"But where the hell have you been?" he asked again. "Officers have been looking for you everywhere."

"It doesn't matter where I've been. What matters is I'm back. I'm back to get my girls, and to see if I might have a second chance with a certain police chief. That is, if I'm no longer a murder suspect."

Quinn smiled. "No ma'am. You are no longer a suspect, but it is my policy to debrief all individuals who have been involved in a case. Would you be available for a debriefing at, say seven o'clock tonight, at my house?"

"I believe I can clear my calendar," she winked.

Quinn gazed at Mary Jane tenderly. "It's good to see you," he said.

"You too."

Sam Rogers walked up to Quinn and announced, "The mayor wants to see you." Sam acknowledged Mary Jane with, "Good to have you back."

"Thanks Sam. Good to be back."

Quinn hugged Mary Jane. "I *am* glad you're back. And that's the truth."

"The truth is what we deal with from here on out."

"Agreed." He didn't want to leave, but the mayor was an impatient man who didn't like to be kept waiting. "I've got to go," he told her.

"I'll see you tonight." She kissed him on the cheek and then watched Sanderson's newest celebrity walk away to his meeting with the mayor.

CHAPTER THIRTY-ONE

Arriving for his appointment with Stephen House, Jake was more melancholy than nervous. House had been good to him and Sanderson had been good to him, but he had to move on. No one had been beating down his door with offers. If he didn't take the Charleston job, he might be stuck in Sanderson for the rest of his life.

As Jake was walking into the Sentinel office, Kenny, notepad in hand and camera dangling from his shoulder, was walking out. "Where are you headed?" Jake asked his young reporter on the sidewalk.

"First Baptist. They're having Vacation Bible School. I'll be able to take lots of photos to help us fill up the pages of this week's paper. How's Maddie?"

"Better. Have you talked to Sunny?"

"No, but I'm going to. I'm going to get her a graduation present. Man, what else can happen to her?"

"Hopefully nothing. She's been through so much. Is Stephen here yet?"

"Yeah, all tanned and talkative. He looks great. I don't think he's missed this place at all."

"I guess he's upset with me."

"Doesn't act like it. He'll be glad to see you."

"I hope you're right. Say hello to Pastor Allen for me."

Inside, Stephen House was leaning on Hazel's desk, engaged in an animated conversation with her about her Master Gardener husband's prize tomatoes. He smiled when he saw Jake and immediately rushed to him for a firm handshake. "Do you make things happen or what," Stephen kidded Jake. "I'm only gone a few weeks and Hazel tells me that you've already got our circulation up seventeen percent."

Going along with Stephen's kidding, Jake said, "I had help. Our city librarian was kind enough to commit three really bizarre murders."

"Janet Wayne is the last person on earth I would have thought capable of something like that. I would have pictured her more as the type who would chain herself to the door of a liquor store to keep people from going in, or to protest against the EZ Shop for selling nudie magazines."

"Me too. Needless to say the entire town is shocked and shaken up. But you look great. Traveling obviously agrees with you."

"I'm having a blast. I've been seeing some beautiful country in California."

"Have you decided what you want to be when you grow up?"

Stephen laughed. "No, not yet, but I understand you've made a decision."

"I have," Jake replied meekly.

"Come on. Let's go back to your office and talk about it."

They made a stop in the break room to pour cups of coffee and proceeded to Jake's office. Stephen sat in a side chair, leaving Jake's regular chair behind the desk for him, and sipped on his coffee. "Believe it or not," he told Jake, "I do miss this place—a little. And I believe you will too when you leave."

"You're right. I will. This is a good town, full of good people."

"Hazel tells me you're sweet on the home economics teacher. How's that going?"

"We were working on a relationship. That's making my leaving very difficult."

"How's Maddie doing after the episode with Miss Wayne?"

"She's better."

"What does she say about you leaving?"

"Not much. I think she would like for me to stay, but she's not going to stand in my way."

Stephen took another swallow of his coffee and looked at Jake. "That's going to be my position too, Jake. I'd love for you to stay, but I'm not going to stand in your way. In the short time you've been here, you've done some great work. You've made an impression on this town. You've made some good friends, Quinn being one of them. But considering my own quest to follow my heart, I understand why you've got to leave. If you want to stay, I'll even sweeten the pot a little more, but I'm not going to beg you."

"I appreciate that. Believe me, leaving is tough enough already."

"When do you want to leave?"

"Soon. They want me in Charleston right after the Fourth of July."

"I'll start making a few phone calls and talk to some folks. So, have you been taking good care of my house?"

"I have, and that's one of the things I'm really going to miss. That and the good home cooking from Hazel and Maddie and all the other ladies. They flat out know how to cook."

Stephen smiled. "You do look like you've put on a few pounds."

Jake smiled back but didn't immediately reply. His eyes wandered around the office before settling on Stephen. "I need to ask you something," Jake started. "And be truthful with me. I've got to know before I leave."

"All right," Stephen said, perplexed by Jake's request.

Jake lowered his head, flexed his right hand and wished he had some of Quinn's Black Jack gum. He looked back at Stephen House and humbly started, "When I first talked to you about this job, I was as low as you could get. I was just out of rehab. I'd lost my wife, my job, my self-respect and the respect of other people. When I started trying to find work, no one would talk to me or return my phone calls. You did. Not only did you give me this job, you made me a deal I couldn't refuse. You said I was the right man for the job, but there had to be a plateful of guys who would have been better." Jake paused and looked down at the floor again. He asked the question before looking up. "What's the real reason you hired me?"

Getting out of his chair, Stephen smiled, picked up the latest issue of the Sentinel from the corner of Jake's desk, glanced at the front page and put the paper down. He leaned back against the wall close to Jake and smiled at him again. "You were the right man, Jake," he started. "The job you've done here proves that, but you were right for another reason. Let me tell you a story."

"When Quinn told me a story recently about Janet Wayne, it started a whole lot of trouble," Jake jokingly warned House.

House smiled, returned to his chair and leaned forward.

"I wasn't always the upstanding, responsible, mature guy you see now. When I was a teenager and in college, I was rowdy. Looking back on it now, I think I was doing it to rebel against my Dad. Everybody in this town loved him and they expected me to be just like him. Back then, I didn't want to be like him. Now, I realize it was an honor that people wanted me to be like him.

"Any way, after graduation from the University of Georgia, three pals and I went to Atlanta to party and celebrate. We were bar-hopping, drinking too much and acting like idiots. At our fourth or fifth bar, we started mouthing off at some jerks and things got out of hand. The next thing you know, I've got a knife headed straight for the side of my face. About the time I'm about to get cut from my ear to my Adam's Apple, this hand shoots in front of my face and gets sliced instead of me. Bouncers break things up, but there I am about to piss in my pants, and this guy who saved me is on his knees on the floor, blood gushing out of his hand.

"I asked the guy if I could take him to the hospital or at least give him some money to get stitched up, but he said no. All he did was hand me his business card and say that I might be able to do him a favor someday. I've still got his business card. Want to see it?"

Before Jake could answer, Stephen had his wallet out, pulled out the ragged card and handed it to him:

Jake Martin

Senior Reporter

Atlanta Advocate

Surprised and embarrassed, Jake looked at the card for several seconds before handing it back to Stephen. Jake held out his right hand and flexed it. "I'm sorry," he apologized to Stephen. "I don't remember. I don't remember a lot of things about that time in my life."

"That's O.K. I remembered for both of us. I couldn't believe it when I got your resume' a few months back. It was like fate was drawing us together. I knew then if you could walk straight and put two sentences together, I was going to hire you."

His face reddening, Jake got out of his chair and turned his back to Stephen to compose himself. Turning back around, Jake said, "I don't know what to say, except thank you."

"No, Jake. Thank you. That night changed my life. Coming so close to being disfigured or even killed made me realize I had no business in a place like that doing crap like that, and I had to get my act together or I would end up in jail or dead. I haven't been drunk since that night. I came home and started working hard for my Dad and the Sentinel. Dad and I started getting along. He told me he was proud of me." Stephen's eyes started watering. "Jake, everything I have today, I owe to you. I really do. I'm going to keep this card, and whether you are in Charleston or floating down the Amazon on a bamboo raft, if there is anything you need, you call me."

Jake's eyes were getting misty as well and he was trembling. "Your Dad had every right to be proud of you," he told Stephen. "I would be proud to have a son like you."

The two men hugged and the tears were flowing freely.

CHAPTER THIRTY-TWO

Ready to deliver her graduation present, Kenny called Sunny on her cell phone. She suggested he meet her at her old house, where she was collecting a few things to take back to Maddie's. Sunny seemed happy to see Kenny and invited him in to have a beer, which he accepted since it was late afternoon and he was off work. Sunny knew he was underage to be drinking, but she joked that she wouldn't tell if he didn't. Kenny suggested she open the small package containing her gift, but Sunny said she would in a few minutes and went to the kitchen to get the beer out of the refrigerator.

Kenny looked around the quiet, deserted living room. He suspected Sunny didn't have many fond memories of the place, and would be glad when a buyer was found and the For Sale sign could be taken out of the front yard. He quickly noticed there were no family photos, and that reinforced his opinion that for Sunny, the place had been merely a house and not a home. It made Kenny thankful for his parents, even though he had frequently accused them of being too strict and overprotective. And least they cared. He had never had any doubts about his parents' love for him.

Sunny returned with two foamy beers, which had been poured out of cans into frosted mugs. "Dad claimed beer is better in a cold mug," Sunny smiled as she handed Kenny his beverage.

"Can, mug or bottle, beer is beer and I like it!" Kenny proclaimed and proceeded to drain half the mug. Sunny took a single slow tip of hers. Kenny finished his in two more gulps, and politely declined Sunny's offer for another.

Kenny had initially balked at the idea of coming to Sunny's house, anticipating their private meeting might get uncomfortable considering how their relationship had ended. She quickly made him feel at ease though, asking numerous questions about his plans for the fall and even wanting to know more about Callan. Thirty minutes passed quickly.

Kenny looked at his watch and realized his vision was blurred. He rubbed his eyes and then the back of his neck. "Man, I am so tired," he admitted. "All of a sudden I can't keep my eyes open. My head feels like it weighs a hundred pounds." He tried to focus on Sunny but couldn't. "Can I lie on your sofa a minute?" he asked without waiting for permission. He was out before his head hit the cushion . . .

. . ."Wake up, Kenny." Groggy and disoriented, Kenny thought he heard someone calling his name, and he had the sensation he couldn't move. He had felt that way several times before when he was so tired his sleep was restless. The feeling was frightening and he hated it. Two firm slaps to the right side of his face made Kenny realize he wasn't dreaming. Someone *was* calling him, and he *couldn't* move. Panic set in when he realized he was tied sitting up in a straight back dining room chair.

"Wake up Kenny." His vision was still blurry but he could see Sunny standing directly in front of him.

"Where am I? What am I doing tied to this chair?" he asked, trying to come out of his stupor.

"You are at my house. Did you enjoy your beer?"

"Did you spike my beer?"

"When my Dad died, the doctor gave me some powerful medicine to help me sleep. I had some left. I'm glad you don't weigh too much. That made it easier getting you in the chair and wrapping the packing tape around you."

"Why? What's going on, Sunny?" Kenny wriggled violently to try to free himself, but there was too much tape and it was too tight. He was as much angry as frightened.

"Why? Because it's payback time."

"Payback time? For what?"

"For my miserable life in this little hell of a town. For you breaking up with me. For your parents hating me. For your new girlfriend, the bimbo cheerleader!"

"But . . . you told me the other day all of that was all right, that it was time for the two of us to go on with our lives."

"I lied."

Kenny's anxiety was building. "I said I'm sorry! What else do you want me to do? Let me go and I'll get down on my knees and beg your forgiveness. I'll talk to my parents. I'll tell Callan to get lost." He wriggled in the chair again, so hard that it almost toppled over.

"Too late. Besides, you really wouldn't do any of that."

"What are you going to do? You can't leave me like this."

"I wouldn't think of leaving you like this. I'm going to kill you."

His heart skipped a beat. Kenny was beginning to realize how serious Sunny was and that he was in desperate trouble. "I don't believe you," he said defiantly.

"Believe it. I'm going to kill you just like I killed my Dad."

Her admission took Kenny's breath away. "You killed your Dad? I thought Miss Wayne did."

"That's what I wanted everyone to think. I copycatted her. I figured that if I made my Dad's murder look like the first two, no one would suspect me. They would think the same person committed all three. And they did. This town is full of morons who have no idea about what is really going on."

"Why did you kill him?"

"Why? That's a stupid question Kenny. Weren't there times when you wished he was dead, when you wished you could kill him? He was a son of a bitch. I wanted him dead for two reasons. He had abused me my whole life, and when he wasn't abusing me, he was ignoring me. I needed his life insurance to help me get away from this graveyard of a town and start a new life. You want to know how I was able to lure him to the cemetery? He was into kinky sex . . . with me. Tying him to that cemetery marker turned him on. Killing him was a piece of cake. I enjoyed every second of it. I loved watching him squirm and suffer!"

"God, Sunny, I'm so sorry. I suspected he was abusing you and I didn't do anything to stop him. You're right. He deserved to die. Cut me loose and we'll see about getting you some counseling. I promise." Kenny was struggling to find the words that would convince Sunny to let him go. Sweat was pouring down his forehead and his shirt was soaked.

"I don't need your help. The insurance money and the highway leading out of this dump is all the counseling I need. As soon as I take care of you, I'm out of here!"

Kenny closed his eyes and prayed. At this point, he was convinced Sunny was going to kill him. He just didn't know how.

While Kenny's terror was multiplying by the second, Jake was ending his day at the Sentinel. He stopped by Hazel's desk to let her know he was leaving two letters for the next day's mail. About to step out the front door, he stopped and looked back at Hazel. "Are you wearing a different perfume?" he asked.

"Hard not to notice, isn't it?" she smiled.

"Yeah, it gets your attention. A bit strong for me. But I've smelled it before. I just can't place where it was. Maybe the prom. Maddie was wearing some potent stuff that night."

"It's Sunny's favorite fragrance. It's too much for an older, mature lady like me, or even Maddie, but I can see how a young girl would like it. Kenny is giving it to Sunny for a graduation gift. He's gone to see her now. He let me sample it."

"Sunny was at the prom. She and Kenny sat with us. That has to be it. Well, see you tomorrow, Hazel. Have a good night."

With the fragrance following him, Jake walked the few feet to his car, contemplating asking Maddie out to dinner at the little town's one Mexican restaurant. Putting the key into the ignition, Jake stopped and blurted out, "Damn! The city cemetery!" Jake suddenly made the connection. The scent on Regal Krause's body and the scent Hazel was sampling were identical! There was no doubt. The fragrance was too strong to mistake. Jake had an immediate sickening feeling Kenny was in trouble. He tried calling Kenny's cell phone but got his voice mail. Rushing back inside, Jake asked Hazel if she knew where Kenny was meeting Sunny. He was out of breath and panting. "At her old house. What's wrong?" Hazel asked, upset at Jake's frantic state. Jake was out the door in a flash. Backing out of his parking space on Main Street, he almost hit a minivan, and then laid down black streaks as he jerked the transmission into drive and sped off to the Krause house, where Sunny was gleefully engaged in emotionally torturing Kenny. She had popped all the buttons on his shirt and was rubbing his chest. Grabbing a handful of hair on the back of his head, she tilted Kenny's head back and french kissed him. Next she put her hand over his heart. "My goodness Kenny. You heart is going a mile a minute. Are you afraid, or have I got you excited?" She put her hand on his crotch and squeezed. "Oh Kenny," she moaned into his ear. "You don't know what you missed. I learned a lot of sexual tricks from my Dad!"

"Let me go and you can show me."

"Nice try, but I don't think so." She ran her fingers through his hair. "Well. Let's get this over with. It's time for me to say goodbye to you—and this damn little town—forever! I wish things could have turned out better, Kenny, but there's no use crying over spilled milk." Sunny walked to a roll top desk a few feet away, opened a drawer and pulled out a hammer and two ten penny nails. Returning to Kenny, she placed one of the nails against his right temple and tapped it lightly with the hammer, just enough to draw blood. A single small drop trickled down the side of Kenny's face. He closed his eyes, bit his lip and started praying again, harder than he ever had in his life.

Sunny lightly tapped the nail with the hammer again. "Like mother, like daughter," she announced playfully.

"What?" Kenny asked, his eyes popping open, his heart about to explode.

She answered with, "*She put her hand to the nail, and her right hand to the workmen's hammer, and with the hammer she smote Sisera, she smote off his head, when she had pierced and stricken through his temples. Judges 5:26.*"

"Don't do this, Sunny, please!" Kenny's body was quivering, as much as being tied to the chair would allow.

"Goodbye Kenny." Sunny put the nail to Kenny's temple again, pulled the hammer back and brought it forward. Kenny screamed at the top of his lungs.

Which is exactly what Jake was doing in his speeding car. "Damn it! Damn it! Damn it!" he screamed. He felt as if he was in the second chapter of a bad dream. Not that long ago he had been speeding to the abandoned Kingman plant to keep Maddie from getting hurt, and here he was now, driving like a lunatic to get to Kenny. Perhaps he had jumped to a huge conclusion about Sunny's perfume, but so far in this town, nothing had turned out to be coincidental. Everything and everyone was tied together. He was dead certain Kenny was in trouble.

Jake squealed his car to a stop in the cracked concrete driveway of the Krause house. Kenny's yellow Mustang was the only vehicle there. Breathing heavily, Jake rushed to the front door which was locked. He pounded on the door, but got no response, and he tried looking in the windows, but all the blinds were drawn. Returning to the front door, he tried to kick it in, but it was too sturdy. Scampering back to his car, Jake pulled a tire tool out of the trunk and used it to smash one of the front windows. Even though he was careful, Jake gashed his right arm crawling through the window. Stepping on crackling glass as he slipped into the living room, Jake let out a giant sigh of relief when he saw Kenny still tied to the chair, packing tape over his mouth, still struggling to get loose.

Jake yanked the tape from Kenny's mouth. "Ow, damn it!" Kenny yelled.

"Got yourself in kind of a mess here, don't you?"

"Man, am I ever glad to see you. I thought I was history. How did you know I was here?"

"Perfume."

"Perfume?"

"Yeah, perfume. Your graduation gift to Sunny. I'll explain later. She did this to you? That sweet, shy retiring little girl?"

"You mean the devil in disguise? She killed her father and was about to kill me. Man, talk about your life flashing in front of you!"

"I'm sorry this happened, but thank goodness you're all right. I figured out the part about her Dad on the way over here." Jake started pulling the tape away from Kenny's torso. "What's that smell? It's not perfume."

"I crapped in my pants. The thought of having a nail driven through your head will cause you to do that. Do you realize your arm is cut?"

Jake glanced at his arm where blood was seeping out at a steady rate. He slapped the packing tape that had been on Kenny's mouth over the cut.

"Why didn't she go through with it?" Jake asked.

"I really thought she was going to drive the nail into my head, but she pulled back the hammer at the last possible split-second. She said that I had been a good friend to her, in spite of the way our relationship ended, and that she couldn't bring herself to kill me. She said he would be content with scaring the crap out of me, and as you have already noticed, she was successful in doing that."

"Where did she go?"

"Don't know. All she said was she was leaving this damn little town."

"We'll find her," Jake promised as he removed the last strand of tape from Kenny's leg. "You go clean up in the restroom and I'll see if there's a pair of Regal's pants around here."

They left the house a half-hour later, with Kenny much calmer and more presentable, even though he was wearing a pair of jeans he could have used as a camping tent.

CHAPTER THIRTY-THREE

Fondly studying the faces of the waitresses, cooks and customers at the crowded Waffle House, Jake sighed and admitted, "I'm going to miss this place," before he finished off the last swallow of his coffee.

"It's only a Waffle House," Quinn told his friend. "I'm sure there are Waffle Houses in Charleston."

"But these people won't be there. I'll miss you. I'll miss our talks where we vent our frustrations and solve all the world's problems."

"For this to be a little old town in the middle of nowhere, we have had a lot to talk about, haven't we?"

"Indeed," Jake agreed as he watched the grey-haired waitress refill his cup. "Any word on Sunny?"

"Security at the Atlanta airport found her truck abandoned in long term parking. We checked with all the airlines, and none of them had her listed as a passenger. We couldn't spot her on any of the airport security cameras either. I'm guessing she changed her appearance, bought some bogus identification and left the country. By now, I bet she's sunning on the beach on some lovely tropical island, laughing at all of us."

"You know what's funny? All Sunny wanted was a new start for her life, a second chance, just like you and me," Jake suggested.

"But we went about it in totally different ways. You and I end up in Sanderson, scratching and clawing to regain our self-respect. She commits murder and gets away with it—not to mention a bundle of cash from her Daddy's insurance."

"Yeah, Sunny is smart. She had to be smart to plan her Dad's murder and pull it off. We certainly found out she's not the sweet little innocent thing we all thought she was. And Janet Wayne gave Sunny the perfect set-up to get away with murder."

"Jake, you really should write a book about all of this."

Jake nodded in agreement. "I just might do that."

"Well, Jake, do you think this town can get along without us?"

Jake looked at Quinn over the rim of his coffee cup. "What do you mean *us*?"

"I'm leaving too. I made my mind up this morning. I'm headed for Kentucky. I'm going to be the lead homicide detective for the Lexington Police Department. An old friend I visited on my way to Ohio offered me the job. I've still got a few hoops to jump through, but he assured me it's a done deal."

"That's great Quinn! I'm happy for you. You deserve this."

"I'm taking Mary Jane and her girls with me."

"Are you sure you want them to go with you?"

"Absolutely. I've never been more certain of anything in my life."

"Her past is going to follow her, you know that, don't you?"

"So will mine. We'll deal with it."

"Then I'll be pulling for you. I wish you—I wish both of you—nothing but the best."

"Thanks Jake. You too. Good luck in Charleston."

Jake smiled, finished his coffee and looked at his watch. "I've got to go. Maddie's waiting."

The two men stood up and Quinn tossed a couple of dollar bills on the table for a tip. "Jake, you've been a good friend. You were always there to push me when I started doubting myself."

"And you put me on to the wonderful calming powers of plastic baseball bats and Black Jack chewing gum."

"Speaking of which . . . ," Quinn took two packs of gum out of his pocket and gave them to Jake. "A going away present," he nodded.

The two men hugged and patted each other on the back, and neither wanted the other to see they were about to get emotional. Quinn made an excuse about needing to see the Waffle House manager, which allowed Jake to walk out to his car alone. Jake stopped at the door, and the two friends waved one last time.

Stepping into the parking lot, Jake noticed his trip to see Maddie was going to be delayed a few more minutes. "What are you doing here?" he asked Kenny, who was seated on the hood of his Mustang.

"I came to talk you into staying in Sanderson. I've got three good reasons why."

"You do?" Jake asked, folding his arms.

"Yeah. Reason number one: Maddie. Reason number two: Maddie. Reason number three: Maddie."

"I see. Those are all very good reasons, but I have three why I should leave," Jake said as he hopped on the hood next to Kenny. "One: Charleston is one of the South's great cities, full of history and tradition. Two: the chance to work with a loyal old friend. Three: more career opportunities. Lots more career opportunities."

"O.K. Your reasons are good too. Being honest, I didn't think I'd be able to talk you into staying, so as much as anything, I came to say thanks."

Jake cocked his head and waited for Kenny to continue.

"You've been great to work with. I've learned so much from you. Plus, you kept quiet about my loss of body functions during that little adventure at Sunny's."

"I'm sorry about Sunny," Jake told Kenny. "In spite of how things ended, you did a lot for her. You really were her only friend."

Kenny sighed. "Thanks, but that doesn't make me feel any better. I feel like I let her down. And you know what, Jake? I can't blame her for killing her old man. If I had been in her situation, I might have done the same thing."

"Maybe. People tend to do desperate things where they are desperate." Jake paused and smiled. "The one thing I hope you've learned from this is to stay away from beer. It can get you into serious trouble, especially with a whacko ex-girlfriend."

"Brother, you've got that right!" They both laughed.

"I'm expecting great things from you, Kenny. You go off to the University of Georgia and work hard and study hard. Maybe one of these days you can give me a job like Stephen House did."

"It would be my honor. Take care, Jake."

Another hug and Jake was off to see Maddie. Saying goodbye to Quinn and Kenny had been hard, but parting with Maddie was going to be downright gut-wrenching. From the moment he hit town, Maddie had been his biggest supporter, not judging him on his past and helping him to deal with his present. He thought about taking the coward's way out and heading out of town, calling Maddie on the phone, but he wasn't going to do that. She deserved better.

Jake did make one concession. He didn't go into Maddie's house. That would make leaving too difficult. Instead, he asked her to sit with him on her front porch. She had prepared a basket of goodies for him to take. "Just like the students in my home economics class would make," she said proudly.

"That bad, huh?" he joked.

"All of your favorites are in the basket. It will be something you can remember Sanderson by."

"I'll have many fond memories of this town and you'll be my best memory. I can't leave, though, not yet. I've got to ask you a question."

"O.K." Maddie agreed with slight hesitation. She had no idea what Jake was about to ask.

"Are you all right? Are you over everything that happened with Janet Wayne?"

"I'm O.K. I'll never forget what happened and I still have some bad moments, but I can function. I have my parents, my friends, my co-workers and my church family for support."

"I can't go until I'm certain you're all right."

"I'm fine, Jake. I really am." She took Jake's hand and squeezed it. "Besides, it would be so selfish of me, to cause you to lose this wonderful opportunity."

"Are you sure?"

"Yes."

Jake looked at his watch. "I guess I'd better go. I've got a long drive."

Maddie looked out at Jake's Maxima. "Where are all of your belongings? Don't you need a trailer?"

"No. Everything's in my car. I travel light," he told her just as he had Stephen House months before.

"Goodbye Jake." Maddie hugged him and kissed him on the cheek. She didn't want to let go, but gently broke away and handed him the basket of treats. "Have a safe trip." Maddie waved at Jake from her porch as he drove off. He wasn't happy with their goodbye. It seemed so antiseptic, so impersonal, so inadequate for everything they had been through. But perhaps parting that way was best for both of them. It was certainly less painful.

Jake drove through town one last time, past the little city park, past the Sentinel office, past City Hall and the Police Station. He turned the radio to the town's only station, the 1,000 watt Big Country Machine that was playing Trisha Yearwood's *How Do I Live Without You?* Jake quickly turned the radio off and slipped a chocolate chip cookie out of the goodie basket. Munching on the cookie, he drove past the Waffle House and Jabbo's Garage before getting to the Sanderson City Limit sign, which urged *Come Back To See Us.*

Jake drove another mile before he realized he was gripping the steering wheel tighter than a tick sticks to one of George Howell's hunting dogs. Pulling on to a dirt road that led to three shabby mobile homes, Jake got out of his car but left the engine running. He wadded every piece of one of the packs of gum Quinn had given him into his mouth and began chomping as he paced up and down the dirt road. Once all the flavor was gone, he spit the gum into his hand, rolled the rubbery concoction into a ball and fired it into a thicket of pine trees. He got back in his car and hit the highway again . . .

. . ."Jake?" Maddie asked when she opened her front door. She stepped out on to the porch.

"Do you think the people of Sanderson would give me a second chance if I want to stay at the Sentinel?" he asked.

"Hmmm. Let me think. Since you've been here, my two favorite students were in a fatal car accident and another turned out to be a killer. We've had three murders and two attempted murders, including one where I was stripped down to my birthday suit and tied spread-eagle between two iron posts. Some folks say you brought a black cloud with you to this little town." Then she smiled. "But most everyone thinks you're a pretty good guy. I believe if we put the matter to a vote, the kind people of Sanderson would allow you to stay. The vote might be close, but they'd let you stay."

"Good, because that's what I really want to do."

"Good, because that's what I want you to do. I really, really want you to stay!"

They kissed, and this time, there was nothing antiseptic, impersonal or inadequate about it. "Sit down while I make a phone call," Jake requested. "I've got to call Stephen House before he gives my job to someone else."

Maddie softly laid her hand on Jake's cheek. "You make that phone call," she smiled. "I'm going to make some sandwiches."

While Jake remained on the porch to talk with Stephen House, Maddie started humming *Jesus Loves Me* on her way inside to the kitchen. Taking a serrated knife out of a drawer, she started slicing a vine-ripened south Georgia tomato. Her humming became louder and a smile spread across her face as she gazed out the window over the sink and watched the teenage boy who lived next door cutting grass. She had plenty to smile about. She had won Jake's heart and executed wicked sinners Todd Monroe and Joe Lambert. Sunny had saved her the trouble of dealing with Regal Krause. And all of Maddie's secrets, thanks to Janet Wayne's antics and Quinn's tunnel vision about the librarian being guilty, would forever be safe from the world.